"Listen, just because you kissed me, that doesn't change anything between us,"

Megan said.

Alex thought a moment, then answered. "You kissed me back. Heartily. Lengthily."

Megan wished she could stop the blush she felt warming her cheeks. "All right, so it was a two-way street. The whole thing took me by surprise. Suddenly we were up close and…and it had been a long time since…" She cleared her throat. "At any rate, I shouldn't have behaved like that. I'm not usually so…so…"

"Responsive? Passionate? Abandoned?"

Why in the world had she begun this conversation? "No, I'm not any of those things," Megan stated flatly. "I was acting out of character."

Alex moved to sit next to her. "Don't bother trying to convince me you're not all of those things. Because I know.

"I've kissed you, and I know."

Dear Reader,

Have you noticed our special look this month? I hope so, because it's in honor of something pretty exciting: Intimate Moments' 15th Anniversary. I've been here from the beginning, and it's been a pretty exciting ride, so I hope you'll join us for three months' worth of celebratory reading. And any month that starts out with a new book by Marie Ferrarella has to be good. Pick up *Angus's Lost Lady;* you won't be disappointed. Take one beautiful amnesiac (the lost lady), introduce her to one hunky private detective who also happens to be a single dad (Angus), and you've got the recipe for one great romance. Don't miss it.

Maggie Shayne continues her superselling miniseries THE TEXAS BRAND with *The Husband She Couldn't Remember.* Ben Brand had just gotten over the loss of his wife and started to rebuild his life when...there she was! She wasn't dead at all. Unfortunately, their problems were just beginning. Pat Warren's *Stand-In Father* is a deeply emotional look at a man whose brush with death forces him to reconsider the way he approaches life— and deals with women. Carla Cassidy completes her SISTERS duet with *Reluctant Dad,* while Desire author Eileen Wilks makes the move into Intimate Moments this month with *The Virgin and the Outlaw.* Run, don't walk, to your bookstore in search of this terrific debut. Finally, Debra Cowan's back with *The Rescue of Jenna West,* her second book for the line.

Enjoy them all, and be sure to come back again next month for more of the best romantic reading around—right here in Silhouette Intimate Moments.

Yours,

Leslie J. Wainger

Leslie J. Wainger
Senior Editor and Editorial Coordinator

Please address questions and book requests to:
Silhouette Reader Service
U.S.: 3010 Walden Ave., P.O. Box 1325, Buffalo, NY 14269
Canadian: P.O. Box 609, Fort Erie, Ont. L2A 5X3

STAND-IN
FATHER

PAT
WARREN

Published by Silhouette Books

America's Publisher of Contemporary Romance

SILHOUETTE BOOKS

ISBN 0-373-07855-2

STAND-IN FATHER

Copyright © 1998 by Pat Warren

All rights reserved. Except for use in any review, the reproduction
or utilization of this work in whole or in part in any form by any
electronic, mechanical or other means, now known or hereafter
invented, including xerography, photocopying and recording, or in
any information storage or retrieval system, is forbidden without
the written permission of the editorial office, Silhouette Books,
300 East 42nd Street, New York, NY 10017 U.S.A.

All characters in this book have no existence outside the imagination of
the author and have no relation whatsoever to anyone bearing the same
name or names. They are not even distantly inspired by any individual
known or unknown to the author, and all incidents are pure invention.

This edition published by arrangement with Harlequin Books S.A.

® and TM are trademarks of Harlequin Books S.A., used under license.
Trademarks indicated with ® are registered in the United States Patent
and Trademark Office, the Canadian Trade Marks Office and in other
countries.

Printed in U.S.A.

Books by Pat Warren

PAT WARREN,

mother of four, lives in Arizona with her travel-agent husband and a lazy white cat. She's a former newspaper columnist whose lifetime dream was to become a novelist. A strong romantic streak, a sense of humor and a keen interest in developing relationships led her to try romance novels, with which she feels very much at home.

This book is dedicated to Dr. Beverly S. Tozer, Internal Medicine, one of the most compassionate and caring physicians I know, and to Dr. Barbara J. MacCollum, Gastrointestinal Specialist, for willingly sharing her knowledge and expertise regarding transplant surgery, and to the many transplant teams and thousands of brave transplant recipients across the country.

Chapter 1

Alex Shephard opened his eyes, blinking at the hazy white glare. There was no pain, only a floaty feeling, almost surreal. Memory came drifting back. He was in a hospital bed, of course, in Intensive Care in a private cubicle surrounded by machines bleeping and clicking and the nurses' station visible through sliding glass doors. He'd spent a lot of time in hospitals, mostly in Emergency, and had always hated them.

But not this time. Waking up this time meant he'd beaten the worst odds he'd ever been given.

Damned if he wasn't alive. Alex closed his eyes and felt a rush of emotion clog his throat. Funny, he hadn't known how much he wanted to live until he'd almost died. Funny also because he'd almost bought the farm half a dozen times with what some would call his reckless way of life, his insatiable thirst for new adventures, and he'd never once considered dying.

This time had been different because this time he'd not had even a modicum of control over his fate. The disease had hit fast and hard, escalating rapidly. Hepatitis C, the most serious strain. The doctor had been blunt. Without a new liver, he'd die in less than a month. Alex had felt helpless, angry, impotent. Then suddenly, a new liver had been located, surgery scheduled.

They'd said his chances were good, that his otherwise healthy body would most likely accept the newly transplanted organ. However, Dr. George Benson had warned that there were never guarantees with major surgery. If he made it through surgery, that would be the biggest hurdle. Six weeks afterward, his chances would improve dramatically, and if he survived five years, he'd likely live a long life.

Alex was determined to do just that. He still had a lot of living to do.

A nurse came into his private cubicle on silent shoes. Her dark hair was pulled back from a round face into a neat bun at her nape. "Good. You're awake."

Alex looked up, read Donna Campion on her name tag and swallowed around a dry throat. "Thirsty," he managed, his voice sounding rusty to his ears.

"In a moment." She turned his hand over and pressed two fingers to his wrist, her eyes on her watch. Moments later, she made a notation on his chart, then popped a thermometer in his mouth.

Curious, he raised one arm, trying to see the needle taped to the inside of his elbow, testing his mobility.

"It's best if you don't try to move just yet," Donna admonished him. "You're in ICU, still heavily medicated." She withdrew the thermometer, marked down his temperature. After opening a fresh straw, she poured water into a glass, bent the straw and held it to his lips. She allowed him two brief sips, then set the glass aside and straightened his bedding, adjusted his pillow.

She was used to running the show and stingy with the water, Alex thought, but he was too weak to protest. There was something more important on his mind. He hated to ask, but needed to hear the words spoken out loud. "The transplant took, then?"

Her face softened. "So far, so good."

Alex let out a relieved sigh and closed his eyes.

The next time he opened them, his father was standing beside his hospital bed. Alex had no idea how long he'd been out this time, but the worry lines on Ron Shephard's forehead had eased slightly. Lord knows he'd put a lot of creases on his father's face through the years. However, this time, this illness, hadn't exactly been due to carelessness.

He'd been competing in a sailboat regatta and his team had come in first as it usually did. A bunch of the guys were going out to celebrate and he'd borrowed someone's razor, then cut himself in his haste. Who'd have dreamed you could get a fatal disease from something so ordinary, so seemingly safe?

Ron Shephard took hold of his son's hand, squeezed gently. "You're doing well, Alex," he said, his voice thick. "Real well."

"You talked with the doctor?" Ordinarily, he wasn't a skeptic by nature, but this wasn't exactly an ordinary happening.

"Absolutely." Ron smiled reassuringly. He'd spoken with Dr. Benson earlier and found him to be "guardedly optimistic," a phrase medical personnel used often enough to become a cliché. Benson had gone on to say that Alex wasn't out of the woods yet, for his body could still reject the new liver, but that his son was doing as well as could be expected at this phase.

Reject the new liver? No, that couldn't happen, *wouldn't* happen, Ron thought emphatically. He'd already lost his wife and buried one son. He couldn't lose Alex, too.

"You're going to be fine, just fine. Won't be long and you'll be out of here with a new lease on life, a second chance."

Alex heard the words his father didn't say: Don't screw up this time. How many lives you think you have?

"Maddy can hardly wait to start fussing over you," Ron went on. "She's dying to fatten you up."

Just what he needed, Alex thought. Recuperating at his father's home in La Jolla with both Dad and the housekeeper who'd all but raised him hovering over him for weeks. But he'd promised he wouldn't go home to his condo on the beach until he was well enough. Of course, he'd been so damn sick when they'd admitted him he'd have promised anyone anything. Still, it was probably for the best. He felt weak as a kitten.

"Want some water?" Ron asked. "Or your bed raised?" He felt uneasy in hospitals, a legacy from twenty years ago when his wife had battled for months against the cancer that had finally won. Alex had been only twelve.

"No, thanks." Alex felt a vague heaviness in the area of his abdomen. He'd been told the incision could be as much as a foot and a half long. Shifting slightly, he tried to push back the sheet to check it out, but there were too many tubes running in and out of his arms, preventing easy movement, and the covers were too heavy.

"What is it? What do you want?" Ron asked.

"The incision. I want to see—"

"You don't need to be worrying about your incision." The nurse entering was younger than Donna but equally no-nonsense, firmly placing his hand outside the sheet and light blanket. "We've got you bound up good and tight. No way you can see that incision for a while." She glanced over at the older man. "Your five minutes are up, Mr. Shephard. It's time for my patient's medication."

"Sure thing." Ron stroked his son's bare arm, smiled down at him. "I'll be back next hour, Alex. You rest now."

"Later, Dad." He closed his eyes as a wave of nausea had him swallowing hard.

"Not feeling too great, eh?" She picked up the syringe from the tray she'd brought in. "This'll fix you right up."

Alex focused on her name tag as she injected his medication. Andrea Owens, R.N. She had big brown eyes and curves her white uniform couldn't hide. He watched her replace one of his drip bags, and before she was finished, he felt the warmth of the medication flood his system. "You've got great legs, Andrea," he whispered, then drifted off into oblivion.

Whispering voices, muted but definitely close by, drew him out of a drugged sleep. But his eyelids felt too heavy to bother opening his eyes. Two nurses shuffled about his cubicle, gathering data from the machines behind his bed. He was getting used to the hourly routine. Alex drifted in that pleasant place halfway between being awake and sleeping, yet aware of their movements and snatches of their conversation.

"He's definitely one of the lucky ones." Donna Campion's voice had the lilt of her English background. "His vitals are holding steady even sooner than Dr. Benson thought."

"That's good," Andrea commented. "I'm glad. He's too young to die." She remembered him commenting on her legs yesterday and took a moment to study him. Blond hair bleached by the sun, a great tan and green eyes she'd noticed earlier when he'd been awake. A square jaw with a stubborn tilt, full lips she wouldn't mind sampling. He had the kind of face no woman would easily forget. Her slender fingers settled on Alex's wrist, her touch gentle as she shifted her gaze to her watch.

"I don't expect he'll die with that father of his ready, willing and able to help him out, no matter the cost." Donna jotted his blood pressure reading on the patient's chart.

"What do you mean?" Andrea whispered.

"The transplant, of course. I heard tell this one's name wasn't next on the list." Coming around to the other side of the bed, she spoke in hushed tones. "The word is that his rich father bought him a liver."

Andrea was clearly shocked. "You mean he bypassed the other patients on the list?"

"Only one that I know of, but still…" She tucked the sheet in more tightly, her round face disapproving.

"Maybe this patient was more critical. That's how it's supposed to go, isn't it? The most critical gets the next transplant?''

"Age and probable recovery play a part, but I didn't know that powerful, wealthy relatives could move a waiting recipient to the top of the list." The experienced nurse shook her head. "Medicine isn't what it used to be."

Andrea wasn't so quick to condemn. "Maybe we don't have all the facts. Maybe there were extenuating circumstances."

"I doubt it. I overheard Benson talking to the transplant team post-op. This guy's daddy's a prominent San Diego businessman and a big donor to this hospital. What chance does a poor ordinary slob have against all that?''

Reluctantly, Andrea set down her patient's hand, her eyes on his handsome face. "I'll bet he doesn't know what his father did."

The English nurse snapped her pen into place on the clipboard. "Right. And I'm Florence Nightingale. Let's move along. The sooner we finish, the quicker I can take my break."

Alex waited a long minute before opening his eyes. The room was still hazy, as was his mind. Had he heard correctly? Maybe he was dreaming, or foggy from all the drugs he'd been given. Surely they couldn't be right. Dad wouldn't...

Alex swallowed. Yes, it was exactly the sort of thing his father would do. The nurses' words had the ring of truth. Because of two devastating tragedies in the past, Ron Shephard had been protective of Alex to the point of smothering. Alex had reacted predictably, by defying the gods full speed.

There'd been only two years separating him and his brother Patrick, but they'd been very different. Patrick had been steady as a rock, rarely taking chances, content with quiet pursuits while Alex viewed life as one big challenge, wanting to taste it fully. From skydiving to scuba diving in remote places, from mountain climbing to sailing across distant seas, he'd lived a wild and carefree life. Although Ron had objected, Alex pretended not to hear. His mother's premature death at thirty-two had taught him that it was foolish to waste time, that you only go around once and you'd better enjoy the trip.

Alex's philosophy had been reinforced when Patrick had drowned in a minor boating accident off San Diego Bay a week before his twenty-seventh birthday. To die because of a probable misstep on a sailboat, a mast swinging around, clunking him on the head and sending him overboard in the early-morning hours with no other boaters nearby to help out, had been so...so ignominious.

As it would have been to die because he'd borrowed a guy's razor, Alex thought. When he'd heard the doctor's prognosis, he'd realized he didn't want to die, had struggled against the very thought. But he hadn't realized the depth of his father's concern until he'd heard the nurses' discussion just now.

Despite his escapades, Alex knew he'd always conducted himself honestly and honorably. He'd knuckled down at his father's company, Shephard Construction & Development Corporation, and made himself into a real asset, only indulging his pursuit of pleasure on weekends and vacations. He'd asked for no special treatment, working his way up, never taking a promotion he didn't feel he deserved. To learn that his father had evened the odds for him was a shock.

What could he do now, after the fact? Confront his father? Yes, he would do that, but Alex thought he probably already knew the answer. Ron wouldn't lie to him, nor would he apologize. He was a man very successful in business and used to calling the shots, of having his way, of removing obstacles to get what he wanted done.

Even if it meant riding roughshod over some poor unlucky person next in line for a liver transplant, someone neither of them had met.

Alex felt a shiver take him despite the warmth of the ICU cubicle. He'd have to think about this new wrinkle, learn to live with it. But first things first. He needed to get well, and for that he'd need all his energy right now.

Closing his eyes, he let the lingering medication take him back under.

"I'll be damned if I'll apologize for doing whatever it takes to keep my only son alive." Ron Shephard poured himself iced tea from the pitcher on the glass-topped wrought-iron table and drank half of it down without pausing.

Alex lay back on the padded lounge chair on the covered patio of his father's home in La Jolla. Just ahead were three hundred yards of sloping green lawn, then stone steps that led down to the beach and the sea beyond. Gulls dipped and rose over the whitecaps on this bright morning in mid-August, the noonday sun overhead warm and welcome. He'd been out of the hospital a week and finally decided to confront his father.

"What about the person I replaced on the list, Dad?" Alex asked, his voice not accusatory but rather questioning.

Ron sat down on the edge of the companion chair, looking momentarily troubled. "Don't you think I've thought of that person many times since I...persuaded the hospital staff to help me? But if he or she was as sick as you—and he'd have had to be to be next in line—then he's probably had the surgery by now and doing as well as you."

Rationalization. He'd thought of that argument, too. "How do we know that for a fact?"

"We don't." A scowl appeared on Ron's strong face. "Listen, I don't want you to be thinking about this. You need to concentrate on getting well, on recovering. What's done is done, and if there's blame somewhere in this, it rests clearly on my shoulders."

And perhaps the hospital staff and the doctor in charge, for caving in to financial pressure, to hospital politics. However, Alex wasn't naive. These sweetheart deals were made all the time in business. And running a hospital, he knew, was exactly like running a business. Sometimes difficult decisions had to be made for the overall good.

But a life had been involved here, a poor, unsuspecting,

very ill victim of liver disease. He'd been there and knew how that felt, how the unfairness of it all ate at you. Only that person hadn't had a guardian angel in his corner.

He decided to make one more stab at it. "I thought there was a regional transplant registry, plus a national one. Isn't shuffling people around on the list against the rules?"

Ron's face took on a stubborn look. "You let me worry about the rules."

And that, Alex knew, would be the last Ron would say on the matter. Wearily, he ran a hand over his unshaven chin. He'd gotten lazy lying around, reading, napping daily, letting Maddy spoil him with special meals and freshly baked cookies. The doctor had said it would likely be several months before he could get back to work. Although he didn't mind his enforced rest now, he was sure that as soon as this incredible weakness left him, he'd be anxious to get back. He'd been too active all his life to enjoy being idle for long.

Ron touched his son's shoulder and squeezed. "Don't hate me for this, Alex. I simply couldn't lose you, too." His voice was thick with emotion.

Alex gripped his father's hand. "How could I hate you? You saved my life. I'm grateful."

Ron leaned over and grasped his son into a rough hug, then straightened. "Got to get back to the salt mines. I'll see you at dinner."

"Hey, Dad, will you ask Mitch to come see me? If I can't get back just yet, I'd kind of like to hear what's going on in my department." Alex was in charge of the land acquisition and development end of the business, while the construction division was Ron's responsibility. Mitch Franklin was Alex's right-hand man, an old college buddy.

"All right," Ron said, his reluctance obvious. "But I don't want you concerned about the company just now. We're doing just fine. You need to heal."

"I'm healing, I'm healing." He waved his father off, wishing for the day he could put all this invalid stuff behind him. Shifting on the lounge, he felt the pull of the staples still in his incision. Eighteen inches long from left to right across the top of his abdomen just under the sternum. Not a pretty sight.

Alex heard the patio door open and saw Maddy coming toward him with a small tray. His afternoon medication, no doubt. Fourteen pills a day including the newest antirejection drug. He'd be on most of them the rest of his life.

But at least he was alive.

Resolutely, he set aside his thoughts about the person who'd moved to second place on the transplant list and smiled a welcome to the housekeeper who'd been like a mother to him.

Mitch Franklin was as dark as Alex was fair, with brown curly hair and eyes that were almost black. He was also a good four inches shorter than Alex's six-two, but he was muscular and strong, a former college wrestler.

In shirtsleeves and his trademark paisley suspenders, Mitch walked into Ron's den and found his friend watching an old Hitchcock movie. "Man, what a life you lead!" His smile wide, he shook hands with Alex and dropped down onto an oversize hassock, propping his elbows on his knees.

"Yeah, it's great. I've memorized the dialogue from a dozen movies and read nearly every book up there." He waved at the far wall of floor-to-ceiling bookcases.

"Ah, come on, it's only been a month."

"Feels like longer." Using the remote, he turned off the television. "You have no idea what boredom can do to you. I'm considering taking up needlepoint. What do you think?"

"I think you're a natural. Great hands, lots of patience." He grinned at his friend. "No kidding, you're looking good."

They'd talked on the phone several times, but this was Mitch's first visit. "No, *you're* looking good. Tanned and healthy, while I look like hell."

"I wouldn't say that. A little pale maybe, but better than being golden yellow," Mitch commented, referring to the jaundice Alex had had before his transplant.

Alex sighed and sat up. "I guess you're right. How're Jan

and the kids?'' Unlike Alex, with his brief marriage that had ended in divorce after less than a year, Mitch was happily married, a real family man. Jan was a tall, dazzling blonde who adored her husband and had given him a son and daughter so far. Alex dropped by for dinner every few months, but he knew the domestic scene wasn't for him.

"Great. Cheryl's taking ballet and Toby's in Cub Scouts, which means I have to be a group leader. Ten six-year-olds. I wish I had their energy.''

"Me, too, especially these days. So, how're things at the office? And don't give me one-word answers like 'fine' and 'okay' the way Dad does.''

Mitch shoved long fingers through his thick hair. "But things *are* fine and okay. We locked up that parcel outside Fallbrook. We should have water approval in another week. Oceanside condos are completed. Not much else simmering right now.''

"So then you don't really need me. I can jump on my boat, live on board, sail around the world.''

"Oh, I wouldn't go that far. There are always problems. Electricians are on strike, but you probably read about that already. That might put us behind on the Del Mar project if they don't settle soon." He glanced out the window. "And this unseasonable heavy rain's slowing things. Plus two people are out this week and I'm buried in paperwork. Same old, same old.''

Alex was quiet, not commenting right away, staring out at the rain slithering down the window. A day as gloomy as his thoughts. He'd been pondering something for weeks. It was time to act. "Mitch, I need you to do me a favor.''

"Sure. Name it.''

"I want you to hire a private investigator to find out something, and I don't want anyone else to know about this.''

Mitch didn't bother to hide his curious frown. "All right. What's it about?''

"I don't know if you're aware of this, but organs for transplant are available first in the area they're harvested. The hospital in each area has a recipient list, names waiting for a donor. When an organ becomes available, the man or woman who gets first crack is determined by age, probable recovery and by how sick they are, how needy. By some fluke, I found out that I shot to the top of the list because…because of Dad's influence." His eyes on Mitch, he waited for a reaction.

Mitch shrugged. "I'm not surprised. Ron's pretty aggressive, which can't be news to you."

"No, but sometimes he crosses the line."

"How'd you find out?"

"I overheard two nurses talking. I want you to hire this guy to get me a copy of the list at the time I went into surgery."

Mitch looked perplexed. "Why?"

Alex ran a hand along the back of his neck. "I just need to know. Because of Dad, someone who was scheduled next got shoved to second place. I want to know that someone's name and as much about him or her as this P.I. can dig up."

Drawing in a deep breath, Mitch shook his head. "I fail to see why you need to know. It's not going to change a thing."

"I'm aware of that. I…I just want to know. And tell him no fudging. I want the truth. Also, I'll pay the guy in cash. I don't want Dad to know about this."

Rising, Mitch stuck his hands in his pants pockets and rattled his change as he studied his friend. "I'd like to talk you out of this, Alex. There's no way this information is going to help you put all this behind you and move on with your life."

Wearily, Alex leaned back. "Maybe you're right. Nevertheless, I want it done. Will you find someone?"

Still frowning, Mitch nodded. "I'll get right on it. Might take a bit of doing. Hospitals guard that sort of information."

"Get someone good. Call me when his report's in." Alex watched his friend walk away, then shifted his gaze out to the rain-washed yard and beyond to the gray skies.

Was he doing the right thing? Who was to say? He only knew he wouldn't rest until he got some answers, right or wrong.

* * *

It felt great being back in his own place among his own things, Alex thought. His father had been against his leaving, as the hovering housekeeper had been, but he'd insisted. His condo was only ten miles up the shoreline from Ron's house, so it wasn't as if he'd be far away. Of course, he couldn't drive yet, but he was only a phone call away.

Maddy had insisted on stocking his kitchen, so he was well set. Alex yawned expansively. If only he felt like doing something more strenuous than a leisurely swim in the community pool or his evening stroll on the beach. Dr. Benson had ruled out ocean activities for now, but he seemed pleased with Alex's progress. The ennui would gradually fade, his energy would return and his need to nap disappear altogether, they'd promised him. So far, none of that had happened.

But his appetite had returned. Finishing the sandwich and glass of milk he'd prepared for lunch, Alex put the dishes into the dishwasher just as the doorbell rang. Moving slowly, as he did most things, he went to answer.

Mitch strolled in, a manila envelope under his arm and a hesitant look on his face. "Ron says you're jumping the gun by moving back here so soon."

Alex closed the door behind his friend. "Dad's become an old woman. I had to get out of there before he and Maddy drove me nuts. And I'm fine." He nodded toward the envelope. "Have you finally got something for me?" It had been three weeks since their last meeting. Each time Alex had phoned, Mitch had told him to be patient, that good investigations take time.

"Yeah, but I really wish you'd reconsider. This is crazy, Alex." He faced his friend, concern plain on his tanned face. "What possible good will this do?"

"It'll set my mind at ease." He held out his hand.

"I doubt that." Reluctantly, Mitch handed over the envelope before wandering into the kitchen. "Got any coffee made?"

"Yeah, in the pot. Warm it in the micro." Walking to his

favorite chair by the large picture window, Alex sat down and opened the envelope.

The first sheet listed ten names. His name was second in line. In the number-one position was a Neal Delaney. Alex felt a muscle in his jaw clench. It was one thing to think about this for weeks now, but quite another to put a name to the man he'd replaced.

The second sheet contained two short paragraphs. Alex read them quickly, then a second time more slowly. The third, topped by the private investigator's letterhead, was a bill for services rendered plus expenses. Alex scarcely glanced at it, returning instead to the information sheet on Neal Delaney.

Thirty years old, had a congenital liver disease that was apparently inherited from his grandfather and known to skip generations. Diagnosed first week of July, immediately put on the list. Became critical two weeks later, moved to top position. Died on July 29 before an organ became available.

Shaken, Alex lowered the pages as Mitch walked in, sat down and looked at him. "I told you this wasn't a good idea."

Alex didn't know what he'd been expecting to see, what he'd *hoped* to learn. Probably that the guy had gotten a good liver right after his own surgery and that he was doing well. That would have eased his conscience a great deal. But this…this was a shocker.

Neal Delaney had died two days after Alex's surgery.

Wordlessly, he read the second paragraph. Neal's widow, Megan Delaney, was twenty-six, his son, Ryan, was seven. They lived in Twin Oaks, twenty miles northwest of Los Angeles where Megan now operated Delaney's Bed & Breakfast alone. Neal had had two insurance policies totaling $275,000.

Mitch glanced down at the sheet Alex had just read. "At least she's not broke, eh?"

Alex nodded, setting the packet onto the table alongside his chair. He pushed on the lounge chair's arms until the footrest rose and then stretched out. He felt uncharacteristically numb.

Sitting down opposite his friend, Mitch leaned forward, his dark eyes worried. "Chances are the man was too sick, Alex. He might have died *during* surgery, or maybe right after."

But Alex wasn't buying that. "They wouldn't have considered him if they hadn't thought he had a good chance. But every patient has a narrow window of opportunity. If no replacement organ shows up in time…" He let his words trail off.

"Damn it, I never should have hired this guy, never should have gone along with your cockamamy request." Angry with himself, with Alex for asking him, with the Fates, Mitch got up and paced the room.

That brought Alex around quicker than anything could have. "Look, it's not your fault. It's mine. My fault."

"No, it isn't!" Mitch became louder as his anger grew. "It's Ron's fault, but how can we blame him? I've got kids. I'd do it for them in a heartbeat. Think about it. Wouldn't you, if you had a kid?"

Alex's eyes were grave. "Maybe." But he didn't have a kid. Neal Delaney had had one, and now that boy had no father. Because of him. Absently, he rubbed his incision through his clothes.

Mitch got up and stood looking down. "You've got to put this aside, forget what you read. Think about it this way—if you'd died, your father would probably have given up and been dead inside a year. He'd have no one to live for after his other losses." He stepped closer. "Remember that saying that goes change the things you can and learn to live with the things you can't? That could've been written for you."

Alex drew in a deep breath. He had no business thrusting his concerns on Mitch. With no small effort, he made himself smile. "You're right. I'll try."

But that evening after the rain had stopped, Alex walked along the sandy shore and watched the waves roll in, wondering if he'd ever learn to live with what he'd learned today. He'd inadvertently been the cause of a man's death. It was one thing to risk his own neck countless times for the thrill of it or for God-only-knew what reason, but quite another to risk someone else's.

He wondered what kind of woman Neal's wife was. Was she bitter, lonely, angry? The insurance money wouldn't go very far over the long haul, not with a business to run and a growing child to raise. A fatherless child at that. And how much could she take in running a bed-and-breakfast? There were dozens along the California coast.

Damn, but this wasn't like him, focusing on others to the exclusion of most everything else. He'd always been a man who wanted to be responsible only for himself. He'd been more or less a loner all his life. Yet since his surgery and now since learning about Neal Delaney, his concerns had shifted somewhat. He couldn't seem to stop thinking about Neal's widow.

He couldn't help wondering if somehow she'd learned that another man had gotten the organ meant for her husband. Did she blame that faceless, nameless individual for living while Neal had died? Did she worry how she'd tell her young son the truth one day? And what was the boy like? Had he been close to his dad and was he now suddenly feeling lost and abandoned? Who'd take him to ball games, tell him about girls, teach him to drive?

But most of all, Alex wondered if he'd ever be able to get the Delaneys out of his mind.

In Twin Oaks, it was still raining, a quiet, steady September rain. Good for the flowers, Megan Delaney thought as she stood looking out her kitchen window. They'd had a dry spell, so rain was most welcome. Tomorrow, time permitting, she'd get out there and do some weeding, pick some wildflowers for the tables.

She finished washing the cookie sheets and baking pans, left them to air-dry, then moved to the counter to wrap up the evening's baked goods. In the morning, Grace would take the cookies, the zucchini bread and banana loaves to the Cornerstone Restaurant in town to be sold. The baking she did afforded her a good side income and she really didn't mind doing it most evenings.

Glancing over at her son stealthily reaching for another warm chocolate cookie, she smiled. His hair was as dark as hers, a lock falling onto his forehead. His eyes were a deeper blue than hers, large and round and inquisitive. An altogether handsome boy, Megan thought, as only a mother does. But she was also a mother who had to worry about cavities and dentist bills. "Hey, kid, I told you two was your limit."

"Just one more, Mom? I promise I won't ask again." Ryan made the sign of the cross over his heart, his mischievous grin revealing a space where his two front teeth were missing.

How could she refuse that face? "All right, but that's it." Just to be sure, she removed temptation from the table and began stacking cookies in the tall jar shaped like a clown. From long experience, she knew that even out of sight didn't necessarily mean out of mind for Ryan when it came to his favorite dessert.

"Is your project ready for tomorrow?" It was the third week of the new school semester and Ryan's third-grade teacher had already assigned a project. Each student was to make a dinosaur of his choice from papier-mâché. Megan had helped Ryan with his before dinner, but he was to have added the finishing touches.

"Yeah, I glued it into the shoebox I decorated yesterday. I even made some hills out of clay and stuck them around him to look like rocks. You think I'll win a prize, Mom?" Ryan washed down his last bite with milk, eyed the full-to-bursting cookie jar his mother finished filling and wondered if he dare push his luck and ask for one more. Nah, probably not. He didn't want her to get upset 'cause he had a favor to ask her. A big favor.

"I think you've got an excellent chance of winning a prize." Megan knew that all of the kids would probably receive some kind of prize. It was usually done that way in the lower grades to encourage participation.

"Mom," Ryan began, climbing down and putting his dish

and glass in the sink the way he'd been taught, "you know those kittens that Tommy's cat had last month?"

Megan almost groaned aloud, knowing exactly what was coming. "Uh-huh."

"Are you *sure* we can't take one? I mean, we'd be doing Tommy's mom a real favor 'cause she's got the mama cat and three kittens left and four are just too much work. This one is really cute, black with white paws and all cuddly. He likes me, Mom."

Megan steeled her heart and stood firm. "Sweetheart, we've talked about this. You know with so many guests coming and going around here, we can't have a kitten underfoot. He might get stepped on or maybe run away when someone leaves the door open. And some people are allergic to animals and can't stay where cats live. I can't afford to lose business because of a kitten, Ryan. Please try to understand." Living in a bed-and-breakfast had its drawbacks if you were a young boy.

Ryan heaved a dramatic, long-suffering sigh. "Okay. Only one day, can we, Mom? I mean one day when we don't have to have all these people living with us, can I have a kitten or a puppy?"

Megan felt a lump form in her throat. How could she explain the necessities of life versus a boy's desire for a pet to her son? "One day, Ryan, I promise."

His face brightened immediately. Basically a happy child, he was seldom sad-faced long.

She pulled him to her, hugging him fiercely, blinking back tears. Why were her emotions still so close to the surface? Of course, Neal's funeral with all its accompanying problems were part of the reason, but that had been weeks ago. For Ryan's sake, she needed to get a grip.

She buried her face in the sweet little-boy curve of his neck. He allowed it for all of five seconds, then pulled away, his attention roaming. "I love you, punkin," she whispered.

"Mom! You said you wouldn't call me that anymore. I'm almost eight, you know."

Megan smiled down at him. Too soon, Ryan was moving toward independence. Though in her head she knew that was as it should be, her heart wasn't ready to let him start the journey. "You're absolutely right. I forgot. But you won't be eight for another three months."

"Close enough. Can I go watch Looney Tunes?"

Glancing at the kitchen clock, she went back to packaging her remaining baked goods. "All right, but I'll be up to run your bath right afterward. School tomorrow."

"Okay." Ryan's white Nikes pounded up the uncarpeted back stairs leading to their third-floor living quarters.

"Was that the 101st Airborne Division marching upstairs?" Grace Romero asked as she came into the kitchen carrying an armload of clean dish towels and table linens.

"Sure sounded like that, didn't it?" Megan turned to smile at her assistant. Chief cook and bottle washer might fit better. Grace helped out in everything from the front desk and bookkeeping to upstairs maid, running errands and keeping an eye on Ryan. But mostly, Grace was her friend, a woman who'd saved her sanity on more than one occasion. "Think you can drive Ryan to school tomorrow morning? He's got a dinosaur project he has to take in, and I know if he rides the bus, he'll smash it somehow. I've got two couples from Oregon checking in early and I probably won't be finished with breakfast till late."

"Sure, no problem." Finished putting away the linens, Grace took a flat cardboard out of the cupboard and began shaping it into a box. "I can drop these at the Cornerstone on the way back."

Megan set aside the last loaf and reached out to hug her friend. "You're a godsend." Grace had answered her help-wanted ad shortly after she and Neal had bought the big older house and set out to remodel it into a bed-and-breakfast. Childless and divorced twice, Grace had no family this side of the border and only a few cousins in Mexico. She'd pitched in from the start and become like a member of the family.

Megan was certain she couldn't manage without her and told her so.

"You got that right." Grace grinned as she packed the box with baked goods.

Hurrying so she could spend a little time with Ryan before his bedtime, Megan quickly did a mental inventory, checking to make sure she had everything she needed for breakfast in the morning. When her Oregon guests arrived, all seven of her rooms, including the two larger suites, would be full. And three couples were staying a week. Maybe, just maybe, she'd be able to think about getting a new washer soon. The old one was on its last legs and small wonder since it struggled through at least ten loads daily.

Absently, she jerked open the cupboard to put away the cookie sheets and gasped as the door fell off into her hands, one of its hinges broken loose. Ruefully, she stared at the bent screws. "Not again. If it isn't one thing, it's another."

"What we need around here is a handyman, if there is such a thing somewhere on God's green earth. Or maybe just any man." Grace moved over to hold the door for Megan. "If only—"

"Don't! Don't you dare say if only Neal were here, he'd fix it. You know better, and so do I."

"You're right about that. I kept hoping he'd grab hold." Grace's opinion of Neal Delaney had never been high, not even during the early days. She'd spotted his aversion to work, his champagne tastes on a beer budget and, unfortunately, his wandering eye long before Megan had.

She'd hoped he'd grab hold, too, Megan thought, but he never really had. "You and I can fix this. We don't need a male around here except the one upstairs watching Looney Tunes."

Megan walked to the laundry room and reached for her toolbox. *Her* toolbox. Neal had had trouble pounding a nail in straight. During his many absences, she'd slowly gathered a small assortment of tools for minor repairs and learned how to use them.

Back in the kitchen, she rummaged around and found the correct anchor, then shoved it into the hole left by the bent screw. While Grace held the cupboard door, Megan threw away the old screws, put a new one through the hinge and, using her automatic screwdriver, fixed the first hinge, then tightened the second. Pausing to look at the repair, she nodded satisfactorily. "Good as new. Until the next time."

"Until you yank it too hard again, you mean. Honey, you move at double time. You've got to slow down." Grace nodded her russet head toward the window. "There're roses out there you've never smelled. And snapdragons and peonies and all manner of growing things. You need to get out there and smell the flowers now and again. All work and no play makes Megan a pale and tired little innkeeper. You need to have some fun. You remember what that is?"

Megan frowned. Did she? Not really. "Fun for me is getting the bills paid, keeping the rooms filled, being with Ryan and you. I don't need anything more than that."

"The hell you say, sweetie. A woman needs a man. No child or girlfriend or full house can match that kind of fun." Grace's dark eyes danced with excitement, with memories.

Grace was still a very attractive woman, Megan thought, with her thick auburn hair that she usually wore in a twist during working hours and down around her shoulders when she went out. Which was far oftener than Megan did, even though Grace was on the far side of forty. Odd how the woman was still looking for Mr. Right after two disastrous marriages, the first to a man who robbed her blind and the second a drinker whose reckless antics nearly bankrupted her. Hope springs eternal for some, she supposed.

But not for her. "No, thanks. I've tried that kind of fun and the cost is too high."

Grace sobered. "Honey, every man's not like Neal. Or my exes, for that matter. Somewhere out there is a guy who'll—"

"Sweep me off my feet? Whisk me away to paradise? Puh-leeze. I'll leave the romantic daydreams to you."

Grace's unlined face moved into a gentle smile. "I know

how you feel, honey. I just don't want life to pass you by.
You're young. You need something besides working all day.
If not a date, then go shopping, take in a movie, get your hair
done. You know I'll watch over things here.''

Megan shook her head. ''I don't need time off. I need to
know that this place is turning into a success, that we're safe
and secure.'' A feeling she hadn't experienced in far too long.

Grace knew the reasons Megan felt so strongly about
hearth and home, so she didn't argue anymore. ''Okay, I give
up. I'm going up to my room to watch 'NYPD Blue.' That
Jimmy Smits makes my juices flow.''

Smiling, Megan turned out the kitchen light. ''Grace, honestly.''

Grace's lusty laugh preceded her up the stairs.

Chapter 2

Alex tossed down his pen and swiveled in his desk chair so he could look out at the sea. The corporate headquarters for Shephard Construction was on the fourth floor of a high-rise on the western shore of San Diego. It was a beautiful spring day, the 27th of April, the sun was beaming down on the breakers, and he could see over a dozen sailboats gliding through the water.

He ached like the devil to be out there with them, skimming along on his boat, *Black Sheep,* free as a bird. Alex sighed. Exactly nine months since he'd had his transplant surgery and he was bored out of his gourd.

He'd been back in his office since the first week of December, though only half days until mid-January. He'd done mostly desk work, leaving the scouting and traveling to Mitch, on doctor's orders. Benson was as much of an old lady as his father.

Finally, by March, the good doctor had graciously agreed that he could gradually resume some of his former pursuits, though not too many until he had at least a year or more under his belt. Even so, he'd attached several caveats.

Don't overdo, don't get overtired. Don't engage in strenuous physical activities. Just don't do anything stupid. And above all, don't get an infection.

He might as well have said don't live, just exist, Alex thought. Hell, he wasn't exactly planning to walk a tightrope across the Grand Canyon. He'd gone hiking on Cowles Mountain last month, even though those trails were nothing compared to most others he'd climbed in the past. And last weekend he'd gone exploring in Anza-Borrego Desert State Park and even slept out under the stars.

But he longed for something more challenging, like a week in Death Valley, horseback riding on an open stretch of hard-packed sand, maybe scuba diving in some remote lagoon. However, since none of his friends was available to go on any of these treks with him and he'd decided going alone might be pushing the envelope, he'd postponed any adventurous trips for now. One day, though, he'd hopefully be able to do those things again, and more. It was high time he resumed his life at full tilt. Past time.

Rising, he walked to the bank of windows and stared out at puffy white clouds. A Santa Ana was in the making, bringing hot, dry winds and unseasonably warm weather for late April. There were a few hardy souls in the water upshore, probably tourists. Except for a few surfers, the locals rarely wandered into cold ocean water even though the air temperature hovered around eighty.

Surfing. Something else he'd enjoyed once upon a time.

Alex rolled his shoulders, then patted his hard, flat stomach. His twice-daily walks that had gradually turned into jogs along the beach had paid off. He'd regained the weight he'd lost and was lean and trim. The scar had faded to a pinkish hue, no longer an angry red. He took his medications religiously and hadn't experienced any of the side effects of bloating and increased hair growth he'd been warned of, not so far anyway. He wasn't restricted to a special diet, nor did he feel he should be hampered by Benson's limitations after all this time.

In other words, he was about as healthy as he would ever be and it was time to stop acting like an invalid. And time to look into something that bothered him. A lot.

Turning, Alex strolled back to his desk and picked up the newspaper article he'd been reading. A parcel of land had become available for possible development either as a residential or a commercial building site. It was his job to scout out such parcels and ascertain if any would meet the requirements of Shephard Construction. The fact that this land was located in a small city twenty miles from Los Angeles made it appealing since Ron didn't like to acquire too far from home base. But that wasn't its greatest appeal.

The fact that the city was Twin Oaks was.

Twin Oaks where Neal Delaney had lived and died almost a year ago. The city where Neal's family presumably still lived. The town where Delaney's Bed & Breakfast was located.

Obviously, Alex needed a place to stay while scouting locations for his company. Most likely there were hotels and motels in and around Twin Oaks. But on the trips when he stayed for a week or so, he tried to book a room at places that had a cozy, home atmosphere. He'd never liked motel chains or formal hotels. A B and B would be perfect.

Sitting down, Alex sighed. Who was he kidding? The site inspection was a secondary reason for going. For months, as he'd recuperated at home and even after he'd returned to the office, not a day had gone by that he hadn't thought of the Delaneys. He wasn't sure what he hoped to accomplish by visiting Twin Oaks, but he knew he had to go. He had to find some sort of closure to this whole thing before he went stark raving mad.

Both his father and Mitch would think he'd gone around the bend if he told them his plans. So he simply wouldn't, saying only that he planned to drive up the coast on a scouting expedition and he'd check in from time to time. The two men had fallen into the habit of humoring him since his surgery, and while it often annoyed him, today he would use it.

Alex studied his calendar a moment, then picked up the phone, checked with Information and dialed the number before he could change his mind.

When he hung up four minutes later, he was frowning. The voice at the other end had been female with a definite hint of Spanish. A name like Megan Delaney didn't sound Spanish. Of course, she could have sold the business by now, added the check to her insurance money and relocated to any number of places.

He should have asked for her directly, he thought, scowling at the phone. But what would he have said if she'd asked where he got her name? Maybe the woman was only the desk clerk. Oh well, it was only a two-hour drive. He'd made an open-ended reservation, so if the Delaneys were gone, he'd check out the parcel of land, then cut his visit short. But if she and her son were there...

What? What would he say, do? Nothing, Alex decided. It wouldn't be wise to reveal who he was, how he knew of her. If she was aware of the list, she'd toss him out on his rear. Even if she didn't, any explanation would sound lame. Best to play it by ear.

Quickly, Alex packed his briefcase, tossed in the newspaper article and snapped it closed. He'd pop into Dad's office and let him know he was off on a scouting trip, drop by his condo to throw a few things in a bag and be on his way.

If nothing else, it was a great day for a drive.

Skimming along the coastal highway, Alex kept his mind firmly on the gorgeous scenery, the rocky cliffs, the black rocks slippery with dark green moss, the Pacific endlessly smashing onto the shore. He passed sunny beaches with white sand and cliffside homes with breathtaking views, the scent of the ocean teasing his nostrils. He had the top down on his blue Porsche, his hair blowing about in a stiff breeze and the sun warming his face.

Life was good.

It wasn't until he had to veer east onto the inland road, following the sign toward Twin Oaks, that he allowed himself to focus on his undoubtedly misguided mission. And he still couldn't figure out just why he wanted to meet Neal Delaney's family.

Ostensibly, it likely was to make sure they were all right at least financially so he could appease his nagging conscience. What if they weren't? Would he then drop anonymous check donations into the widow's bank account monthly? Would that help him sleep better?

At a curve in the road, Alex spotted a roadside billboard advertising Delaney's Bed & Breakfast two miles ahead. He followed the directions, his powerful car climbing the winding, hilly road with ease. Minutes later, he pulled into a circular driveway where a discreet sign read Welcome To Delaney's Bed & Breakfast.

Someone had a green thumb. A colorful bed of California poppies bloomed within the driveway circle. Pink bougainvillea trailed up the stucco fencing from the side yard to the back. On the far right was a patch that seemed to be an herb garden beneath three tall royal palms that looked as if they'd stood there since the beginning of time.

Alex parked in the paved area next to a four-wheel drive. The only other car was an older tan Mustang off to the side. Either the house wasn't fully up or nearly everyone was away somewhere. Getting out, he took a moment to stretch and look around.

The main building was three stories high with a center entrance and two wide wings, topped by a slanted black roof. The pale gray wood could have used a touching up, he thought, along with the shutters and trim painted a Wedgwood blue. It didn't yet look shabby, but it might soon. Thick and healthy green vines trailed along each side, winding along the third-floor windows. Wisps of smoke curled upward from a redbrick chimney, maybe from a fireplace. Twin Oaks was at a much higher elevation than San Diego, though he didn't really think it was chilly enough for a fire.

A country-style mailbox painted poppy red was near the entrance. A small two-wheel boy's bike leaned against its post. Did it belong to Neal Delaney's son? Alex wondered.

All things considered, Delaney's Bed & Breakfast wasn't bad, he thought as he walked toward the arched front door. He'd been right; there was a cozy, countrified feel to it.

Alex stepped into the spacious foyer and onto a red Mexican tile floor. A chest-high walnut check-in desk flanked by twin rubber tree plants was against the far wall facing the door. A stately grandfather clock stood off to one side. The scent of warm apples and cinnamon had him remembering that he'd skipped lunch.

Through the archway off to his right was a comfortable room furnished in pastels, Southwestern-style. Two women were watching Oprah on a large-screen television while an older couple played chess at a table by the window. At the far end, glowing embers smoldered in a large stone fireplace. The colorful Indian carpet was a bit faded, but the room was neat and clean.

To his immediate left was a large dining room with a long buffet table near double swinging doors. Half a dozen maple tables filled the room, some with place settings for four, others two and a larger round one for six. Here the carpeting was a rich red, the tablecloths checkered and the earthenware chunky and casual. The chandelier was heavy wrought iron and smoky glass. A woman with auburn hair, her back to him, was arranging fresh flowers in several vases. Altogether inviting, Alex decided.

Since no one seemed to notice him, he was about to ring the small bell on the desk when a woman straightened from behind the desk where she'd obviously been stooping down to search for something. Shoving the box of printed forms she held under the countertop, she checked her watch, looking worried. But she erased her frown as she raised deep blue eyes to his and gave him a welcoming smile.

"Can I help you?"

"I'm Alex Shephard. I believe I have a reservation."

"Oh, yes. We're glad to have you with us."

"Glad to be here." Not for the first time, Alex wondered why people who worked in hotels and such often spoke in the plural.

She reached for a registration form from a slot in the desk and turned it toward him, then handed him a pen. "If you'd fill this out for us, please."

He watched her make several notations in red ink on a card. Was this Megan Delaney, or was Megan the woman in the dining room? No, the flower arranger seemed older than the wife of a man of thirty, though he couldn't rule her out.

More likely this one, he decided, since she looked to be in her mid-twenties. She had a great face, oval with high cheekbones, and then there were those sky blue eyes. Her mouth was wide and inviting, but right now her lower lip was caught between her teeth. The frown was back on her face. A rush of guilt had Alex wondering if the loss of her husband and all that that meant had given her a perpetual frown.

He began filling out the registration form while continuing to study her from under lowered lashes. There was a small, interesting depression in her chin, less of a dimple than a dent. She had a distracted air about her as she again glanced at her watch, then toward the front door.

"Is something wrong?" he asked, pausing, more to make conversation than because he needed to know.

Megan swiped at wispy bangs that reached to her eyebrows. "I hope not." She shot him a quick smile, then looked pointedly at the unfinished form in front of him. "Are you having trouble with that?"

His turn to smile. "Not really." He resumed writing as running footsteps sounded behind him, coming closer. Thundering now, accompanied by heavy breathing. Curious, Alex swung around.

A small boy with dark windblown hair came racing in, dragging a dripping backpack by one soggy shoulder strap.

His once white Nikes were muddy, his beltless jean shorts were at half-mast, and his yellow polo shirt was streaked with dirt. His round face was twisted into a comically nervous look. "Mom, don't be mad," he began.

Megan skirted the desk, so relieved to see her son that she had trouble not smiling at his forlorn appearance. He had only one short block to walk from where the school bus let him off along with two other children, but still she worried, especially when he was more than ten minutes late like today. She had a pretty good idea what had happened as she stood looking down at him. "Again?"

Eyes downcast, he nodded dejectedly. "Me and Bobby were wrestling when I slipped in this mud puddle." Looking up, he gave her a hopeful smile. "I won the match, though, and I'll clean my backpack all by myself, honest. Probably nothing inside got wet 'cause I grabbed it right out."

It was the third time in as many days. The morning showers never dried up enough by afternoon and were magnets for small boys. Ryan's best friend, Bobby, was as prone to puddle hopping as her son. "If you'd carry your backpack the way you're supposed to, using the shoulder straps, you wouldn't always be dropping it."

A horrified look screwed up the boy's face. "Mom! Only geeks do that."

Megan dabbed at a muddy spot on his cheek, needing to touch him after her anxious ten minutes to reassure herself he was all right. "Maybe, but geeks don't have wet backpacks." She dropped her gaze to his Nikes, then to the muddy footprints trailing in his wake. She'd have to get the mop, again. "Take your shoes off here and go upstairs. I want you to wash up and change *clothes* before you hit the kitchen, okay?"

"Okay." Relieved she wasn't mad, he gave his mother a quick hug, then stepped out of his untied Nikes, the shoelaces trailing mud. Turning, he noticed the tall man watching him. "Hi. I'm Ryan. See you later." Flashing a sunny grin, he grabbed his backpack, the movement liberally spraying Alex with drops of brown water. Ryan's eyes grew wide. "Oops. Sorry." With an anxious glance at his mother, he ran in his damp stocking feet through the dining room. "Hi, Grace," he yelled out as he bounded through the swinging doors.

Amusement on his face, Alex stared after the boy. He wasn't used to children of any age, hadn't spent much time around them since he'd been one himself. The occasional dinner at Mitch's house with his two kids around the table was enough, even though they were quiet and shy. Unlike Ryan Delaney.

"He's like a small tornado," he commented, brushing off his pants.

"That he is." Gingerly, she set Ryan's muddy shoes on a paper towel behind the desk, then walked around to inspect his slacks. "I'm sorry you got splashed. Can I get those cleaned for you?"

"No, thanks. I'm washable." Alex let his gaze trail down her curves from shoulders to breasts to slender hips and hoped the effect she had on him didn't show on his face. She was definitely nicely put together.

Still, Megan felt the need to explain. "He usually goes around back to our private entrance. He's been taught to stay out of the way of guests." She was never certain how strangers felt about children, especially a man alone. Then again, if he objected to a child on the premises, he could find another place to stay. She needed the business, but not as much as she needed Ryan to feel secure. Pen poised, she eyed him as he stared thoughtfully at the muddy footprints on the tile. "You look a little uncertain. Do you have a problem with children?"

"No, no problem." Alex bent to finish his form. Not as long as they weren't his.

Megan took a moment to study Alex Shephard now that her concern for Ryan's safety wasn't a distraction. Tall, over six feet, with football shoulders and a lean, tanned face. Sun-streaked hair and big sea green eyes with long lashes many a woman would kill for. He was wearing tan khakis and a denim shirt. Not exactly business attire. Most open-ended Monday check-ins were business people. Then again, he could be on vacation.

Aware of her scrutiny, Alex put down the pen and met her eyes. "Do I pass inspection?"

Instead of looking embarrassed, Megan laughed. "Sorry. Occupational hazard. When you allow people into your home, even paying guests, you kind of like to check them over. I didn't mean to be rude."

"You're not. And I'm not an ax murderer." He took a business card from his pocket and handed it to her. "I'm scouting locations for possible land development and construction for my father's firm. I'm not sure how long my business will take, which is why I left the departure date blank. Probably at least a week, if you can accommodate me."

Megan read the card and nodded. "Matter of fact, we have two rooms available. Our French provincial bedroom in back on the first floor and our Southwestern suite on the second, which is larger and has a sitting area, as well. Both have private baths. Your choice."

"The suite will do just fine." French provincial wasn't even close to his first choice.

She reached behind her for the key and held it out to him. "We don't have air-conditioning, but the windows open and there's always a breeze this far up the mountain. Breakfast is served from seven to nine. Picnic lunches are available if you let us know the night before. We do offer some dinners by special arrangement." She'd begun the dinner practice three years ago when she'd noticed quite a few repeat guests, some honeymoon couples, others celebrating anniversaries and special events. It had been a big hit from the start.

"Sounds good."

"Great. There's no elevator. Do you need help taking up your bags?"

Lifting one golden eyebrow, he let his eyes roam down her slender frame and back up, wondering if she was putting him on. Did she honestly carry up guests' luggage? "I think I can handle it, but thanks."

"All right, then. I'm Megan Delaney and my assistant, Grace, is around here somewhere. Please let us know if there's anything you need. I hope you enjoy your stay with us." Turning, Megan busied herself straightening papers.

Megan did carry the bags for a few folks, older people and some who just looked frail. It had become a habit to ask, but obviously, a macho guy like Alex Shephard would never allow a woman to help with his luggage.

As the man in question walked out to his car, Grace came from the dining room and joined Megan at the desk, her eyes following him. "Now, there's a fine specimen. Was he wearing a wedding ring?"

Megan sent her a cool look. "Don't start."

Hunger had Alex leaving his comfortable suite after settling in to wander off in search of food. He decided to walk the two miles into town, remembering a small café he'd spotted on the drive through. Half an hour later, he found the restaurant he'd been seeking.

The Cornerstone had four booths and six tables, served three meals a day according to the sign on the door, accepted all major credit cards and sold freshly baked goods from an appetizing display case—pies and cookies and assorted loaves of bread, all homemade. Though he was not usually much of a dessert eater, the assortment nonetheless had Alex's mouth watering as he slid into a vinyl booth by the window.

It was early, not yet five, and only one other booth was occupied. The two women sitting there were obviously lingering over coffee, perhaps after a late lunch. He studied the handwritten menu as a middle-aged redhead wearing a pink uniform with a huge, lacy white handkerchief trailing out of a breast pocket walked over.

"Coffee?" she asked, the carafe poised in her hand.

"That'd be great." He held out his cup. "How's the pot roast?"

"Wonderful. I made it myself." She grinned, revealing a crooked eyetooth. "I'm Emily, the owner. You just passing through?"

Alex had been in dozens of restaurants just like the Cornerstone in dozens of small towns up and down the coast on his scouting expeditions. He knew that the owners, usually friendly, knew everyone in town and were the best source of information around. "Pretty much. I work for a land development firm. We're interested in the parcel at Grayson and Thomas at the east end of town."

Emily nodded. "I know the one. Been vacant forever. Old man Parsons owns it. His wife died last year and his kids put him in a nursing home just last month. Guess they want to sell the land to pay for his stay. Elderly care can get real expensive."

"So I've heard." The Parsons kids had a need to sell and weren't just testing the waters. That would be helpful to know when it came time to negotiate.

"Where you staying?"

"Delaney's Bed & Breakfast."

Emily's smile was genuine. "No finer place around here." She nodded toward the menu. "What'll it be?"

Alex ordered the pot roast and was amazed when the heaping plateful of meat and vegetables was set before him in a matter of minutes, along with a generous salad and warm rolls. Nothing stingy about Emily's place. He dug in.

He was scooping up the last of the rich, dark gravy with a piece of roll when Emily sauntered back to refill his cup. "That's the best meal I've had in months," he told her honestly.

Emily beamed a smile at him as she poured. "I like to see a man eat hearty. How about a piece of rhubarb pie?"

"Did you make that, too?"

"No, sir. Megan Delaney makes all our baked goods. It'll melt in your mouth, I guarantee."

Alex didn't bother to hide his surprise as he gazed at the

display case. "She baked all that? You'd think she'd have enough to do running the bed-and-breakfast."

"Megan bakes like an angel. I'd buy from her even if she didn't need the money." She glanced up and smiled as the two ladies got up to leave. "I donate the day-old stuff to the church."

Even more puzzled, Alex frowned. "It wouldn't seem she'd need the money. Her place is nearly full up on a Monday night, only one vacancy left after I checked in. Not bad for a small, out-of-the-way place. I...heard her husband died, but surely he had insurance." Alex felt a bit squeamish inquiring behind Megan Delaney's back, but the reason for his trip was to make sure she and her son weren't in need.

Emily shrugged. "I suppose there was insurance, but then they did a lot of remodeling when they first bought that place and probably ran up some hefty bills. Plus it's a big house to keep up. I don't know, really. Megan's real closemouthed. I do know she's grateful for every crumb I sell here."

Alex shoved aside his empty plate and leaned back. "You've known her a long while, then?"

"Sure have. She's never had it easy, poor girl."

"How's that?"

Since the place was empty, Emily sat down across from the young man uninvited, one hand rubbing her sore back. "Her family rented a house in town, only a block from mine. Her mom and two sisters still live there. My daughter, Katie, is a good friend of Megan's. The father just up and drove off one day, leaving his wife with three girls to raise alone. Megan was about ten. Dottie, her mother, had to struggle ever since. It was awfully hard on Megan since she was the oldest."

Alex could relate somewhat since he, too, had lost a parent at an early age. But at least his family hadn't had to struggle.

"And now," Emily went on, "since Neal's gone, Megan's got to raise that sweet little boy all alone. She's a wonderful mother."

Guilt washed over Alex and he wondered if it showed.

"She seems too young to have a boy that age. He must be seven or so." He sipped his coffee.

"Ryan's eight now, I believe. But you're right. My Brian was interested in Megan back in high school, but she had eyes only for Neal. 'Course he was handsome and a real charmer, but you'd think a smart girl like Megan would've seen through all that. But then, she was young. We make a lot of mistakes when we're young."

Here was his chance to find out what kind of a man Neal Delaney had been and Alex didn't hesitate to take it. "You didn't care for her husband?"

Emily topped off his coffee before answering. "I don't wish anyone an early death like Neal had, but from what I could see, he wasn't much of a husband or father. Couldn't hold down a job even though he had himself a fancy college degree. Everyone liked him 'cause he was good-looking. But charm don't put bread on the table. Megan worked almost up to the day that boy was born and went back the week after. Then Neal's folks died in a car crash and they bought that big old house with the insurance money. Megan's idea, I'd wager. Neal would've frittered away the money. Good thing they did, too, or she and Ryan might not have a roof over their heads today. At first, I thought Neal was going to finally be happy running that place. He did a lot of the renovating himself with Megan working alongside him, scraping, painting, replanting the grounds." Emily ran a hand through her short red hair.

"I imagine it took a while to get the business going." Most new businesses took several years to show a profit, Alex knew.

"They didn't have too many guests right off, but within the year, things picked up. Megan's awfully hospitable and no one can beat her cooking. Word spread and folks kept coming back, telling others. 'Course there's only seven rooms to let, three down and four on the second floor. The third's for the family and Grace. With a small place, you got to keep those rooms filled every night to show a profit."

Emily looked up as a family of four, parents and two young children, came in and headed for a table. She gave them a familiar wave—probably regular customers. "Anyway," she said, sliding out of the booth, "Megan's going to make it, I'm sure. She's a hard worker and a real sweetheart." She nodded toward the desserts. "How about that pie, or something else?"

Alex shook his head. "I'm stuffed, but thanks."

Emily pulled his check from her pocket and slipped it onto the table. "Come back and see us, you hear?"

"Thanks, I will." Rising, he placed several bills on the table, including a generous tip, and left the Cornerstone. Strolling back up the hill, he was thoughtful.

Megan Delaney, he'd learned, was a great innkeeper, hospitable, a terrific cook, a wonderful mother and a hard worker who had, according to Emily, led a difficult life. Neal Delaney, a man with a degree who couldn't seem to hold a job, hadn't been much of a father or husband, but he'd been handsome and fun. Yet Megan had had eyes only for Neal even back in high school.

What had their marriage really been like? Alex wondered. Had Neal been so charming she'd overlooked his job difficulties? Had Megan loved him enough to forgive his shortcomings as a family man? And what about the insurance money? Had $275,000 not stretched enough to pay off all the bills? Could Megan no longer afford to finish renovating? Was that why the place had a slightly shabby air about it and why Megan had to do baking on the side?

A lot of questions, Alex thought. And he meant to find some answers.

"Not bad, Ryan, but the second one's wrong," Megan told her son. "How do you spell *impossible?*"

Seated at the kitchen table, Ryan wound his feet around the chair legs and screwed up his face thoughtfully. "*I-m-p-o-s-i-b-l.* Impossible." He gazed up at his mother hopefully.

Removing freshly baked cookies from the sheet with a

spatula, Megan looked over her shoulder at him. "Not quite. Two *s*'s."

"Two? Why two? Why do they double letters anyway? It just confuses everyone." Reluctantly, he stuffed in another *s*. "I'll mention that the next time Webster rewrites his dictionary . One more thing. There's a silent *e* at the end."

Clearly exasperated, Ryan bent his head and propped it in one hand. "That's another dumb thing. What good are silent letters?"

Lips twitching, Megan thought the kid had a point. "I don't know, but we have to learn them. Erase the word and write it over."

"Ah, Mom…"

"Ryan." She watched until he blew out a frustrated breath before picking up his pencil. Perhaps *impossible* ought to be spelled *R-y-a-n*, Megan thought. Hearing the swinging doors open, she glanced over.

"Hi," Alex said, smiling. "I hope I'm not intruding. I was wondering if I could have a glass. There isn't one in my room."

"Oh, sure." Megan set aside the cookie sheet and spatula, reached into the overhead cupboard and got down a glass for him. "Sorry about that."

"Thanks."

Gazing about, Alex noticed a warmth to the kitchen that had nothing to do with the heat from the ovens. The floor was covered by hand-painted Spanish tiles, the walls pale blue, the curtains a sunny yellow. Pictures obviously drawn by her son and a variety of reminder notes were attached to the large refrigerator door with assorted magnets in the shape of mushrooms. Half a dozen African violets lined the windowsill above the double sink. A kitchen witch in gingham was next to the stove and a wooden plaque declaring this to be Megan's Kitchen hung on the opposite wall. *Homey* was the word that again came to mind.

Alongside the table, he glanced down at the boy painstakingly printing on a smudged paper. "Homework, eh? I used to hate homework."

Recognizing an ally, Ryan nodded his agreement. "Me, too. Were you good at spelling?" Anything to put off working.

"So-so. Do you need help?"

"He's just finishing, thanks," Megan told him. She set the cookie sheet and spatula in the sink and stepped to the table, wiping her hands on a towel.

Looking over the boy's shoulder as he carefully wrote a word, Alex smiled. "I always had trouble with *impossible,* too. I never knew if I should double the *m,* the *s* or the *l.*"

One hand on her hip, Megan cocked her head at him. Had he been listening on the other side of the door. "Is that a fact?"

"Maybe we should double them all, just in case." Ryan giggled at his own joke.

Alex couldn't help noticing the four loaves of some kind of nut bread, the two pies and the three boxes of cookies stacked on the long counter. He turned to find Megan's frankly assessing gaze on him. "I had dinner tonight at the Cornerstone. Emily speaks very highly of you and your baked goods."

"Emily's very kind." But she had a tendency to talk too much, Megan thought, wondering what all she'd told this stranger. The woman meant well, but gossiping was second nature to her.

Finished finally, Ryan wanted back in the conversation. "You've got a really neat car. What's it called? I've never seen one like it before."

"A Porsche 930 Turbo."

"Wow! My dad used to have a red Corvette convertible, but we had to sell it when he died. Can I have a ride one day?"

"Sure thing," Alex said before Megan could comment. "If it's all right with your mother, that is."

"Can I, Mom?" His eyes were dancing with excitement.

"We'll see. It's time for you to go up and take your shower. Tomorrow's a school day."

"One more cookie, please?" He looked over at his ally. "Mom makes the best chocolate chip cookies in the whole world."

"So I've been told." He, too, looked expectantly at Megan. "They're my favorite."

"Mine, too," Ryan answered. "And peanut butter."

A smart woman knows when she's outnumbered and out-maneuvered. "All right, but just one." She handed Ryan a cookie in a napkin. "Now scoot—and remember, the dirty clothes go in the hamper, not on the floor."

"Thanks, Mom." He turned to Alex and caught the wink, then grinned. "Bye." Already chewing, he marched up the stairs.

Turning to the co-conspirator, Megan held out the plate. "Would you care for a cookie?"

"Thanks." Alex took one and noticed it was still warm. He remembered eating cookies warm from the oven before his mother died. Later, Maddy had made cookies often, but always when he was at school, so they were cooled by the time he got home. He took a fragrant bite and almost purred. "Emily's right. You bake like an angel."

Megan raised a brow at that. "She's a bit prejudiced, I think." She turned to the sink, then filled it with soapy water. She never liked putting her baking things in the dishwasher.

Alex felt he had to say something. "I apologize for coming in if the kitchen's off-limits to paying guests."

She spoke over her shoulder as she worked. "It's not. Our guests have the run of the first floor and the grounds. As long as you don't mind if I finish up here." She rinsed a muffin pan and set it on the counter. She wasn't used to a man in her kitchen. For that matter, few guests took up her offer to freely roam about except in the lounge off the lobby.

"Go right ahead." Alex glanced at his watch, saw that it was nearly eight. She would have had to be up by at least six to start serving breakfast at seven. Yet she looked as fresh as when he'd arrived, her yellow slacks and blouse spotless. She'd taken off her shoes, though, and he saw that her toenails were painted a bright pink. "You put in some mighty long days, what with the inn and doing all this baking."

"I don't mind." She set another pan to drain, cocked an ear and heard the shower upstairs go on. Good. Ryan was following orders without being reminded for a change.

Finished with his dessert, Alex walked over and grabbed the towel he spotted hanging on a hook, then picked up a pan and began drying it.

Surprised, Megan paused. "Oh, no. You can't do that. You're a paying guest, for heaven's sake." She reached for the towel.

He wouldn't let her have it. "Listen, I'm a guy who can't sit still. I don't feel like going anywhere or watching TV. Please, let me do this." Up close to her, he caught her scent, a light floral, perfectly suiting her, mingled with the baking smells. He also noticed a flour smudge on her cheek just under one eye. He almost reached up to dust it away, but stopped himself. After all, he hardly knew this woman. And he had the feeling she wouldn't welcome his touch.

Megan glanced toward the swinging doors, wishing Grace hadn't gone out tonight. "This is really unusual. I feel awkward having you helping out in the kitchen."

Alex set the first dry pan aside, picked up another. "Please don't. I can't sit back and watch someone work and not pitch in."

Megan forced herself to relax. He was awfully nice and easy to talk with. But he still made her nervous.

"What about your husband? Didn't he help out in the kitchen?" Watching her expressive face, he saw her mouth tighten slightly and her eyes lower.

"No." Neal hadn't been fond of kitchens. Or of work, period. But she wouldn't think about Neal right now. She was certain chatty Emily had told this man that her husband had died last year. No secrets in small towns. Well, not many anyway.

Alex wanted to keep the conversation rolling, so he searched his mind for a more comfortable topic. "Are you familiar with the parcel of land at Grayson and Thomas? I believe the Parsons family owns it."

Megan's features relaxed. "Yes, I know where that is. Is that the land you're here about?"

"Yes. I've got an appointment tomorrow with a representative of Mr. Parsons. First, I want to go take a look at it, walk the area, so to speak."

Finished with the last pan, she rinsed and dried her hands before moving to the table to begin packaging the loaves. "And what would your firm be building on this land?"

"I'm not sure. I have to go to the courthouse and check on the zoning, maybe hire someone to do a feasibility study. Twin Oaks is kind of a sleepy little town. Do you think it could handle more housing in that neighborhood?"

Megan measured plastic wrap and worked as she considered his question. "There's a lack of middle-income housing here, I think. There are plenty of big homes, older ones, along the cliffs. Most have been in the same family for generations. And there's some low-income housing on the far side of town near the railroad tracks. Nothing much in the middle."

Alex set down the last pan and dangled the towel in his hands. He was fascinated by her eyes, a deeper shade of sapphire blue tonight. He'd noted that they crinkled at the corners when she'd gazed at her son and almost glowed. What kind of a fool had Neal Delaney been not to be a good husband to this woman, nor a good father to that sharp little kid? Maybe the guy had married before he'd been ready. Alex could relate.

Clearing his throat, he returned to the subject. "But if we build that kind of housing, will they come? Will enough middle-income families migrate to Twin Oaks?"

Megan shrugged. "Good question. I don't know the answer."

"You've lived here all your life, or so Emily said. What made you stay while others have left?"

Blowing her bangs from her forehead, Megan shook her head. "Another good question. Lots of reasons, none very interesting." His questions were bordering on the personal, on things she didn't want to discuss with him or anyone else. She wrapped the last loaf and put the roll of plastic wrap away, then moved to the back door. "Want to check out our gardens?" she asked, slipping bare feet into her sandals.

She was back to talking in the plural again, Alex realized, as if Neal were still alive and they were a couple working this little inn together. That sort of thing was hard to turn off, he supposed. As he stepped outside with her, he also realized she was good at changing subjects without seeming to.

The air was mildly cool and fragrant with the scent of shadowy purple wisteria vines along the stucco fence. There were two nearly overgrown paths between the rows of rosebushes and marigolds and azaleas. The dew was heavy on the leaves as Alex followed Megan along one trail to a large smooth rock at the end.

A night bird called to a mate as Megan sat down on the rock, gazing up at a half-moon playing hide-and-seek among the clouds. "Looks like we'll have rain again tonight or tomorrow morning."

Alex was busy studying the plantings, noticing that the rosebushes needed propping up with sticks, that the alyssum needed thinning and that weeds had all but taken over the ice plants. Hands on his hips, he stood surveying the garden. It was obvious that Megan didn't have time to keep this up along with everything else she did. He wondered if she'd welcome his help. It wasn't much, but it was one thing he could do to lighten her load. And lighten his conscience.

"I like gardens," he began. "My mother loved flowers. I used to help her all the time. She'd explain each variety to me, tell me whether it would do well in the sun or the shade, how much water it needed, how much sun it could handle. After she died, I kept up our garden until I went away to college."

A strange admission from a man she'd thought was probably a well-to-do businessman who'd hire such things done. She watched him bend, pick a daisy and hand it to her with such casual ease you knew he'd done it many times before for many other women. He looked like a California surfer with that tan and that flashy car and that killer smile, more interested in fun than flowers. Still, a man who spoke sentimentally about his mother and enjoyed gardens couldn't be one of the boys in black hats, could he? However, bad news came in many shapes, she'd learned.

"How old were you when she died?"

"Twelve."

"That's rough. I lost my dad when I was ten." That's how Megan always thought of her father's departure. To say he'd walked out on his entire family made her too angry.

He caught the small lie and didn't blame her for it. It was hard to admit that a parent had chosen to leave. Stooping, Alex tugged at a weed that lifted easily out of the moist ground. "Maybe tomorrow, after my meetings, I can come out here and do a little pruning and weeding. I had surgery not too long ago. Gardening's good therapy."

Megan felt her back stiffen. "Thanks for the offer, but there's no need. I'll get to the garden by week's end."

He looked up at her, at the rigid way she held herself, her eyes averted. "I didn't mean to insult you. I don't have all that much to do and—"

"No." She never should have allowed him to dry her pans, to invade her kitchen, to critique her yard. "My guests don't weed my garden. I'll get to it when I have the time. Until then, they'll be fine."

"Are you always so stubborn, so independent?"

"Yes, when I think I'm doing the right thing."

Straightening, Alex dusted off his hands. Apparently, he was going about this all wrong. Time to rethink his approach. Tomorrow. Tonight, he was a little tired from trying too hard. "All right. Good night, then." Retracing his steps, Alex went back inside.

Megan watched him go, her eyes narrowing. Who was this

man, this stranger, coming here and overstepping his boundaries as a paying guest? The trouble with a guy like him was that if you gave him an inch, he wanted a mile. He had the air of confidence that always having had money gives a man. Some might even call it arrogance.

Well, he'd soon find out that his unsolicited offers didn't cut it with Megan Delaney. She was never going to be beholden to a man ever again. Not any man. She and Ryan would manage just fine without any outside help.

There was something different about him, however, something that shadowed those dark green eyes. She'd give him a wide berth, she decided. Of course, everyone had their secrets, Megan thought, rising and walking slowly toward the house.

She had a few herself.

Chapter 3

Alex drove the short distance from town to Delaney's Bed & Breakfast automatically, his mind still on the meeting he'd just had. The two Parsons daughters had seemed reasonable enough and anxious to sell the land he was interested in. And he *was* interested in it after having spent the best part of an hour walking the parcel. It was ideally located, near town but yet not downtown. The land was six blocks from a grade school, ten from the town's only high school and within walking distance of two churches.

But there was a snag, and his name was Jimmy Parsons.

The elderly owner's only son wanted to hold out for big bucks, which could squelch the whole deal. However, Alex wasn't one to judge too early. He'd indicated interest, but not eagerness. They'd talk again, he'd told the three of them, then strolled away, leaving them wondering, he supposed.

Time was on his side, since one of the sisters had blurted out that they hadn't had any offers as yet, nor had any other builder asked to speak to them. Of course, the ad had only recently appeared and would undoubtedly spark more interest.

Fortunately, acquiring the parcel wasn't a do-or-die kind of thing with Alex, an attitude that usually put him one up on anyone else who badly wanted to purchase.

Chances are, he thought as he turned the Porsche onto the winding road leading to the inn, that Jimmy Parsons was just testing the waters, showing off in front of his sisters, trying to prove he was a mover and shaker. He wasn't. Alex had seen the young man's nervous swallowing, the slight trembling of his hands. Although Alex was willing to pay fair market value, there was no way he would overbid so the kid would look good.

Parking under the large California live oak shading the far end of Delaney's lot, he decided he'd go in and make a few phone calls, see if he could round up a few comps, make appointments with some local lenders for comparison and look into ordering a feasibility study. Although Megan had told him she thought the area could handle some middle-income housing, he felt she was too far out of the loop to make a solid judgment.

Megan. Getting out of the car, Alex stared up at the sky, clearing after the morning rain, and thought about the woman who'd sat in her garden last night, wearing her stubborn streak like a badge of honor. Her resistance to any proffered help seemed more than independence. More like a strong determination to make it on her own. Why? he wondered. What could it have hurt if she'd have let him pull up a few weeds? Did all that track back to Neal and their relationship?

He supposed the prudent thing would be for him to quit offering. Even his wiping a few pans had upset her. At breakfast this morning, she'd been polite and smiling, but in an impersonal way. She hadn't once let her eyes linger on him or spoken to him directly unless he'd asked her a question. Apparently, he unnerved her and again he wondered why.

Alex stepped into the lobby and saw the reddish-haired woman who'd been arranging flowers yesterday behind the desk today.

"Ah, Mr. Shephard," Grace Romero said, catching his eye.

"Just the man I want to see." Her gaze roamed over him appreciatively.

Alex knew a flirt when he saw one, no matter her age. He read her name on her badge. "Well, here I am, Grace. What can I do for you?"

"It's more what we can do for you." Grace ran a hand over her smooth hair, wishing she'd have worn it down today. Men, all men, liked long hair, she'd discovered long ago.

There was that *we* plural stuff again. "And what might that be?"

"Megan's decided to put on a barbecue dinner tonight. The couple in our upstairs green room is celebrating forty years of marriage, so all the guests are invited. Chicken, ribs, potato salad, beans, fresh corn and, of course, something lovin' from the oven. About six on the back lawn, if you'd care to join us." Her dark eyes watched him think the invitation over.

"Sounds good. I believe my evening's free. Tell me, are you and Megan doing the cooking or are you having it catered?"

Grace's laugh was full-bodied and rich. "Catered? Oh, my saints, no. We're doing it all. Finger-lickin' good, I promise you. And no charge."

Alex raised an eyebrow. "No charge?" Not a very good business practice, but perhaps Megan had a reason.

"Walter and Jean have spent every wedding anniversary with us since the year we opened," Grace went on to explain, "and sent many of their friends to us, as well. Megan wanted to do something nice for them. There'll be music, too. Do you dance, Mr. Shephard?"

Hands in his pockets, he smiled at her. "The woman who dances with me has to wear steel-toed shoes, Grace. And please call me Alex."

"Thank you, Alex. Too bad. About the dancing, I mean."

She was wearing a gauzy, full-skirted dress in bright turquoise. He could picture her swirling in it. "I'm certainly looking forward to watching you." He decided to give it one more shot, this time with a woman who seemed more amenable. "If you and Megan need any help setting up tables out back or whatever, I'm available."

"Oh, thanks, but we can handle things just fine. We never let guests help."

"So Megan told me last night." He glanced through the dining room at the double doors leading to the kitchen, surmising that Megan was probably in there right now, slaving away on the dinner. "I don't know why not. Guests are people, and people don't offer unless they really want to help."

Grace shook her auburn head, causing her large gold hoop earrings to all but brush her shoulders. "No, guests are to be waited on, not do the waiting on others. House rule." She flashed him a wide smile.

But Alex wasn't one to give up easily. "Can I bring something, then? To add to the menu. I passed a store in town just now. Out-of-season watermelons. They're almost a requisite at an outdoor barbecue, don't you think?"

Grace considered his suggestion. The man was persistent; she'd give him that. Megan might not like it, but really, what could it hurt? "All right, but remember, I didn't ask you."

He gave her his most charming smile. "No, you didn't."

"See you later." She saw him walk out toward his car as she hurried off, her list in hand. She'd invited all the guests and everyone had accepted except for one couple who'd made other plans for the day. In the kitchen, she found Megan putting the finishing touches to a huge pot of baked beans. "Okay, I got to all of them. It'll be ten for dinner, plus the three of us. Manageable."

"Yes, and thank you." Megan brushed the back of her hand across her damp forehead. Her next purchase would have to be a large ceiling fan for this kitchen the moment she had extra cash. The washer would have to wait. She was about to melt in this heat. "Lord, but it's hot today. Does the weatherman know the first of May hasn't even arrived yet?"

"It's not hot outside, only in here with two ovens on, several pots bubbling away and a big dishwasher running."

Grace noticed that Megan's face was flushed with heat. "Honey, why don't you go out and cool off?"

"Oh, Grace, there's too much to do." She sighed, mentally running through the list. The barbecue was a good idea, and certainly Walter and Jean deserved the extra treat. But it made for a very long day, what with getting breakfast to cleaning all the occupied rooms, then shopping for groceries and now cooking and baking all afternoon. She hoped she didn't nod off during dinner.

Grace walked over to Megan and yanked off the towel she'd fastened around her waist in lieu of an apron, something Megan refused to wear. "Enough. I don't want you pooping out on me. You've been running around all morning like a crazy woman. Go and grab some fresh air while I frost the cake. Half an hour won't put us behind. Scoot! Go!"

"Oh, all right." Megan went to the door, paused with her hand on the knob. "The decorative tips are in the—"

"Third drawer. Don't you think I know this kitchen by now? Get outta here, woman!"

Smiling, Megan stepped out and drew in a deep breath of air heavy with the fragrance of flowers. It was cooler out here, the ground still damp from the morning shower. She intended to cut some irises for tonight's centerpiece, but not until later. This would be an ideal time to do a little weeding. And to check on a sickly rosebush, a hybrid that had been a gift from Emily. No matter what Megan did, the poor thing always seemed to be struggling just to survive.

Moving along the grassy path, she bent to her task.

Some twenty minutes later, she'd just finished cleaning out under and around the rosebushes and bagging the weeds when she heard the front gate into the garden open. Straightening, she saw Alex Shephard walk in carrying a huge watermelon. His strides along the brick walk were long and confident until he spotted her. Pausing, looking oddly uncomfortable for a man who exuded self-assurance, he gave her a sheepish smile.

"For the barbecue," he said, indicating the melon. Though he'd known her but a short time, he recognized that stubborn tilt to her chin. Aware of the frown forming on her face as she strolled toward him, he went on, "Grace told me you had plenty of food, but I spotted this in town at the Green Grocer and couldn't resist." He pointed to a small plug at one end. "The owner cut out a wedge so I could taste it. Heavenly. Want to try some?"

Megan watched him try to talk his way out of a situation he had to know she wouldn't like and almost laughed at how nonplussed he was. Almost. She stopped several feet from him and met his eyes. "Tell me, were you always this good at following directions as a child or is this something new?"

He grinned, shifting the melon in his arms, relieved she didn't appear truly angry. He wondered if she knew how appealing she looked with her dark hair tied back with a blue ribbon, her face smudged not with flour this time but rather dirt from her weeding, and the knees of her well-worn jeans grass-stained. Appealing and very young. "Oh, I was worse, much worse. My father's hair was totally white by the time I started high school."

"I believe it." She gazed at the huge melon. "Well, I suppose since you went to all that trouble, we should chill that." Dusting off her hands, she led the way into the kitchen, holding the screen door for him.

Just finished with the cake, Grace was at the sink drying her hands. "That's what I call a giant melon." She smiled at Alex and caught his wink as Megan bent to the sink to wash up, then went to the refrigerator to make room.

"Wow, what is this, thirty cubic feet?" Alex asked, standing behind her as she poked inside the huge refrigerator.

"More like forty, industrial-size," Megan answered as she pulled out several bagged chickens, then straightened. But she hadn't realized Alex was so close behind her, so she bumped squarely into him, her backside bumping his hip—and lost her train of thought.

Quickly, Alex shifted the melon, tucking it into one arm like a football, and slipped his other arm around Megan to steady her. She was so soft and more fragile than he'd have guessed. The swell of her breast just grazed his arm. Up close, he inhaled her womanly scent and felt her tense.

At first contact, Megan's eyes leaped to his face. Why did she get the feeling he'd planned that maneuver even though his expression was painfully innocent? She couldn't help noticing that he had the greenest eyes she'd ever seen. His hand on her bare arm was large and very warm, strong and protective. His touch aroused a flare of heat within her, one she didn't welcome. Enough of this. She sidestepped him. "On the bottom shelf, please," she instructed, her voice just a shade unsteady.

Carrying the fryers to the sink, she dropped them in before checking his progress over her shoulder.

Alex closed the door and turned to find both women watching him. "There. What else can I help with?" As soon as the words were out, he regretted them as Megan's frown returned.

"Nothing, thanks," she said firmly. Even her glance at Grace was somewhat irritated. Why couldn't this man busy himself elsewhere?

"I'm shucking corn," Grace announced, dumping the contents of a large bag onto the butcher-block table. Her movements efficient, she went to work, watching Megan and Alex through lowered lashes. There seemed to be an odd tension between the two, strange for people who scarcely knew each other.

Annoyed but loath to rudely order Alex to go away, Megan reached into her knife drawer, searching for the one she wanted to use to cut up the chickens. She looked up as he stepped over to the counter, wondering why he was moving closer again, then cried out as she nicked her finger on a sharp blade because she wasn't paying attention. "Darn!" She sucked at the small cut.

"At the risk of having you impale me with one of those knives, may I *please* give you a hand cutting up those chickens? I learned how years ago." His father's housekeeper had felt it her duty to teach both Alex and Patrick a few basics about cooking so they could survive on their own. Man chores, she'd called them, like grilling outdoors, making a mean omelette and cutting up chickens.

Megan slammed the knife drawer closed and opened the second one, searching for a bandage, her temper rising. Apparently, she'd have to hit this guy over the head before he'd get the message. "I'm sure you can truss, debone and probably teach a chicken to whistle 'Dixie,' Mr. Shephard, but this is *my* kitchen and you're a guest in *my* inn and I'd prefer it if you'd leave the cooking to Grace and me. Thank you for the offer and the watermelon. We'll see you at dinner tonight at six."

As dismissals went, it was barely polite and quite insistent. Alex watched her give up the drawer search, wrap a napkin around her bleeding finger and resume looking for the correct knife. Not only lovely and independent, but stubborn as hell. He noticed that she'd dropped the plural, not wanting to include Grace in her temper tantrum. Frankly, Grace looked as if she wouldn't have minded his help.

"As you wish, Mrs. Delaney," Alex said, matching her formal tone. With another wink at Grace, who grinned at him, he went through the swinging doors.

Bleeding all over the sink, Megan closed her eyes for a moment and prayed for patience. The cut was deeper than she'd originally thought. "Grace," she said, her voice low with frustration, "where in hell are the bandages?"

"Coming right up," Grace said, moving to the cupboard. She'd seen Megan Delaney through thick and thin, through sad times and fun days. But she'd never seen her unnerved or flustered by a man yet, guest or not. There was only one reason Grace could think of for her friend's odd behavior.

Megan was attracted to Alex Shephard and it scared her mightily.

Yes indeed, it was going to be an interesting barbecue.

Stretched out on a lawn chair he'd found in the side yard, Alex had his briefcase on the grass and a pile of papers he needed to go through on his lap when he noticed that the sun was moving into his eyes. Rising, he decided to shift the angle of the chair just as Ryan Delaney came into sight. The boy was wearing a baseball mitt that nearly swallowed his small hand and smacking a softball into it as he cautiously walked over. Alex settled back into the chair.

It was nearly four, so Alex guessed that the bus had dropped him off a short time ago. "Hi, Ryan. How's it going?"

"Okay." Slam went the ball into the mitt.

"Uh-huh. What grade are you in? Second? Third?"

"Third." Two more slams.

"Uh-huh." What in the world does a grown man talk about with an eight-year-old? He glanced around the yard, remembered the day they'd met. "No puddles to jump in today, eh?"

"Nope." Ryan dropped the ball, picked it up, kept his eyes averted, wondering how to talk to this guy. He wished he'd had more practice with grown-up men. Maybe he should've brought him a cookie. He'd been real happy that time in the kitchen. Maybe he was pretending to impress his mom like that creep, Eddie Jenkins, who came around to fix the washer and didn't really like boys.

Alex looked down at his papers, knowing he should get back to work, but it was hard to ignore Ryan thunking his ball into his glove. He searched his mind for a kid topic. "You like to read?"

"Not much." He glanced toward the kitchen window. "I'm not allowed to annoy the paying guests," Ryan quoted, sounding as if the warning had been drummed into him. But his blue eyes were hopeful.

"Is that a fact? Then I'll be sure to let you know when I'm annoyed." He smiled, suddenly anxious to put the boy at ease. He nodded toward the ball and glove. "Are you a ballplayer?"

Pleased not to be sent away and because his mom wasn't at the window, Ryan plopped down on the grass next to

Alex's chair. "I'm on a Little League team. The Marlins. I'm the shortstop."

Impressed, Alex raised his brows. "Hey, great. Why'd you pick shortstop?"

"'Cause you get more chances to get the ball, to make outs." His young face grew cloudy. "Only I don't get to play that much. Coach said I need more practice."

A by-now familiar guilt swept over Alex. "I guess your dad used to help you practice, eh?"

"I'm not supposed to talk about my dad."

More no-no's. "Why is that?"

"Mom says if you can't say something nice about someone, you should keep quiet."

Alex mulled that over, thinking that Megan had revealed a great deal by giving that warning to her son.

Squinting up at him in the sun, Ryan wondered if this guy knew anything about baseball. He seemed neat enough, but maybe he was too busy, like his dad had been. "You like the Dodgers or the Padres?"

"I'm from San Diego. The Padres, of course."

Ryan grinned. "Me, too. Only I'm about the only one on my team who likes them. Most everyone likes the Dodgers." He pounded the ball into the glove. "We had pizza day at school today. You like pizza?"

"Who doesn't?"

"Yeah. I build model cars. Neat ones like yours."

"Really? Takes a lot of patience." Alex watched the boy chuck the ball and decided to climb out on a limb. While it was true that he didn't know much about kids, he remembered feeling like Ryan when he'd been a boy, wanting to connect to another male adult when his father hadn't been available. And Ryan's father would never again be available. He should by all rights finish updating his file, read the others. Instead, he dropped the stack of papers into his open briefcase. "You want to toss a few?" he asked, indicating Ryan's ball.

The boy's face lit up. "Yeah, sure." He scampered up and

walked out a ways on the grass. "I don't have another glove."

Estimating the approximate distance between bases, Alex paced it off. "That's okay. Come on. Throw me one." The throw was loopy and fell short. Alex scooped it up, ignoring Ryan's embarrassed face. "Ready? Here it comes." He tossed one to him, slow and easy, and Ryan managed to grab it, but just barely. "Good. Now throw it to me, only put your arm into the pitch." Assuming the stance, he waited.

Grace stood at the kitchen window looking past the rows of flowers to the grassy area where a small boy and a tall man were playing catch. Through the screen, she heard Ryan's whoop of delight when he caught one on the skid, followed by Alex's cheer. Well, well, she thought, smiling.

Megan straightened from basting the second batch of chicken with barbecue sauce and returned the pan to the oven before walking over to the sink. "What's so fascinating out there?" she asked, then felt her spine stiffen when she realized her son was playing catch with one of the guests. The meddlesome guest, as she'd come to think of Alex Shephard. "What is with that man?" she asked softly, almost to herself. "First the weeds, then the watermelon, then the chickens and now Ryan. Why doesn't he know his place like our other guests? Does he stay at a Hilton and offer to do the dishes or change the sheets?"

Crossing her arms over her chest, Grace shifted her gaze from outdoors to the woman beside her. "Remember the McPharlins? They brought you fresh peaches from their orchard in Georgia the last time they stayed with us, and she insisted on baking up a couple of pies right here in this kitchen. And what about that traveling salesman from San Francisco who entertains all the guests by singing in the lounge at least one night of his stay? These are folks who pick this place because they feel comfortable and at home here, and they don't at a Hilton. So why do you suppose this one guy bothers you so much?" Her long friendship with

Megan involved many such questions through the years, and Grace felt no qualms asking now.

Megan narrowed her gaze, watching as Alex stood behind Ryan now, showing him the proper way to wear his glove, how to hold his hands waiting for the throw. The blond head bent to the dark-haired boy. The question was, why was he being so nice to her son, so anxious to please? She couldn't pigeonhole the man. Handsome to a breathtaking fault, undoubtedly as rich as Trump, yet here he was, playing catch with Ryan. Go figure.

So, why *did* he bother her so much? "He's different, Grace," she said quietly. "It's as if he wants something and I don't yet know what that is. He's so confident, so sure he's right, so...so..."

"Handsome and sexy?"

Frowning, Megan turned. "That's not at all what I was thinking." *Liar,* said that small inner voice.

"Maybe it should be. Maybe he's interested in Ryan's mother and that's what scares you."

Interested in her? She doubted it. A man like that could have most any woman he wanted. He certainly didn't need a small-town woman who came with a child attached. "I have to think of Ryan." She swung her gaze back to the unlikely twosome and watched her son leap into the air to try to catch a fly ball. He caught it though he fell to the ground with the effort. Alex gave him a thumbs-up. "He's going to be here at least a week, he said. Two days and Ryan's already getting attached. How will he feel when the man leaves?"

"Honey, you can't wrap that boy in cellophane and keep him from reaching out to people just because they may walk out of his life. Ryan's dying for male attention. Has been all his life. You don't give him enough credit. He knows the people who stay here come and go. He'll handle it. Let him enjoy a little male bonding while he can." She stepped closer, watching out the window as Alex leaned down explaining something. Ryan nodded solemnly, his face a study in concentration. "If you ask me, he's doing something for that boy you and I can't do."

Hating to admit defeat, Megan sighed. "I suppose you're right." The truth was, Alex Shephard was doing something for her that no one else had done in a very long time, either.

At the barbecue dinner table, Alex was seated between Ryan, who'd insisted he sit beside him, and Mrs. Julia Kettering, a widow in her eighties who'd taken a shine to him. A small, thin woman wearing a floral print dress and tennis shoes, her snow-white hair in a long braid down her back, Mrs. K, as she liked to be called, wore granny glasses and smelled of talcum. She could also talk the wings off a butterfly.

"My poor departed husband, Horace, used to make ribs now and again," Mrs. K went on. "You didn't need teeth to eat them, they were so tender." She leaned closer to Alex. "These run a close second."

Alex set down a clean rib bone and picked up his napkin. "They're mighty good." He reached for a piece of chicken. "So, are you staying here for long?"

"You could say that. It's been over a year now." The old woman dug into her corn with false teeth clicking.

"A year? You mean you live here?" A permanent resident? Alex hadn't been aware that a bed-and-breakfast could be someone's home. "Are you a relative of the Delaneys?"

Swallowing, Mrs. K shook her head. "Might as well be, as good as Megan treats me." She dabbed at her thin lips with her napkin. "I used to live across the street from Megan and her mama, used to baby-sit her and her sisters a lot. My husband was sick for years and our insurance money ran out. I had to borrow, then sell my little house to pay our creditors when he died. By then, Megan already had this place, and when she heard, she came to get me, moved me in that day. I got no other family." She gazed at Megan through her thick glasses. "Hardly lets me pay for a thing from my small pension. That girl's a saint, is what she is."

Small wonder she had to sell baked goods to make ends meet, Alex thought, if she takes in a poor little widow and puts on free barbecues. There wasn't that much profit in small businesses. His gaze drifted to the lady in question, his eyes narrowing as he studied the dent in her small, stubborn chin.

But what had happened to the insurance money?

"You like crossword puzzles, young man?" Mrs. K asked.

"Yes, I do," Alex answered.

"Me, too. The one in this morning's paper stumped me. What's a Buddhist movement in ten letters?"

"Hmm. I'll have to think about that." Then a noise at his elbow had Alex glancing at Ryan, who was fiddling with his silverware. "How come you're eating everything but your potato salad?"

"I don't like potato salad."

"Really? Too bad. You ever hear of Tony Gwynn, right fielder for the Padres?"

"Sure. Everybody's heard of him."

"I hear he eats potato salad three times a day sometimes."

Ryan's expression was skeptical. "You kidding me?"

"Would I lie about potato salad?" Alex took a heaping forkful, chewed away. "Man, this is good. Builds muscles, too."

From across the table, Megan watched her son gamely take a small bite, then another. She saw Ryan look up at Alex and tell him it wasn't so bad, he guessed. Mrs. K on the other side of Alex clawed at his arm with her long, thin fingers, wanting his attention again. His fair head bent to the old woman as he listened closely.

All right, so the man was a charmer. Billy the Kid probably had been, too. And Neal. Charming and totally irresponsible. There was something definitely unnerving about Alex Shephard. Whatever it was, Megan imagined it would come out soon. Secrets had a way of being revealed at the darnedest times.

Neal had taught her that.

Grace and Megan got up to clear while the anniversary

couple, Walter and Jean, danced on the brick patio to a golden
oldie from the portable radio, then held court reminiscing
about their wedding day. The Donahues, married only a year,
were listening intently, probably finding it hard to imagine
being married for forty years. The businessman from Sacramento who was leaving in the morning thanked them and
excused himself. The two middle-aged couples from Spokane
who were staying in the center connecting rooms upstairs
smiled and interjected marital anecdotes of their own.

By the time Grace set out dessert plates and Megan placed
the beautifully decorated cake in the center of the round table,
everyone was in a jolly mood. Megan lifted her glass of iced
tea and gave a warm, sentimental toast to Walter and Jean,
and the rest followed suit.

"Mom, where's the watermelon?" Ryan asked. Cake was
great, but he positively adored watermelon.

"I'll get it," Grace said, passing out dessert forks.

"Please," Alex said, rising, "allow me. It's really heavy."
Not looking at Megan or waiting for a reply, he left the yard
and hurried to the kitchen.

Megan poured iced tea, milk or coffee all around, very
aware of Alex at the buffet table slicing watermelon and
Grace serving.

"This cake's delicious, dear," Jean said to Megan. "But
then, everything at your table always is."

Passing her chair, Megan touched the older woman's shoulder. "Thank you, Jean." She carried the tea pitcher to the
buffet table where Alex had just finished. All right, bite the
bullet, she told herself. "Thanks for helping."

"My pleasure." Stepping closer, he took her hand in his,
turned it over to examine her bandaged finger before she
could pull away. "How's your cut? Those knife slices can
hurt like the devil."

There were four tiki torches placed around the backyard.
They'd been enough at twilight, but nearly two hours later,
the lighting was dim and romantic from the flickering flames.
The radio played softly in the background. Overhead, tree

branches swayed in a gentle breeze and a lone cricket could be heard serenading nearby. For a long moment, time seemed to stand still as Alex watched Megan's blue eyes darken, saw awareness leap into them as their look held.

"It's fine, thanks." But she didn't pull her hand back.

She was wearing a scoop-necked white peasant blouse with a multicolored full skirt and white sandals, her hair falling softly to her shoulders. He felt a crazy urge to touch the ends to see if her hair was as soft as it looked. His free hand started up and...

Alex cleared his throat and stepped back. What the hell was he thinking?

Megan swallowed hard and prayed he couldn't tell how her heart was pounding beneath the thin cotton material of her blouse. Moving aside, she busied herself getting extra napkins and the bowl of lemon slices.

Why did Alex Shephard have to come here and upset her nice, safe, boring life? She liked boring. It sure beat having her husband come home drunk as a skunk, embarrassing her in front of their guests, or forget to come home for days at a time. Yes, she'd choose boring every time.

Only she'd bet that no one around Alex Shephard was ever bored for long.

Within ten minutes, the party had broken up, the guests going off to their rooms or wherever. Though he knew she didn't really need the assistance, Alex offered to walk Mrs. K to her room, listening to her chatter all the way. Walking back out, he passed Ryan, who'd been sent up to get ready for bed. "See you tomorrow, sport," he called after the thundering feet on the back stairs.

Ryan stopped. "Hey, Mr. Shephard, my next game's tomorrow night. Maybe you could come?" The small voice was hopeful.

"I'll see what I can do. Good night, Ryan." He opened the screen just in time for Grace to walk through, her arms laden with bowls of leftover food. "If you've got a tray, I can start bringing in some dishes." He caught her dubious look. "What, you, too? You want to spend half the night cleaning up here?"

"Not especially, but Megan doesn't—"

"Grace, give me a tray. I'll handle Megan."

She handed him a tray, then smiled to herself as he went back out. So he was going to handle Megan, eh? This should be good.

Out in the yard, he didn't wait for permission, but started stacking plates onto the tray. He had only a moment to wait for the anticipated reaction.

"What are you doing? I thought I told you that—"

"Yeah, you did." He was ready for her. Stopping, he turned to face her. "You told me it was your kitchen, your flower garden, your bed-and-breakfast. That's fine because I have no intention of taking over. But look at you. You've been working since six this morning and now it's nine at night. You're ready to drop you're so tired and your finger's wet all the way through the bandage and probably throbbing like hell. Why can't you accept a little help?"

She didn't have the energy for this right now, Megan thought. "Listen, Mr. Shephard, I can handle this without your help, like I've been doing for years. I take my responsibilities very seriously."

"That's very admirable, Mrs. Delaney. But right now, you're exhausted. Please, go inside and upstairs to your son. Grace and I will finish up here. You can yell at me tomorrow if it'll make you feel better."

To his surprise, she set down the towel she'd been holding, turned from him and went inside. Letting out a big breath, Alex went to work.

Moments later, Grace came out carrying two plastic trash bags. "If I hadn't seen and heard that with my own eyes and ears through the open window, I'd have bet good money against it ever happening. Alex Shephard, I think I'm going to have to rethink my opinion of you."

In the dim light of a glimmering tiki torch, he smiled at

her. "All right, but when you do, as they say, please be kind."

Her robust laugh rang out in the evening air.

Cruising along in his Porsche, Alex spoke on his car phone. "The bank's not going to give us any trouble, Dad. But I need you to order a feasibility study for me. I'd like our people on it instead of using someone up here. It's a good parcel and wouldn't require much clearing. There's gas and electric at the street. But I'm not sure that this town can support an influx of middle-income residents." He'd already talked earlier with his secretary and Mitch, but Alex knew his father liked a personal report.

"I'll get right on it. Did you meet with the owner?"

Alex turned, heading up the hill. "Owner's incapacitated. I met with his three adult children. The one with the power of attorney's giving me a bit of a hassle, but I think he'd come around if we got serious."

"Good. So you'll be heading home?" Ron Shephard still wasn't happy having his son away too long. Transplants were tricky.

"Not yet. I'm checking a few other things out." Namely one widow and her son.

"But you're feeling all right, taking your pills?" He knew it would irritate Alex to be asked, but he couldn't stop himself.

"I'm feeling fine and being a good boy, so stop worrying."

"Yeah, all right. Just take it easy."

If he took it any easier, he'd be comatose. "Talk with you later." Alex hung up and swung into Delaney's lot. He'd gone running this morning, skipping the inn's breakfast, hoping to give Megan a little more time before facing him. He wasn't sure just what reaction he'd get after her surprising turnabout last night.

After showering, he'd gone into town, walked through the shops and had an early lunch before meeting with a couple of bankers. So he hadn't seen Megan at all, or even Grace.

Strolling into the lobby, he noticed Walter and Jean playing gin rummy in the lounge and waved to them. Grace was behind the check-in desk punching in figures on an adding machine. "Hi," he said.

Grace glanced up and smiled. "Well, if it isn't the miracle man."

Alex glanced toward the kitchen. Since it was nearly five, he figured that Megan was probably there either fixing Ryan's dinner or already starting her nightly baking. "How is she today? Happy as a clam or gunning for me?"

"Nah, she's fine. A little subdued. Still tired, I'd guess."

"She works too hard."

"You don't have to tell me." She paused, her fingers poised over the keys. "What I would like you to tell me is why you're so concerned."

The woman was blunt, but Alex knew it was probably because she cared a great deal for Megan. "I hate to see anyone, especially a young, attractive woman, bury herself in work day after day. When did Megan last take some time off?" When Grace shook her head, he knew he was right. "See what I mean?"

"Yes, I do, and I agree. But I still can't figure you." Pointedly, she glanced outside toward his blue Porsche, then at his gold Rolex watch, his casually expensive clothes. "I'd wager you're pretty well off, your daddy owns the store, and you're here on a business trip, one of many in your travels around the state. What's it to you if Megan, or any of us, for that matter, work hard or not at all?"

Guilty knowledge had Alex jamming his hands into his back pockets and gazing down at his shoes. *Because if it wasn't for me, Megan would have her husband here beside her and she wouldn't have to work so hard.*

"You're right, Grace. My daddy owns the store. But he started off as a young apprentice carpenter and worked his way up. He still puts in more hours a day than most men half his age. Before my mother got sick and died, she used to work in the office. Both my brother and I started doing odd jobs on his construction projects after school as soon as we hit our teens. I know what hard work is and that it can take you over. I've always believed that you need to balance work with pleasure. And I don't think Megan takes much time out to play. Am I right?''

"You're right. She runs around here at top speed. I'm always telling her to slow down. But I repeat, why do you care whether or not she does?''

Alex saw the shrewd way she was watching him. "Are you trying to make me say something here, Grace? All right, you caught me. I find her attractive and I'd like to show her some fun. Is that so wrong?''

Grace pursed her lips thoughtfully a moment, feeling certain that Alex Shephard could show a woman all manner of fun things. "No, as long as you don't hurt her. Anyone who does will have to answer to me.''

He smiled. "I'll remember that. Is she in the kitchen?''

"No, she's at Ryan's ball game.''

"Oh, right. He invited me yesterday and it slipped my mind.'' He wasn't used to considering an eight-year-old's activities when he thought about a woman. "Where's the game being played?''

Grace told him, then watched him hurry back out to his car, wondering if she'd done the right thing. Sure, she'd wanted someone in Megan's life, but this guy was coming on awfully fast. She'd never been one to trust fast.

Megan held her breath as the boy at bat swung, hitting the ball directly toward her son at shortstop. Ryan saw it coming, moved into position and waited, shuffling his feet nervously, his eye on the ball. His teammates began chanting for him to get it. Some of the two dozen or so parents and relatives in the bleachers rose to their feet. The ball arced high. Ryan took one step closer and trapped it in his mitt.

"Fly ball. You're out!'' yelled the umpire.

It was the third out, putting Ryan's team up to bat. The boys came running in, high-fiving the shortstop, cheering.

One grabbed Ryan's baseball cap and turned it around backward on his head. And through it all, Ryan's grin grew and grew. Finally, he had a chance to catch his mother's eye. She gave him a big thumbs-up and whistled through her teeth. Ryan grinned some more.

"Where'd you learn to whistle like that?" Alex asked as he slid into the empty space on the bleachers beside Megan.

Startled, she jumped. What on earth was Alex Shephard doing here? Was there no place she could go where those penetrating green eyes wouldn't be watching her?

Shifting over, she made room for him on the bench. "I was the oldest of three sisters and the only tomboy. A kid down the street nicknamed Sharkey taught me how to whistle, how to do wheelies and how to shoot marbles. Then he got mad when I beat him and took all his marbles."

Alex laughed. "Poor Sharkey. I'll bet he still doesn't trust women. Teach 'em all you know and they wind up walking away with all your marbles."

"You could be right. I hear he's on wife number three." Megan swung her eyes back to the field and found her son sitting on the bench waiting his turn at bat. "I didn't thank you yesterday for giving Ryan some pointers. Did you see that catch he just made?"

"Yeah, pretty terrific. He's a cute kid." She was wearing a baseball cap, too, with her hair gathered into a ponytail and dangling out the back. He thought she looked way too young to be the mother of any of the boys out on the field and told her so. "You must have been a child bride."

Her face clouded for just a moment. "Pretty much. Barely out of high school. Dumb move. I don't advise it." Megan turned, squinting in the late-afternoon sun, suddenly curious. "I guess you escaped the old matrimonial bug."

"Not really." Alex gazed off toward the field. "I got married right after college. It lasted eleven months."

"I'm sorry."

"Don't be. It never should have happened." He shifted, met her eyes. "Was your marriage a good one?" There he went, nosing around again. But he'd been wondering ever since talking with Emily at the Cornerstone.

It was Megan's turn to gaze off into space, wanting to be fair without lying. "It was, for a while. Things change. People change."

"That's the truth."

"It's never just one person's fault."

"No, it isn't." Oddly, he felt better knowing that at the time of Neal's death, their marriage hadn't been the best. Better, but even more guilty. "About last night," he began. "I apologize if I was too bossy. Dad says I always think I know what's best for people and I don't mind sharing my strong opinions with them."

The way he told on himself made her smile. "Yes, you are kind of like that. But no apology necessary. You were right. I was exhausted, but I couldn't leave Grace there to do it alone. My mother says I always take on too much, then get cranky that I have to finish it."

Alex smiled at that. "Sometimes our parents do know us fairly well." At the sound of his name, he turned his head to look at the field and saw Ryan moving up to the plate, carrying a bat in one hand and waving to him with the other. "Hey, Ryan. Go get 'em."

"Oh, I hope he gets at least a base hit," Megan whispered. "He hates to strike out."

"Who doesn't?" Alex saw the first pitch come and Ryan swung at it, missing by a mile. "How much time does the coach spend helping these kids?"

"They have practice every Saturday, but each man has two teams to coach. There aren't enough volunteers to go around, so no individual boy gets much help. Unless he has older brothers or a father who cares."

A father who cares. *I'm not supposed to talk about my dad,* Ryan had told him. A picture of Neal Delaney was forming, and it wasn't pretty.

Ryan missed the second pitch, as well. Alex could tell by the boy's stance that he was by turns nervous and embarrassed. "I guess Ryan's father didn't have much time to spend coaching him on the side."

Megan sighed. She'd spent most of her married years defending Neal's disinterest and absences to their son and to others, maybe even to herself. Explaining that he was busy, tired, traveling. But with all she'd been through the past two years, she was finding it more and more difficult to maintain the illusion of a caring husband and father. However, Alex was still basically a stranger and she didn't want Ryan to somehow pick up on some ugly truths about his father until he was old enough to understand.

"Neal traveled a great deal, trying to drum up business for the inn. I help Ryan when I can."

The third pitch came. Ryan swung and missed, striking out. Dejectedly, he dragged the bat back to the bench.

Alex was good at reading between the lines. He admired Megan's loyalty to her dead husband even as he wondered at the real story. "You help him, eh? That explains why he swings like a girl."

"Thanks a lot."

"You got a bat around the house somewhere?"

"No." She saw where he was going with this and decided to nip it in the bud. "Look, this isn't your problem. Ryan will manage somehow and—"

"He's quick and smart, eager to learn. If you won't let me help you, at least let me show your son how to hit a ball."

Megan came to a quick decision, for Ryan's sake. "All right, but I'll buy the bat."

"*I'll* buy the bat—you can pay me back. Girls don't know how to pick out bats."

"Listen, mister, girls are good for a lot of things, I'll have you know." The moment the words were out, she realized how they must sound.

Close alongside her, he gazed down into her blue, blue eyes. "Yeah, I do know that. But baseball's not one of them."

She couldn't help it. She blushed, then turned away without another word.

Two more innings, and by some miracle, Ryan's team won. He came galloping over, both shoes untied, his clothes sweaty, his hat crooked. "We won! Did you see that, Mr. Shephard? We won!"

"Good job, sport."

He'd forgotten she was there, Megan thought in amazement. Had to be something to this male bonding. "You were great, sweetie."

"Thanks, Mom." He was beaming ear to ear, his poor showing at bat forgotten.

"A win like that deserves a reward." Alex turned to Megan. "Is there a pizza joint around here somewhere?"

"Pizza! Yes!" Ryan was thrilled.

"There's Pasquale's, but it's about ten miles along the highway and—"

"Aw, come on, Mom," Alex coaxed, making Ryan laugh. "It's not even seven."

Megan was more concerned with the few dollars in her wallet than with the lateness of the hour. However, the excitement on Ryan's face had her giving in. She'd order something small for him and just have a soft drink herself. "All right, you win."

"One more thing," Alex said as they made their way to the parking lot. "Could Ryan ride with me? That is, if it's all right with you?" He knew the kid had been dying for a ride in his Porsche.

Ryan leaped into the air with excitement. "Yeah, Mom, could I? Please, oh, please?"

Megan didn't much care for the way Alex had maneuvered that one, but again she gave in. "Okay, but you stay right behind me at the speed limit."

"Yes, ma'am," Alex said as they arrived at the Porsche. As soon as Alex opened the door, the boy hopped in, squirming with anticipation. Alex climbed behind the wheel and turned on the powerful engine. "Put your seat belt on, Ryan."

Megan stood watching, nervously rattling her keys. "We're going to have a little talk, you and I," she told Alex.

He looked at her, his lips twitching. "I look forward to it."

Chapter 4

The joint was jumping. Pasquale's had Tom and Jerry cartoons playing along the back wall, video games clanging in a side room and four waitresses dressed like mice with floppy ears singing birthday greetings to a table of eight. Just your usual Thursday night happening.

With practiced ease, Alex shouldered his way to a booth with a wide-eyed Ryan and his reluctant mother following. "Now I invited you, so this is my treat," he said, aware of Megan's worried frown. "Tell me what you like on your pizza."

"Everything except anchovies and green peppers," Ryan stated above the noisy din. "I hate peppers."

Alex nodded. "Gotcha." He turned to Megan. "And you, madam?"

"I'm not very hungry, but thanks."

Her stubbornness wasn't going to work tonight. "If you don't want to eat, you can watch us. We're starving, right, sport?"

"Yeah, starving." Alongside his mother, Ryan was craning

his neck, watching all the activity. He'd never been in Pasquale's.

A waitress with pencil and pad poised walked over. "Welcome to Pasquale's. Have you decided?"

"You bet. A large special, but skip the anchovies and peppers. And to drink?" He raised a questioning brow at Megan.

"A small root beer for me and—"

"Make that a pitcher of root beer and three glasses," Alex finished. Noticing that Ryan was looking longingly toward the video games, he dug in his pocket and came up with four quarters. "Ryan, you want to go over and try your luck?"

Ryan looked at the quarters, then at his mother. "Can I?"

Her expression tight, Megan turned to Alex. "That really isn't necessary."

"No, I don't suppose it is. Games are fun, not necessary. Ryan will enjoy playing, and I'll enjoy watching him. Why don't you let him go and we can have that little talk you mentioned?" He pretty much knew what was coming and decided it was best she get it out.

Megan stood up, allowing Ryan to scoot out of the booth. "Stay where I can see you, Ryan."

Spotting a friend from his class, Ryan hurried to the games section.

His mother sat back down. Thoughtful a moment, she searched for a way to get her message across as she toyed with her fork. "I'd prefer if you'd ask me first, out of Ryan's hearing, if you have a suggestion for him." She looked up. "Could you do that?"

Alex nodded. Was it going to be this easy? "Sure. Anything else?"

Elbows on the table, she crossed her arms. "Why are you being so nice to my son?"

That he hadn't expected. Alex shrugged. "He's a great kid, and I'm a nice guy."

"No, really. Tell me why."

The fact was, he couldn't tell her he was driven partially by guilt, a guilt he was afraid to confess. The shadow of Neal

Delaney hung over them. But it was more than that. He who'd not spent much time with children found he got a kick out of Ryan. The boy's enthusiasm was refreshing and contagious. "Can't you take the few things I've done at face value?"

"No. People have hidden agendas. I don't want Ryan hurt. He's already had far too many disappointments for someone as young as he is."

"And you think I'll hurt him?"

How could she make him see without revealing too much? "I don't think you'd mean to, but, well, it's difficult to explain. Ryan's father is gone and he lives mostly with two women. Naturally, he's drawn to a man who pays attention to him. But when you leave—"

"He'll feel abandoned again, like when his father died." Alex drew in a breath, considering that conclusion since it honestly hadn't occurred to him before. "So then you intend to keep him away from all men until you find someone you want to marry. Is that it?"

"No. I don't intend to marry again and—"

"Oh, so then you intend to keep Ryan away from all men, period. Any male teachers, coaches, guests in your home. Anyone he might get attached to, even fleetingly. But women friends are okay, right? Don't women guests ever leave, or teachers move on? Won't he feel bad if a little friend of his moves away? How are you going to prevent that, keep him away from kids, too?"

Put that way, she felt foolish. "You're missing the point."

"No, *you're* missing the point. Ryan's eight, not two. He's smart enough to know that I'm here now, but that I'll be going back home, just like Walter and Jean and your other guests. But that doesn't mean we can't be friends during the time we have together."

Megan sat staring at her folded hands, wondering if she was making a mountain out of a molehill. She'd only wanted to protect her son.

"Listen, I think I know a little of what Ryan feels since my mother died when I was fairly young. Every time I saw my father with a woman, I wondered if he'd marry her. I loved my mother a great deal and I didn't want him to try to replace her. Yet I was drawn to the idea of a woman in our lives again, someone who'd cook my favorite foods and knit sweaters and stick up for me when my dad was too strict. Did you ever think that Ryan looks at me not as a replacement for his father but rather as just a guy he can have a few laughs with and maybe learn something from?''

Except that Ryan's feelings for his father weren't like Alex's for his mother, Megan thought. Neal hadn't had much to do with his son as a baby, and even later he all but ignored Ryan. He'd never helped with his school projects, never attended one ball game, one Cub Scout meeting. No movies or fun visits to pizza parlors. The last year or two of his life, Neal had stayed away more, almost like a familiar stranger to both of them.

But how could she explain all that to a man she hardly knew?

"I see your point, but I hope you also see mine."

Alex reached over and placed a hand over both of hers. "I do. And I promise I'll try not to hurt him."

Ryan came barreling over at that moment, causing both adults to pull back their hands. "Hey, Mr. Shephard, I beat Jamie, this kid from my class, at Pac-Man twice. Can you believe it? Want to play me?"

"Maybe later, sport. Here comes our dinner."

As the waitress set down the steaming pizza and drinks, Megan slid out of the booth. "I think you need to wash your hands before eating, Ryan. Baseball grime all over you. Come with me."

"Aw, Mom, I don't want to go into the girls' room." He changed to a whisper. "My friend's here."

"Ryan, we're far from home and this is a big place. We've talked about stranger danger. I don't want you to go in alone."

The waitress left and Alex got up. "I'll go with him to the men's room. Come on, Ryan."

When they returned, Megan was busily pouring root beer. She noticed that Ryan's hands were sparkling clean. She spoke to Alex without looking up. "I know you think I'm overly protective but—"

"Just a tad, yeah. Hand me your plate, Ryan." He slid a piece on for the boy, then filled her plate and his own. "I also think it's natural to be overly protective when you're solely responsible for your child. You should have seen my dad. The first date I went on, he insisted on driving me to pick up the girl, took us to the party and came back for us. If you don't think I was embarrassed…"

Megan relaxed, surprised yet grateful that he seemed to understand. "How old were you?"

"Fourteen." Alex took a bite and chewed appreciatively. "It was a birthday party for a classmate. Her parents stayed out in the backyard. We played spin the carrot."

Megan swallowed around a laugh. "Spin the carrot?"

"Yeah. We didn't have a bottle so we used a carrot. When it was my turn, the carrot pointed to Norma Doolittle of all people."

"She wasn't your type?"

"She had a problem that became my problem. Braces. The minute I went near her mouth to try to kiss her, these tiny rubberbands came shooting out. Nearly put out my eye."

Behind her napkin, Megan laughed again. "You're making that up." Despite her misgivings about Alex—and there were many—she was beginning to enjoy herself, to enjoy him. *Dangerous!* a part of her mind warned. But for this one evening, she'd ignore the warning.

"You kissed a girl?" Ryan asked incredulously. "Yuk!"

"It was pretty yukky, all right. But things improved as I got older." He grinned at Megan and winked.

As she sipped her root beer, her eyes settled on his mouth and she found herself wondering just how his kiss might feel. That thought, Megan knew, was even more dangerous.

"Star light, star bright, first star I see tonight," Ryan sing-songed as they walked through the graveled parking lot.

"Gotta make a wish. I wish I had a kitten. What do you wish for, Alex?"

"That's easy." Holding the somewhat sticky hand that Ryan had slipped into his, Alex gazed up at a sky full of stars. "I wish I was on a windjammer ship sailing on the South Seas or in Switzerland getting ready to climb Mount Pilatus or in Kenya on a safari. Something fun and adventurous."

Alongside the Porsche, they stopped, and Megan looked up at him as if seeing him for the first time. "You've done those things before?"

"Oh, yeah, and I want to do them again." Alex's expression was filled with yearning. "You feel so wonderfully alive when you're out there—just you and the forces of nature." He remembered it so well with something that resembled nostalgia, then caught Megan's look. "Why are you frowning?"

"I knew someone like you once. He was never satisfied with things as they were, always searching for something new just over the horizon."

Did she mean Neal? "You don't approve?"

"I can't understand such a restless nature, such a fierce pursuit of the next thrill, something more exciting than the last."

"I think of it more as just having fun. Everyone needs some fun in their lives, Megan. You've heard about Jack, haven't you?"

"Jack?"

"Yeah. All work and no play made him a dull boy."

Perhaps she was dull, Megan thought. But that was far better than pursuing the impossible dream.

"What's your wish, Mom?" Ryan asked.

That, too, was easy. Boring, but easy. "I want us all to stay healthy, and I want to keep our rooms filled."

"You always say that, Mom."

Alex looked into her eyes, trying to read through her guarded expression. "Surely you want more than that, Megan. This isn't a dress rehearsal. We only go around once. Life's mighty short.'' Hadn't he almost lost his recently?

"Yes, I know. I buried my husband last year. Like you, he was drawn to new adventures. And he died a very unhappy man.'' She slipped her arm around her son's shoulders, drew him near. "It's time we left, sweetie. Say thank-you and good-night.''

"Thanks for the pizza. And the quarters. I had a great time." Ryan beamed up at Alex.

Unable to resist, Alex ruffled the boy's dark hair. "You're welcome, sport. See you later.''

"And thanks from me, too." Eyes averted, Megan pivoted on her heel, but her sandal got caught on a piece of gravel and she stumbled. She would have fallen if Alex hadn't reached out and steadied her, bringing them in very close contact. So close she could feel his warm breath on her neck.

Heart thudding, she looked up at him, very aware of his strong hands at her waist, the pressure of those long fingers. His eyes were a silvery green in the moonlight, intense, darkly passionate. For a fleeting instant, she wished she could give in to the need she saw reflected there. The sensual pull was much stronger than when he'd touched her by the refrigerator.

Then she straightened and hustled her son to her six-year-old Mustang with the muffler that needed replacing. Inside, she sighed wearily.

She didn't want a man in her life, Megan reminded herself, didn't want to waste energy longing for things she was better off without, for feelings she would only regret. Besides, Alex Shephard was the wrong man to want. He was everything she should run from, everything she'd vowed to never again give in to.

Despite all that, she looked down at hands that trembled and acknowledged that right this minute, she wanted to feel his strong arms around her more than her next breath.

Early the next afternoon, Alex went looking for Megan and finally found her in the laundry room off the kitchen. "I'm sorry to bother you, but do you have a screwdriver handy?''

Straightening from the dryer, she sent him a puzzled look. ''A screwdriver?''

Reluctantly, Alex brought his hand forward from behind his back and held out the doorknob to his room. His key was still in the lock. ''This came off a few minutes ago. I thought I had a screwdriver in my glove compartment, but I don't. It'll only take me a minute if you have one.''

Embarrassed and annoyed in equal measure, Megan reached for her toolbox. ''I'll take care of it.''

''No, I didn't come here for that. I can do it if you'll lend me a screwdriver. Please.'' She was wearing her stubborn face and he was getting exasperated. It had been that kind of day.

He'd met with old man Parsons's son for over an hour this morning and the kid had been arrogant and obnoxious. Alex had half a mind to tell him to take his land and shove it. But then, his reason for staying in Twin Oaks would be gone. Still, he was in no mood for yet another round of sparring.

Grabbing the handle of her toolbox, Megan walked past him and headed for the stairs. ''Just bring it with you, please.''

''No.''

She stopped in midstride, turned around and saw the hand holding the doorknob slither around behind him. ''What?'' she asked, hanging on to her temper by a thin thread.

''This is such a minor repair, Megan. Why are you turning it into a major altercation?''

''I make minor repairs around here and hire someone to do the major ones. If you fix it, I'll have to pay you.''

Damn fool stubborn woman. Two could play this game. ''All, right, what do you think would be fair payment for five minutes work?''

Megan wished with all her might that she'd have handed him the damn screwdriver, but she was in too deep now. ''Five dollars.''

Alex raised both brows. "Five dollars? You pay a dollar a minute for minor repair jobs? I may quit my job and come work for you."

"Yes, I'm sure that's far more than you make." She was so rarely sarcastic, yet he'd pushed her. Hadn't he?

Slowly, Alex brought his hand around, walked over and gave her the doorknob. "Here, you win. Are you happy now?" He walked past her through the swinging kitchen doors.

In the hallway, Megan leaned against the wall and breathed out a rush of air. What had she done to deserve Alex Shephard here in her own home tormenting her? When would he finish his business and go back where he came from?

And why did everything he said and did get under her skin?

By four in the afternoon, Megan was dragging. She hadn't slept well the night before after that close encounter with Alex in Pasquale's parking lot. Her restless dreams had awakened her repeatedly and irritated her mightily. To top it all off, her washer had broken down again after only six loads. This time, no matter what she did, even resorting to giving it a swift kick, it refused to start again.

She'd given up and called Eddie Jenkins, the repairman.

Fortunately, she'd finished most of the essential laundry including Ryan's clothes. Climbing up to the third-floor family quarters, she wished she could indulge in a nap.

Walking past Grace's room, then her own, she stopped halfway down the long hallway. There were voices coming from Ryan's room. That alone was odd, for he never invited anyone in to his private sanctuary. She usually had to struggle to get him to allow her to vacuum it. The door was ajar. Megan paused, listening.

One voice was definitely Ryan's, but the other didn't belong to his friend, Bobby, the only person who visited occasionally. No, it was a deeper voice and much older. She heard two people laughing out loud and pushed open the door.

They were both seated cross-legged on the floor with newspapers spread out between them. The parts to a model car in the making were scattered about and the smell of construction glue was noticeable.

"Hi, Mom," Ryan said, smiling.

"Hi," Alex said, also smiling as if they hadn't all but come to blows earlier today.

"What are you two up to?" she asked, even though it was obvious.

"Putting together the new racer Alex got me." Ryan held up the box with the picture on the front. "A Stingray. Neat, eh?"

"Positively neat," Megan answered, sidestepping them and placing the stack of Ryan's clean clothes on his bed. "Ryan, I thought I told you not to call adults by their first name."

"He told me to call him Alex. He said that I call Grace by her first name."

He would come up with that, she thought. "Yes, but Grace is a friend, an old family friend."

Alex looked up. "You don't think I could be a family friend?"

Unsure what to say to that, still in shock that her son had invited this relative stranger into his domain, much less was now on a first-name basis with him, she stood watching them. Alex held the tube of glue while Ryan used a toothpick to spread it along the back bumper.

Feeling her eyes on him, Alex decided to speak up as he glanced at her over his shoulder. "Are you going to come down on me about buying this model, too? We've been over this ground, but if you're uncomfortable about—"

"No, no." Megan waved a dismissive hand. "If you want to spend your afternoons buying model cars and putting them together with an eight-year-old, far be it from me to stop you."

"Hey, we're having a good time here." He'd thought to say it to put her in her place, but suddenly, Alex realized he meant it. Ryan Delaney was a super kid. "Building model cars is important and educational. Hand-eye coordination, you know. Like batting practice—and we'll get to that after we're finished here. That reminds me. I bought a bat. You owe me $10.37. I accept checks, Visa or plain old cash.'' He turned back in time to shift the tube of glue so Ryan could attend to the front end.

"I see.'' But she didn't, not at all. "I'd have thought you'd rather climb a mountain or go on a safari than do kid things.''

"Not today.'' It was one of his dragged-out days, when he tired easily. The doctor had said he'd have them occasionally.

Megan considered the man in front of her thoughtfully. She'd had a few men try to win Ryan over in order to get her into bed. She was, after all, young and fairly attractive and suddenly available with Neal gone. But not stupid. And she'd seen through the short list of friends, neighbors and traveling salesmen. But although she'd caught Alex looking at her with hungry eyes, he hadn't made a pass or even hinted at anything. And he honestly seemed to enjoy being with Ryan.

She was totally at a loss.

"Megan? Are you up there, Megan?'' Grace's voice came up the stairway.

Megan moved to the open door. "Yes, right here, Grace. What's up?''

"Eddie Jenkins is here to see you.''

"All right, I'll be right down.'' She turned back to Ryan. "Do you have any homework?''

"You already asked me that when I first came home, Mom. No homework tonight.'' Concentrating hard, Ryan stuck his tongue out of the corner of his mouth. "Does this part go over here?'' he asked Alex.

"Yeah, right above the grill.''

"Okay, then. I'll see you two later.'' Feeling like a fifth-wheel when neither of them even glanced up, she left the room.

As soon as her footsteps receded down the stairs, Alex looked up. "Who's Eddie Jenkins?''

"This geeky guy who likes Mom.''

"Likes Mom. You mean, like in boyfriend, girlfriend?"

Ryan dropped the tiny piece and bent to retrieve it before the glue dried. "Yeah, I think he'd like to be her boyfriend."

"How does she feel about him?" Alex hated pumping the kid, but he needed to know. Funny how another guy on the scene hadn't occurred to him. But after all, Megan Delaney was a lovely woman and her husband had been dead nearly a year. He should have guessed there'd be guys coming around.

Not that it mattered to him, really.

"I don't think she likes him very much."

"Does he come over a lot?"

"Only when the washer's broken. He's a repairman. He always brings me candy, but I can tell he only does it on account of Mom."

So, a washer repairman. Maybe he should just wander downstairs and...nah! "Okay, that's about all we should do for now. Let's leave it to dry, then finish it tomorrow."

"Okay." Rising carefully, Ryan carried the half-finished model over to his desk.

Getting to his feet, Alex crumpled up the glue-spattered newspapers and tossed them into the wastebasket. "You've got a real nice room here."

"Yeah. No one ever uses it, guests, I mean. Except my dad when he was here last time. Mom didn't want him in her room, so I slept with her."

"Really? I wonder why."

"She said 'cause they were always fighting."

Interesting. Alex noticed a couple of pictures on Ryan's bulletin board. One was a picture of Megan, a younger Ryan and a tall, smiling man waving from the deck of a sleek speedboat. "Is this your dad?"

Ryan walked over. "Yeah, that's him. He sure loved that boat."

"Where is it now?"

"Mom had to sell it."

That had to have netted her a pretty penny. The only other

snapshot stuck among his Little League schedule and other kid stuff was a close-up of Megan looking uncomfortable standing in front of the Delaney's Bed & Breakfast sign alongside a beaming Neal Delaney.

"That's the day they opened this place," Ryan explained. "Isn't Mom pretty?"

"She sure is." An expensive speedboat that she probably also sold. But what had she done with the money? Alex wanted in the worst way to ask her, but did he have the right?

And if he started delving into her secrets, what about the secret *he* was hiding from her?

Early afternoon the next day, Alex was stretched out on his bed feeling bored and restless. The third and final banker he wanted to meet with was out of town. Of course, since it was Friday, he could check out of the inn, drive home and come back after the feasibility study was complete, provided it was favorable. There was no reason for him to hang around this tiny burg all weekend. Back in San Diego, he could phone half a dozen friends and get as many invitations. Or he could call someone in his little black book for a date, maybe have dinner at the Del or take in a play.

Or get Maddy to pack one of her special picnic baskets and take a date out on the *Black Sheep*. It was about time he tried out his sailboat. He'd bet the weather would be perfect this time of year. He'd been taking his medication on time and was feeling healthy and strong. He hadn't napped once since arriving, although yesterday he'd felt a bit droopy.

Suddenly, a mental picture formed—Ryan on his boat and Megan beside him at the wheel, all of them in orange life jackets. They could go over to Catalina, picnic there, sleep overnight on the boat. He could rent a car and drive over to the buffalo ranch. Ryan probably had never seen a buffalo. They could...wait!

Alex swung his legs over and sat up. What in hell was he thinking? Megan wouldn't leave this place for a couple of hours much less a couple of days. And she'd never let him take Ryan alone. Besides, he'd only come to check things out, make sure Neal Delaney's family was doing okay, not to get involved.

Not for the first time that day, Alex ran a hand through his hair in frustration. But he hadn't accomplished what he'd come to do. He didn't know enough about Megan's financial affairs to make an honest appraisal. She certainly hadn't revealed much and he couldn't very well question local bankers and Realtors. People talked in small towns and she'd surely find out and wonder why he was going around asking questions.

He couldn't walk away until he knew more, until he was satisfied she could keep her head above water. He knew that only two rooms in the inn were currently occupied, other than his and Mrs. K's. Maybe business was slower on weekends. Usually, he'd noticed, travelers only stayed one night, two at the most, at a bed-and-breakfast. How could she show a profit on such sporadic bookings?

Maybe if he got to know her better, she'd loosen up and tell him a bit more. Like she'd paid off the mortgage and all her bills with the insurance money and the sale of Neal's boat. She drove an older car, the place needed sprucing up, and she baked cakes for extra cash. According to the figures Mitch had given him, she'd received over a quarter of a million dollars. Something didn't add up here.

He glanced at the newspaper he'd been reading, then leaned closer for a look at an ad, an idea forming. Smiling, he went downstairs looking for Megan. He found her in the dining room setting the table for breakfast next morning.

"Hi, there." She was wearing a pink oversize shirt and white shorts. Her legs were long and shapely, he couldn't help noticing. Was there no color she didn't look good in?

Cautiously, Megan looked at him. "Hi, yourself." She recognized that restive look, for she'd seen it often enough in Neal's eyes. "Going somewhere?"

"Maybe, if you agree. You said you wanted to know ahead of time if I want to ask Ryan to do something, so I'm asking you first. How about if I take him to see *Space Jam* at the movies tonight? It's Friday, no school tomorrow. He told me he's a big fan of Michael Jordan's.''

She'd begun shaking her head before he'd finished. ''I'm sorry, but I don't let Ryan go anywhere without me. He's too young.'' She stabbed the air with a fork. ''And don't tell me I'm being overly protective because I know it and I'm not changing.''

He'd known her answer all along. ''Okay, then, you come with us. It starts at seven, we'll be out by nine. The movie got a good review, and let's face it, you could use a little fun time.''

''I have my baking to do this evening.'' Why couldn't he accept no for an answer like a normal person?

''Can't you skip it for one night?''

She shot him an annoyed look. ''Emily depends on me. The weekends are her biggest days. I can't let her down.''

''All right, then. It's only one o'clock. You can bake this afternoon.''

''I've got paperwork to do this afternoon. And the wash I didn't finish yesterday. Thanks, but another time.'' She turned her back and moved to the sideboard for more silverware.

Alex was far from defeated. ''Too bad, really. Tonight they're passing out *Space Jam* posters to the first one hundred kids who buy a ticket. *Autographed* posters. Sure would look neat in Ryan's room. Michael Jordan holding a basketball, ready to shoot. The kind of thing every kid would love. I'll bet half of Ryan's friends will be there. But, okay, if you have to work and you won't let me take him. I can see why—''

''Stop!'' She swiveled to face him, wondering whether to smile or pop him a good one. ''You never give up, do you?''

He grinned. ''I wouldn't say never. Rarely, though.''

Megan sighed heavily. She probably could let the paperwork go till the weekend. She could get the baking done and take it over to Emily on the way to the theater. She had to admit that Ryan, who seldom got to go to the movies, would love it. "Seven, you said?"

"Yeah, but we have to get there early to get a poster. Why don't we go to dinner at the Cornerstone? It's just down the block from the movie and—"

"Don't push your luck. We'll eat early, right here in my kitchen. Five o'clock. You can join us. Burgers. Be on time." Before he could talk her into anything more, she pushed through the swinging doors and left him standing there.

Standing there grinning.

"Man, that movie was awesome!" Ryan was nearly walking on air as they left the theater. He carried his rolled-up poster carefully. "Mom, didn't you just love it?"

Megan smiled at his enthusiasm. "I just loved it."

"What was your favorite part, Alex? Mine was when Bugs Bunny and Michael beat the Cartoon Aliens in that last game. Wow!"

"I kind of liked Lola Bunny, Bugs's girlfriend," Alex said with a teasing smile aimed at Megan.

"How big do you think Michael's hands are, Alex?" Ryan asked.

"Way bigger than mine," he answered, holding his hand out. He watched Ryan put his small hand up to his, comparing.

"I guess I've got a ways to go." Walking between his mom and Alex, he felt good. A Friday-night movie *and* a poster. Cool! Then he thought of something. "Do you think I'm going to be tall, Alex? My dad wasn't real tall and I'm the shortest boy in my class. Even some of the girls are taller." His height was something Ryan worried a lot about ever since they were all measured in gym class.

"I told you that girls mature faster than boys," Megan said.

Alex saw the boy's worried frown and knew how important height was to a boy. "I was pretty short throughout grade school," he confessed. "I had asthma, so I couldn't play team sports or do much running. But I outgrew it around fourteen, and right after that I shot up."

"Really?"

"Sure. No use worrying ahead of time."

They reached the Porsche parked on the street. Megan had suggested they take her Mustang, which had a real back seat, not a tiny, abbreviated one. Naturally, Alex and Ryan had overruled her.

"Hey, look over there. A real ice-cream parlor. The Sweet Tooth. I haven't been inside one of those in years."

"I've *never* been inside one," Ryan said hopefully.

"Because it's new," Megan informed them. "They only opened a month or so ago." She couldn't just keep taking from this man. He'd bought the pizza the other night and the tickets and popcorn tonight. The least she could do was to buy him an ice cream. "Before you two start campaigning, let's go in. Only it's *my* treat this time or we don't go." She glanced up at Alex. "Agreed?"

"Yes, ma'am." She seemed more relaxed tonight, Alex thought as they crossed the street. Her hair was loose and just touching her shoulders. She had on a yellow-and-black-striped top over slim black slacks. He noticed she wore a simple gold chain around her neck.

It took Ryan forever to decide which sundae to order. On his knees on the red plastic booth, he squirmed and pondered, considering and dismissing.

"Are you sure you can handle a sundae after a cheeseburger at home and all that popcorn?" Megan asked, hoping he wouldn't get sick between the food and the excitement.

"Hey, Mom, I'm a big kid. Okay, I've got it. The chocolate marshmallow over fudge ripple with whipped cream and two cherries." Pleased with his final selection, he grinned at both of them.

Alex was enjoying the boy's enthusiasm. "Make that two," he told the gum-chewing teenage waitress.

There goes her tight budget, Megan thought, but joined in and told the girl she'd have the same. Looking around the crowded parlor, she waved at one of Emily's sons seated across the room with his wife and two small children, then at an older couple who ran a corner grocery store.

"You came to a place like this a lot when you were my age, didn't you, Alex?" Ryan wanted to know.

"No, hardly ever. My dad wasn't around much, always working and traveling."

"Like my dad."

"I guess so. After my mom died…"

Ryan's eyes grew wide. "Your mom died?"

"Yes, when I was twelve. She'd been sick for over a year."

"Boy, that's awful." Ryan glanced at his own mother, a fearful thought settling on him.

Megan reached over to hug him. "I'm healthy, Ryan, and I plan to be around a long while." The doctor had told her that when a child loses one parent, especially from as rapid an illness as Neal's had been, he's bound to worry about the other parent. She kissed his dark head reassuringly.

She was really great with the boy, Alex thought, and Ryan clearly adored her. It was something to see, their easy affection. "My brother and I had a nanny and she used to take us to get ice cream once in a while."

Ryan screwed up his face. "A nanny? Like a nanny goat?"

Alex hid a smile and saw Megan do the same. "Not quite. A nanny is someone who watches over kids when the parents aren't around. Maddy came to live with us and she still takes care of my father's house. A great lady."

"But not as good as your real mom, right?" After Ryan heard that Alex had lost his mom, his young heart went out to his new friend.

"No, but she tried. She was really good at building kites and even climbed up our backyard tree once to talk to me when I wouldn't come down." Funny how that memory had popped up. The big old apple tree with its gnarled branches had been his haven, his refuge, when he needed to think or just be alone.

"Mom doesn't like me to climb trees. She says I'll get hurt."

"I guess that's possible, but you have to learn to be careful." He leaned forward confidentially. "You know what I always wanted? A tree house."

"A house in a tree? Do they really have those?"

"You have to build it with lumber and stuff. Get a piece of carpet to put on the floor. That'd be neat, huh?" He felt Megan's eyes on him and shifted his gaze. She was definitely not smiling. "I guess it's not very practical."

"Maybe we could build one," Ryan said, catching the fever but not his mother's frown. "We have a big tree in our backyard."

The ice-cream sundaes arrived in time to save Alex from further frowns. Then all three dug in, and to Megan's surprise not only did Ryan finish his, but she did, too.

Wiping her mouth, she sat back. "I have to admit, that was terrific."

"Stick with me, kid, and I'll show you more terrific." His green gaze stayed on her face and he wished just then that they were alone, that he could reach over and touch her smooth skin, watch her eyes grow dark as they had last night in the graveled parking lot. She made him want to do things like showing her New York in the spring or Paris in the summer or Italy in the autumn. Or just simple things, like taking a walk in the forest or watching a sunset by the sea.

Alex felt she was interested, though she didn't want to be. He recognized the signs. And he was interested, too. But only temporarily, and he had a gut feeling Megan Delaney wasn't now or had she ever been a temporary kind of woman.

No man had ever made her lose herself in his eyes, Megan thought, feeling heat move into her face despite the cold dessert she'd just eaten. Alex had her softening, warming, opening with just a look. How could that be? Neal hadn't been able to do that, not on his best day. What was happening to her?

Alex looked away first. This wasn't in anyone's best interest, he decided firmly. He wasn't a forever kind of guy and he also had no business letting Ryan think he might be around for that long. He'd promised Megan he wouldn't hurt her son and he meant to keep that promise.

They strolled back to the car, a noticeable silence between the two adults as Ryan skipped ahead. Under the streetlamp, Alex unlocked the Porsche and held the seat forward so Ryan could get into the small back seat, then turned to allow Megan to enter. As she stepped around him, he saw that she'd pushed her bangs to one side, leaving a pink scar visible near her left temple. He knew a little something about scars and how long they took to heal.

He reached to touch it lightly. "This is fairly recent," he commented. "What happened?"

Moving away from his touch, Megan's fingers feathered her bangs over the scar. "It's nothing." Averting her eyes, she climbed into the low-slung car.

Nothing? Alex thought as he closed her door and walked around to the driver's side. A three-inch scar that had to have happened less than a year ago, since it looked pretty much like his own, was hardly nothing. And if it was nothing, why hadn't she just explained how it had happened?

Something there, he decided as he started the powerful engine. And he meant to find out what.

Chapter 5

Whistling slightly off-key, Alex strolled up the stairs on the way to his room. He'd spent a lucrative Saturday morning and he was pleased with himself. After breakfast, he'd cruised the town of Twin Oaks, which, given its size, hadn't taken all that long. Not only had he found another parcel of land on the outskirts that might be suitable for upscale homes, but he'd come upon some municipal tennis courts. He loved tennis and hadn't played in far too long.

Since his racquet and shoes were in the trunk, if he could just find someone to play singles with, he might be able to work off some restless energy. Switching songs in midwhistle, he reached the top of the second floor where his room was located and saw that his door was open. Puzzled, he walked in.

There was a grunting sound coming from his bathroom. Peeking in, he saw Megan standing in his bathtub barefoot, her jeans rolled up to midcalf, wrestling with a huge pipe wrench. She was concentrating so hard, she didn't hear him.

He couldn't help but smile at the picture she made. Poster girl for *Plumbers' Weekly Magazine*.

"Ahem." He saw her startled jerk just before she turned toward the doorway. "Do you have a union card, ma'am?"

"Very funny." She dropped her aching arms, wishing she had more strength in her hands. "Grace was in here cleaning the room earlier and discovered that your shower was leaking. Hadn't you noticed?"

Actually he had, but he'd been reluctant to tell Megan since she'd already had the repairman out recently for the washer. He'd planned to sneak a peek into her toolbox when she was busy and borrow a wrench to fix it himself without bothering her. He hadn't felt like getting into a sparring match with her over a drippy shower. "Maybe I just didn't turn it off tightly enough."

Megan sent him a long-suffering look. "You look strong enough to me." She raised the wrench, tried to get a good grip, but it slipped.

"You're right. I am strong enough. Stronger than you." He toed off his shoes, whipped off his socks and stepped into the tub with her. "Move over and let me tighten this."

Surprised, Megan nonetheless let him since she'd been getting nowhere. She leaned toward the tiled wall so she could explain. "The head came off in my hand the first try. See over here? I think the threads are worn."

"Probably. I don't suppose you have any Teflon tape so we can wind it around the threads before trying to tighten it again?" He saw her shake her head. "I didn't think so." He took the wrench and adjusted it, then reached up to set it around the bolt. "Tell me, do you play tennis?"

Her mind on plumbing, Megan frowned. "Tennis?"

"Yeah, you know, racquet, balls, a court, a net. Tennis."

Wondering what tennis had to do with fixing a shower, she sighed. "I used to a long, long time ago, in high school." A lifetime ago, it seemed.

Alex gazed at her over his shoulder. "It can't have been *that* long ago. What are you, twenty-six, twenty-seven?"

"Twenty-seven. That was ten years ago, but it seems like more. Why do you ask?"

"I found these fairly nice courts over by Berkshire Woods. I thought we could go bat a ball around for a while. Good exercise."

Just what she needed after her sixteen-hour days was more good exercise. "Sorry, but I'm way too rusty. I'd probably put your eye out. You know, like that girl's rubber bands did." She almost chuckled aloud remembering his story of spin the carrot.

"It'll come back to you, like riding a bicycle. We could just practice, not play a real game until you warm up. Do you have a racquet?" He tightened the bolt again, putting some real muscle into it.

"Probably out in the garage somewhere or maybe my closet." She braced an arm against the side wall, trying to ease past him so she could step out. Instead, her shoulder hit the handle and the shower spray turned on full blast. "Oh!"

Water surged onto Alex's head, blinding him for a moment. Groping about, he tried to locate the handle with his eyes closed, but couldn't.

Megan was trying to climb out and get away from the cold water soaking her, but the more she struggled to get around him, the less traction her bare feet had on the slippery bottom of the tub. In order to keep from falling, she reached out with both hands and grabbed hold of his shirt, hanging on for dear life.

Behind her back, Alex finally managed to turn off the water. Standing there, drenched to the skin, his hair plastered to his head and a very wet woman clinging to him, he did the only thing he could think to do. He laughed out loud.

Surprised, Megan leaned back, then saw the humor of the situation. She began laughing, too. "I guess," she gasped out between bubbles of laughter, "I should have turned the water off at the source."

"Yeah, I'd say so." Alex raised a hand to brush her wet hair off her face. She was close up against him, very close, and smelled like a mixture of soap and shampoo. A clean, wholesome scent, yet oddly sensual. His eyes drifted to her mouth as she licked water from her lips. Involuntarily, his arms tightened around her and his body tightened in response.

Megan felt her smile slip away. She was trapped in his eyes again, in their sea green depths. She was close enough to see a tiny nick on his stubborn jaw where he'd cut himself shaving. She was close enough that she could almost taste him.

Alex saw a chance to give life to his fantasies. He had to kiss her before he went stark, raving mad. Lowering his head, he touched his mouth to hers.

Megan saw the kiss coming, could easily have stopped it. She knew instinctively that he wasn't the sort of man who'd insist if she said no. But she didn't say no, didn't want to stop him. His mouth grazed hers, softly at first, then he drew in a breath and made a sound deep in his throat as he pulled her closer.

Her eyes drifted shut and she let him take her under as her arms wound around him with a will of their own. She hadn't been kissed in well over two years, and even then not like this. Never like this. He eased back slightly, and when her lips parted in surprise, his tongue entered her mouth. He tasted, he devoured, he plundered, and all the while his hands at her back pressed her closer and closer.

She would pay for this in self-recriminations later, Megan knew. But for now, for once, couldn't she just enjoy the kiss when she'd enjoyed so little in far too long? Couldn't she allow herself to feel things she wasn't sure she would ever feel again? Couldn't she be like other women for just this brief moment in time and know what it was like to be in a man's arms, a man who seemed to want her desperately?

She would pay the price later, but for now, she would just savor.

Alex had known she'd taste like this, sweet and oddly innocent. He knew she'd been married for years, had a child. Yet there was a hesitancy about her just before his mouth touched hers that excited him. She seemed inexperienced and stunned to discover her own sensual need.

Her breathing was labored, warm on his cheeks. She smelled so good and tasted even better. Unable to resist, he placed a kiss in the small dimple in her chin that intrigued him so, then returned to her waiting mouth. Almost tentatively, her tongue touched his and he took over while his hands began to roam.

He found her to be slender beneath his roving fingers, yet every inch a woman. She was wearing a short-sleeved denim shirt two sizes too large, and the soaking wet extra material was frustrating him. He wanted to feel her skin, to touch her. His hands moved between them and under the heavy cotton, searching for her breasts.

The moment his fingers touched her bare flesh, Megan felt as if cold water had splashed on her again. Her eyes flew open and she took a shaky step back, coming to her senses. What on earth was she doing? Whatever was wrong with her?

She was standing soaked to the skin in a guest's room, kissing him as if she couldn't ever get enough, with the door open so anyone could stroll by and see them. Thank goodness Grace had taken Ryan to his Little League practice. That would have been all she needed, to have one of them troop in.

With an audible groan, she moved another step back, shoving her damp hair aside with both hands, beating herself up over her stupid lapse of good sense. Quickly, she stepped out of the tub and grabbed a towel from the rack, pressing it to her flaming cheeks. "I...I'm so sorry."

Alex followed her out, having watched the play of emotions on her expressive face and guessing how she felt. "Don't be. We didn't do anything so terrible or wrong."

But Megan wasn't listening, wouldn't look at him. "What must you think of me? Oh, God!" When he touched her arm, she pulled free. "No, no, let me go." And she hurried out, out of his room and up the stairs, tracking water to her own room, where she closed her door and fell on her bed, still clutching the towel.

Pulling up her knees and rolling to her side, she let the raw emotions buffet her as she sobbed into the towel. What must Alex think of her, brazenly inviting his advances the very first time he touched her, with openmouthed kisses she'd obviously invited? She was the proprietor of the establishment where he was a guest, and her behavior was way out of line. She could have stopped it, could have prevented the whole thing from happening. But she hadn't, hadn't wanted to. What, exactly, did that make her?

Lonely. That's what she was, lonely. Not just for a man's touch, but for a man's companionship, like last evening's trip to the movie and the ice-cream parlor afterward. Laughing together, acting like a family, if only a make-believe one, for a few hours. Despite her protestations to Grace to the contrary, work and friendship and her son weren't enough.

But what did she know about flirting, about attracting men in the nineties? She'd married too young to master the game, then found herself alone again. Alone and lonely for the warmth and touch and special flavors of a man, which she'd had for such a brief time with Neal before she'd discovered his true nature.

But Alex didn't know how rotten her marriage had been. He didn't know what a huge price she'd paid for marrying the best catch of the county. Neal Delaney, handsome, charming, sexy. All the girls wanted him, but *she'd* won him. It had taken her less than a year to realize she hadn't caught the brass ring after all.

But Alex couldn't know about those terrible years when Neal had tried job after job, losing one after the other, always blaming others, getting frustrated, turning to drink. She'd been about to leave him when she'd discovered that Ryan was on the way. But where could she have gone anyway, and how could she have supported herself and her baby with only a high school diploma? Not back to her mother's small house where Dottie was still struggling to raise her other two daughers. Eighteen, pregnant and alone would have been worse than sticking it out with Neal. So she had.

When the insurance money from Neal's parents' death had arrived, she'd managed for the first and only time to convince him that they had to invest in something solid for Ryan's sake. The bed-and-breakfast that bore his name had appealed to Neal at first, mostly because he saw himself as this handsome meeter and greeter at the door, welcoming guests to *his* place. What he hadn't been able to visualize was all the work that went into turning an old residence into a viable guest house and keeping it running. And he'd soon tired of trying.

They'd fought and he'd left, but he'd always come back, sober and contrite, swearing he'd be better. Only it simply wasn't in him. The night she'd learned about the other women had been the last night she'd allowed Neal to share her bed. Even when he'd gotten sick and she'd let him come back for a while, he'd slept in Ryan's room, not with her.

But Alex wasn't aware of any of that. Only Grace knew. He knew only that Megan had buried her supposedly loving and very ill husband less than a year ago, and there she was, in his room, straining through her wet clothes to get closer, to kiss deeper. Small wonder his hands had felt free to wander. He probably figured she did that sort of thing with every single man who stayed at Delaney's.

The truth was far different. No man had touched her in too many months to count, nor had she wanted one. Sex had never been that big a deal for her anyway. Some women just weren't very sensual and she was one of them, Megan had decided. She'd put men and all they represented out of her mind. She worked so hard during the day that by nightfall sex was low on her list of priorities. A shower and a few hours of uninterrupted oblivion in her soft, solitary bed held infinitely more appeal. Any physical longings her body might have entertained in her teens had ultimately disappeared.

Until Alex Shephard had sauntered into her life.

In one way, she'd been shocked in that tub to find herself wanting him so powerfully. It seemed every time she was near Alex, she became edgy with restless desire. It had been inevitable, she supposed, that that strong a need would explode as it had. Still, she shouldn't have allowed it to get so far.

Neal had hurt her so badly with his admitted infidelities that she wasn't sure she could ever want another man, or so she'd tried to convince herself. But she'd been wrong. Alex had awakened a dormant passion in her, and although it was thrilling to know she wasn't dead inside after all, Megan didn't know what to do with this unleashed monster.

She couldn't let it happen again, couldn't take a chance on getting involved. Desiring a man was one thing, but trusting one again was even more difficult. She would have to reach down deep inside herself and find the control she'd somehow lost today.

Megan wasn't certain how long she lay there wrapped in her own mortification. But suddenly, she heard loud footsteps on the stairs and knew her son was back. Quickly, she jumped up, went into her bathroom and turned on the shower.

Ryan couldn't learn what a fool she'd made of herself, she thought, stripping off her wet things, nor could Grace. But the question remained: How was she going to face Alex?

Lawrence Williams rose and stood behind his heavy oak desk in his office at First National Bank, extending his hand to Alex. "I'm impressed with your company's reputation. We'd be pleased to do business with you, Mr. Shephard."

Alex shook the hand of the final banker he'd wanted to meet. First National was exactly the kind of lending institution Shephard Construction liked dealing with—not too large, yet with an impressive reputation and a good name in the community. "Thanks. I appreciate your seeing me on such short notice. After the results of the feasibility study are in, I'll be in touch."

Williams walked around his desk, strolling to the door with him. "I look forward to hearing from you." He ushered Alex out to the bank's main lobby. "Did you drive in for the day or are you staying nearby?"

"I've got a room at Delaney's Bed & Breakfast."

"Ah, yes. Shame about Mr. Delaney dying like that. We do business with Mrs. Delaney. Actually, we hold mortgages on many properties in Twin Oaks, both residential and commercial."

Alex knew the loan officer was still trying to impress him with his bank's volume, but something else interested him more. "Do you hold the mortgage on the Delaney property?"

"Yes, indeed. First and second mortgage."

Two mortgages? His hand on the doorknob, Alex paused. "I understood Neal Delaney had a considerable amount of insurance. I'd have thought his widow would have paid off the mortgages after his death."

Williams adjusted his rimless glasses. "I don't know anything about any insurance settlement. I do know she didn't pay off her mortgages. Matter of fact, well, I really shouldn't say any more. Financial information is confidential, you realize."

"Of course. However, I'm more than just a guest passing through." Alex decided that that kiss yesterday allowed him to take their relationship a step further. "I'm a friend. If Megan Delaney's in some sort of financial difficulty…"

"I didn't say that." Williams shuffled his feet uncomfortably. "As I'm sure you're aware, it's not unusual for a new business to have cash-flow problems and get a bit behind. We at First National Bank believe in working with our customers. We know how hard Mrs. Delaney's trying to make a go of her business. We have every faith in her." Obviously uncomfortable about having said too much, he checked his watch. "Now if you'll excuse me, I have another appointment. Please call as soon as you're ready to discuss particulars."

"Yes, thank you, I will." Alex walked through the lobby and outside, his forehead wrinkled thoughtfully. A second mortgage when he'd thought she'd surely paid off the first.

Cash-flow problems? A bit behind? Just how far behind was that and how large were those payments?

And always he came back to this thought: What in hell had Megan done with over a quarter of a million dollars in insurance money?

A sunny Monday afternoon had tourists and browsers strolling by the shops and boutiques of Twin Oaks. Because he needed to think, Alex ambled along among them, glancing in the windows of a fudge shop, another that featured colorful glassware, and a card and souvenir shop.

Had Neal and Megan run up huge debts renovating the place before they'd opened the doors? he wondered. But Emily had said they'd done much of the work themselves. There would have been large cash outlays for the speedboat, the flashy car. Had they lived beyond their means, led the good life, letting essential obligations like the mortgage go unpaid? That seemed so out of character for the way he knew Megan to be, frugally putting on a barbecue herself instead of having it catered, making minor repairs rather than calling a repairman, even baking to supplement her income.

Had Neal been a spendthrift, then?

Or—and this thought weighed heavily—had they, like many self-employed people with small businesses, had no medical insurance, thereby obliging her to pay off heavy hospital debts with Neal's life insurance money? Fortunately, his father had seen to it that everyone at Shephard Construction had excellent health insurance, so his liver transplant, which could easily have run upward of three hundred thousand, had been paid for completely through insurance. If Neal had been number one on the transplant list, he'd have had to have sufficient coverage or cash, or they wouldn't have considered him. Medicine, after all, was a business.

Heading for his car, Alex realized that every question he asked himself only led to others. If only he could get some answers out of Megan.

She'd had trouble making eye contact with him after that kiss. He'd stayed mostly out of her way since then, giving her time to realize that they hadn't done anything wrong. But when he'd tried to take her aside Sunday afternoon, she'd all but run from him, saying she had things to do.

Bull!

They'd have to talk about this shift in their relationship sooner or later. Ignoring it would only emphasize it, blow it out of all proportion. He unlocked the Porsche and climbed in. Easing out into the noonday traffic, he decided he'd try again today. Somehow he had to get through to her so she'd stop berating herself over a mere kiss.

Well, it had been more than that. It had been one hell of a kiss. In reality, it had knocked his socks off and made him long for more. What Megan didn't know, couldn't know, was that that kiss had stirred Alex in ways he'd been privately, silently worried he might not be stirred again. At the onset of his illness, sex had been the furthest thing from his mind. After the surgery, there'd been long months when he didn't care, when sex was a vague memory, a distant dream, as his body fought to survive, to heal.

As he recovered at home, his interest had slowly come creeping back. Some days, yearnings had overwhelmed him, making him tight and tense. But there'd been nothing and no one in so long that he'd fearfully wondered if things would ever be the same again.

Then suddenly, there'd been a beautiful woman, wet and clinging, in his arms. A very sexy, seemingly willing woman. And Alex had been thrilled to realize he not only wanted her, but he wanted her fiercely.

Megan had pulled away before she'd realized how close he'd been to hauling her onto his soft bed. Something had stopped her, some memory or fear or demon of her own. But she wanted him. He knew it and now she knew it, too. Desire had been tamped down, but it would flare up again, Alex was certain.

And why not? They were both single, unattached, available. Why shouldn't they enjoy one another and relieve some of the tension? Of course, if he couldn't get her to open up and talk this out, nothing would happen, he thought as he swung into Delaney's lot and parked.

On his way to the front door, he heard a sound from the side yard and wandered over to investigate. There was the object of his mind's meanderings, using an ancient push mower to cut the grass. She was having a terrible time on the lumpy terrain with blades that looked dull and rusty. He strolled toward her.

Megan finished a row, turned the mower around and glanced up to see Alex walking to meet her. Just what she needed. She was hot, sweaty and tired after struggling with the stubborn mower for half an hour and getting very little done. She had a headache left over from yesterday and the day before, probably because she was sleeping so poorly. There were days, infrequent but nonetheless real, when she wanted to stay in bed, pull the covers over her head and hide from the harsh realities of the world. This was one of them, and the expression on Alex's face told her he was going to add to her problems. She almost groaned aloud.

Blocking her path, he propped his hands on his hips. "This is not something you should be doing. Why don't you hire a handyman?" Maybe a direct question like that would force her to give him a direct answer for a change.

If he only knew how much she'd love to hire a handyman. She had a list that would keep him busy a month. Instead, she put on a smile. "I'm stronger than I look. Besides, this is good exercise. Like tennis."

Alex shot the decrepit mower a disdainful look. "Not with this old thing. It's a struggle every step and you know it." He leaned down and gingerly ran his thumb over one of the blades. "These wouldn't cut soft butter much less this tough grass. Is there anything in that backyard shed that I could use to sharpen them with?"

Wearily, feeling hot and irritable, she used a tissue to mop her damp forehead. "I don't know what all is in that shed. That was Neal's domain." Not that he'd shown any interest in it or yard work in several years.

"I'll have a look. You go inside. I'll finish here."

That got her dander up. "Listen, how many times must I tell you that I either hire work done or I do it myself?"

"Are we going to have this discussion again? Your face is as red as a beet and your eyes look like someone's punched you out."

"Thank you for that complimentary observation." Though she knew he was right, she stubbornly grabbed the mower handle.

Far too easily, he took it from her. "You're not doing this heavy work, not while I'm around. Go inside and make a pie or something." He knew better than to tell her to lie down. He had a feeling she hadn't napped in the afternoon since she was three years old.

Bristling, Megan drew herself up to her full five feet, five inches. "Did I ever tell you I don't respond well to caveman tactics?"

He saw the unyielding set of her mouth, but he also noticed the smudges of fatigue beneath her eyes. "Did I tell you I don't respond well to bullheaded females? Like the song says, you got to know when to hold, know when to fold. You just folded, lady. *Go inside.*" Irritated, he picked up the mower and pulled it toward the backyard shed.

Feeling utterly drained by her morning, by the thought of all she had yet to do today and by the "friendly discussion" she'd just had with a guest she couldn't seem to control, Megan wished she could run away somewhere quiet and have a good cry. She'd done just that the other day after she'd all but ravaged the same guest in his bathtub. This was so unlike her, Megan thought with no small amount of displeasure.

She looked at the shaggy grass again. It wasn't worth the effort of fighting over. It seemed that Alex was hell-bent on cutting it himself, so let him.

Without so much as a glance, Megan walked past the shed where Alex was searching around. In her kitchen, she went to the cupboard and found two aspirins, washed them down with a full glass of cold water.

"Finished already?" Grace asked, coming out of the laundry room with an armload of linens.

"Not exactly." Megan rinsed out the glass, set it to dry. "Alex is going to do it." She raised weary eyes to her friend's surprised face. "Don't ask. Listen, I'm going upstairs to lie down for half an hour to see if I can get rid of this tension headache."

Grace sympathized. "Can I get you anything?"

"No, thanks. I'll be fine. Wake me in half an hour, please." She headed for the stairs.

The rest of the day and evening went by in a blur for Megan. She was downstairs in time to give Ryan milk and cookies after school and listen to his excited chatter about a class outing planned for the following week, but later she couldn't have recited a word he'd said. The damnable headache just wouldn't ease. Grace had volunteered to keep an eye on him while she'd diligently set to work baking three pies and six dozen cookies. About to start on some muffins, she braced both hands on the sink, bowed her head and closed her eyes.

Always one to face facts, Megan decided she must be overtired for this headache to hang on the way it had. She put away the muffin pans and began wrapping the cooled pastries, unable to bake another thing today. She couldn't afford to get a migraine, something she'd suffered with during her last few years with Neal. There was so much to do.

Two of the inn's rooms were empty, but a couple from Minnesota was scheduled to arrive tomorrow and maybe someone would spot her sign and fill the last one. She desperately needed the money. Any day now, the bank would start knocking on her door about the missed mortgage payments. She'd already received two discreet reminders. She'd phoned them about an equity loan, but because of the second mortgage, there wasn't enough equity in the building to warrant another loan.

She couldn't sell her six-year-old car for enough to buy

groceries for a day, much less a week. There were no insurance policies left to turn in, nothing left to sell or borrow on. Where she would turn next, Megan wasn't certain. Something would turn up, she decided with a flicker of her old determination. It had to. She couldn't lose everything she'd worked so hard for.

If only her headache would ease, perhaps she could think of a way out. If only Alex Shephard would end his stay, she could think more clearly. As much as she needed the revenue from his room rental, his unnerving presence was clouding her already befuddled mind.

Finishing, she bagged the baked goods and allowed herself for a brief moment to remember the way he'd held her, touched her, kissed her. Wanted her. Then reality had come crashing back and she'd opened her eyes to find she was cold, wet and ashamed.

The harsh reality was that there were few men who wanted a simple life, to work alongside a woman and her son, to make a life for them all—a dependable man. She could depend only on herself, and Grace, of course. Squaring her shoulders despite the ache, Megan repeated the phrases she so often said to herself like a mantra. *It'll be all right. Things will work out. You can do it.*

The sooner she got Ryan his dinner and saw to it that he was showered and in bed, the sooner she could finally crawl under the covers herself. A full eight hours of uninterrupted and dreamless sleep would bring back her energy and remove the dark circles under her eyes, Megan decided. If she drove the baked goods over to the Cornerstone now, that would be one less thing she'd have to do tomorrow morning.

Hurrying, she ran up the stairs to get her car keys. On the way back down, her thoughts elsewhere, she didn't pay attention to her feet. Five steps from the bottom, she stumbled, grabbed for the railing, but it was too late.

Megan went crashing to the tiled floor, her right foot wrenching miserably under her as she landed unceremoniously on her bottom. "Oh!" she cried out, feeling a sharp pain rip all the way from her ankle and up her leg.

Eyes closed, she sat there, willing the pain to go away as she braced one hand on the bottom stair. Running footsteps could be heard coming in her direction, then suddenly, Grace was there, bending over her.

"Honey, what happened?" Uncertain whether to help her up just yet, Grace frowned.

"I lost my footing on the last couple of steps." Megan set her teeth, determined to stand. "Help me up and..." But the piercing pain had her slumping back despite Grace's strong arm lending support.

More footsteps, two sets, one heavy and one fast and lighter. "Mom, what's wrong?" Ryan asked from halfway down the stairs where he'd stopped, fearful of going farther.

"Just a little accident," Megan said, hoping she sounded more reassuring than she felt as Alex came through the double doors into the kitchen and spotted the forlorn group.

"Let me have a look," Grace said, scrunching down and easing off Megan's sandal. The ankle was already swelling. She heard Megan draw in a painful breath as her fingers lightly pressed along her leg. "I think you've got a bad sprain here."

Alex moved closer. "You want us to call your doctor or go with you to the hospital for X rays?" He could see by her face that neither choice held much appeal.

"The hospital?" Ryan said in a small, trembling voice. He didn't want his mother to go to the hospital. His father had gone there and never come back.

Ignoring her pain, Megan looked up at her son and found a smile. "I'm okay, Ryan. No hospital." She turned to Grace. "If you'll just help me up to my room, I'll wrap it and it'll be fine by morning."

Grace sent Alex a doubtful look.

He noticed it and stepped closer. "Put your arm around my neck," he ordered. When she did without protesting, he figured she had to be hurting badly to have traded her usual feistiness for this unexpected compliancy. He lifted her up into his arms and settled her against his chest.

"I can walk myself...with a little help," Megan said without much confidence.

"I don't think so." Alex spoke to Grace over his shoulder as he started up the stairs. "Since she doesn't want to go to the hospital, call her doctor and see if he'll come out. I don't think he'd want her to put her weight on this ankle until he's checked her over."

Megan struggled in his arms, trying to catch Grace's eye. "No, don't call. I don't want to bother Dr. Lane with a house call. I'll be fine by morning. I have too much to do to be laid up." A house call would cost a fortune, she was certain. She'd known Dr. Lane all her life and knew he'd probably come out, but at what price? She hated having to keep her budget always in mind, but it was a fact of life.

"We'll see. And hold still or you'll have us both on the floor." Alex continued up the stairs with Ryan just ahead of him, the boy still looking worried.

Annoyed as well as miserable, Megan glared at Alex's implacable profile. "Hey, who put you in charge? This is my place, my—"

"Kitchen, my B and B. I know. I assure you it'll be here when you feel better."

Regardless of the indignity of being carried to her room and in spite of the incessant pain, her awareness of the man holding her so close was another unwelcome emotion, Megan noticed. His touch was firm, yet managed to be tender at the same time. She could smell no cologne on him, just the clean scent of soap and the powerful aroma of man. She didn't need this right now, she thought as she wished with all her might that she'd watched where she was stepping.

Alex followed Ryan into Megan's sitting room and walked through the arch into her bedroom, placing her gently on the bed. He saw her wince as he transferred her. He pulled her pillows from beneath the spread and propped them behind her, then watched her lean back and close her eyes. "Where's your aspirin?"

"I know where it is," Ryan announced, wanting to help. He disappeared into Megan's bathroom and quickly came back with the aspirin bottle and a glass of water.

Alex shook two into his palm and held them out. Reluctantly, Megan downed them, although she doubted seriously if aspirin would dull this fierce aching. A sprain she could handle, but please, God, she prayed, let there be no broken bones. She couldn't afford the time that would take to heal.

Ryan walked around the bed, then crawled on next to his mother, his face anxious. Megan reached out and took his hand. "It's okay, Ryan. Just a minor spill." He smiled, but the fear never left his eyes.

Grace came rushing in. "Dr. Lane said he was just finishing up an emergency patient and would be here in about half an hour."

Megan scowled at Grace for listening to Alex instead of her, but took her friend's hand in apology as Grace carefully placed her swollen ankle on a soft pillow.

"I'll get an ice bag and be right back," Grace told her.

Megan saw Alex settle in her rocker and felt like weeping.

Dr. Zachary Lane straightened from examining Megan's foot. "You're lucky, Megan. Your ankle's swollen, but I can't detect any broken bones. I suggest you take aspirin for the pain, alternate heat with cold compresses. When you're resting, you can wrap it with this Ace bandage." He reached into his black bag, having come prepared from the clinic after Grace's call. "If you *must* get up, put on this air cast. It's two plastic pieces held together with Velcro so you can remove it to bathe. It'll help immobilize the foot and hasten healing. However, I strongly recommend that you stay off that foot for three or four days." Noticing her scowl, he shook his head.

In his mid-sixties, Dr. Lane had been a general practitioner in the Twin Oaks area for over thirty years and had delivered

Megan and both her sisters. He was well aware that she was a workaholic.

"I know that sounds like a prison sentence to you, but if you don't follow my instructions, I guarantee it'll take twice as long to heal and you might make it worse."

Megan brushed her hair back with both hands. "Doctor, I appreciate your coming out on such short notice. I honestly didn't think it was necessary—" she frowned at both Grace and Alex "—but I was outvoted." She turned to her son who'd finally lost his worried look after hearing the doctor's diagnosis. "Ryan, get my checkbook from the desk drawer."

"No need," Dr. Lane said, picking up his bag. "I'll send you a bill."

"Thank you, Doctor," Grace said. "I'll walk you out. Ryan, come with me. I'll get your dinner served before carrying up a tray for your mother."

As soon as they left, Alex turned to her, rubbing both palms together. "All right, what do you want first, heat or cold?"

Feeling cross, the pain not easing, Megan squirmed, trying to get more comfortable without much success. "Grace will be back. Thanks for your help up the stairs."

Her terse words were meant as a dismissal, Alex knew. But he wasn't so easily dismissed this time. "Do you have a heating pad up here?" he asked, glancing toward a tall cupboard.

Megan heaved a huge sigh of resignation. Maybe if she let him get her the damn pad, he'd leave. "Cupboard, bottom shelf." To keep her mind off her aching foot, she watched Alex open the cupboard and stoop down. The soft cotton of his shirt stretched across his muscular back as he searched around. She remembered how those muscles had felt beneath her roaming hands that day in the shower. Hard, strong, solid. Like the man himself was—unbending, insistent, stubborn.

Finally, he found the pad, then located the wall outlet and plugged it in. Stretching the cord, he settled the pad over her ankle before handing her the controls. "Maybe you should start off on low and work up to medium or high if it feels good."

"It's not going to feel good for several days." Megan

flipped the switch on low, feeling contrary and resentful that her own body had let her down.

Alex sat on the edge of the bed, sending her a tolerant look. "If you weren't always in such an all-fired hurry, this wouldn't have happened."

Eyes fiery, she glared at him. "Thank you for your insight. I never would have guessed that without your help." Leaning her head back, she closed her eyes.

"People confined to bed usually get surly. They also usually take it out on the ones trying to help them."

Megan mentally counted to ten before responding. "I am *not* surly."

"Uh-huh. Maybe if you got out of your clothes and put on a robe, you'd feel more relaxed. Where do you keep your robe?"

Megan's eyes flew wide open. "None of your business, and I'm *not* undressing." Certainly not with him in her room. Those big hands of his had already wandered over most of her body. At least she could keep his eyes at bay.

"It's stupid to be modest when you're bedridden." He got up and rearranged her pillows. "Did you think I'd jump your bones while you're relatively helpless? I may want you, honey, but I'd prefer you be completely healed first."

Through a haze of pain from her ankle and her headache, she gazed at him. What had he said? her foggy mind wondered.

"You rest, and I'll check on you later."

"Just a little while," she mumbled. "An hour, maybe two."

Right, Alex thought as he left the room, softly closing the door.

I may want you, honey, but I'd prefer you be completely healed first. Had she dreamed those words? Megan wondered as she closed her eyes and invited sleep.

Bending to load the dishes from their dinner into the dishwasher, Grace glanced up as Alex came in from emptying the trash, a chore he'd insisted on doing. Grabbing a towel, she decided it was time she and Mr. Shephard had a little talk. "I must tell you that you are without a doubt the most unusual guest we've had at Delaney's since the place opened. I should know since I've been here almost from day one."

He'd rather thought by the surprised look Grace had given him when he'd picked up Megan that she'd have something to say later. Because Ryan had eaten with the two of them at the kitchen table, the conversation had been lighthearted. Later was now, but he was ready for her. "Is that so?"

"Mmm-hmm." Slowly, she dried her hands. "What exactly are you up to?"

No beating around the bush for this one, he thought, almost smiling. "Where's Ryan?" he asked, noticing that the boy's empty dinner plate and glass were still on the table though he was nowhere to be seen.

"I sent him up to shower. Let's not change the subject."

"All right, then. I'm up to nothing nefarious, I assure you." The fact that he was in Twin Oaks under false pretenses, one his father had unwittingly initiated, wasn't really sinister. And he was sincere about wanting to help both Megan and Ryan. But in order to do that, he needed to know more. "I'm here on business, just like I said. But as I mentioned before, I'm attracted to Megan. You've already warned me not to hurt her. I certainly don't intend to. Satisfied?"

"The road to hell is paved with good intentions, I'm told."

He acknowledged her barb with a smile. "Touché. I don't know why both of you are so suspicious of my motives."

"Maybe we've both trusted before and been burned." She saw his gaze slide to the ring finger of her left hand. "That's right, no rings. Divorced. Twice. Megan only once, but it was enough."

That jolted him. "Megan divorced Neal Delaney?"

Annoyed at her big mouth, Grace tried to backtrack. "Not exactly. She filed for divorce, but then he got sick and died soon after."

Alex decided to store that little nugget of information away for the future. "I see. So every man's a louse because you two married guys who apparently were."

"No, that's not it. I date quite a lot. Still looking for Mr. Right, fairly certain he's out there somewhere. I tell the same thing to Megan all the time. Got to kiss a lot of frogs before Prince Charming shows his face. But—and this is a big but— you seem in a real hurry to impress Megan, and I've never trusted fast."

Alex frowned, perplexed. "I don't follow you."

Grace crossed her feet and leaned against the counter. "You came to us exactly one week ago today. Here you are, cutting the grass, buying and serving watermelon, giving Ryan batting lessons, going to his games and even tucking Megan into her bed. So I can't help wondering just what you're after—an invitation into that same bed?"

"I'd be lying if I said I'd turn it down, but no, that isn't why I've stayed." Hoping he sounded more sincere than he felt, Alex searched for the right words. "My business deal hasn't finalized, so in the meantime I'm simply trying to help out. Is that a concept so hard for you two to grasp?" Now or never, Alex decided. "By the way, I get the feeling Megan's in financial trouble with this place. Am I right?"

Grace shifted her gaze, sure she'd already revealed too much. "That's not for me to say. What if she is? What's it to you?"

Alex knew he'd have to give some to get some. "Listen, I nearly died last year. I was in the hospital for weeks, then recovering at home for six months. Something like that changes a man, makes him realize life is awfully damn short. If I find I like somebody and I can help them out even in small ways, is that a crime?"

At that moment, Ryan, barefoot and wrapped in a blue towel, came racing down the stairs and into the kitchen. "Grace, I can't find my favorite Tasmanian devil p.j.'s. Are they in the wash?"

Still looking at Alex, Grace answered, "In the dryer."

For another long moment, Alex stared into Grace's dis-

ustful eyes, then he turned to the boy. "Come on, sport. I'll
elp you find 'em." He followed Ryan into the laundry room.

"Mom's asleep. Are you going to check my homework or
hould I ask Grace?" Ryan wanted to know.

Alex found a clothes basket and emptied the contents of
ae dryer. "I'll check it. If there are no mistakes, I'll drive
ou to school in the morning in the Porsche."

"All *right!* Wait'll the guys see that!" Ryan found his
ajamas, then hurried from the room. "Good night, Grace."

Grace smiled at his retreating back. "See you later, alli-
ator."

"In a while, crocodile," Ryan singsonged as he stomped
p the stairs.

"Hey, sport," Alex said, trailing after him, "let's not wake
our mother. She's a little grumpy tonight."

She's not the only one, Grace thought as she closed the
ishwasher. We're all a little on edge.

The grandfather clock in the foyer struck nine times, its
himes echoing through the silent house. Long shadows en-
ulfed the rooms from the small lamp left burning in the
ounge for any guests still out and the stove light that stayed
n all night in the kitchen. Upstairs in the third-floor bedroom,
Megan slept fitfully as Alex sat in a bentwood rocker along-
ide the bed, quietly watching her. On his way to his own
oom, he'd detoured and brought up a glass of cold orange
uice and two more aspirin. But finding her still asleep, he
.adn't had the heart to waken her.

She'd changed into a long cotton nightgown, probably with
Grace's help. Restlessly, she'd pushed off the sheet and light
.lanket. Her face was flushed, her thick, dark hair spread out
n the pillow as she lay on her side, one hand curled next to
.er cheek. From time to time, her breathing became a bit
.abored, then she'd cough and settle down again. Occasion-
.lly, she shifted and groaned in her sleep as the pain from
.er ankle made itself known.

He'd been sitting guard for half an hour, just watching her.
So she'd filed for divorce. Interesting. Why? he wondered.

Was it because of Neal's erratic job history that Emily at th
Cornerstone had mentioned? Or the fact that he didn't seen
to take much interest in his son, as Ryan had revealed whe
he'd said that Neal never went to his games? Or was it be
cause he'd wanted to live beyond their means with the bi
sailboat and the flashy car, which didn't seem Megan's styl
at all?

He'd fleetingly wondered how a woman who'd lost he
husband less than a year ago could have kissed him so pas
sionately, and now he had his answer. The glue that had hel
their marriage together had apparently vanished. So they'
been separated when Neal got sick. Had she stood by hin
during his illness anyway, perhaps praying that he'd get tha
all-important transplant? From what little he knew of Megan
he was certain she had, if for no other reason than because
Neal was Ryan's father.

How long had Neal been ill? Had she perhaps even nurse
him for a while until he'd had to go into the hospital? Bu
she hadn't let him into her room, putting him in Ryan's roon
instead. Had his illness drained every cent they had and ex
hausted her besides? Could they have run up a quarter of
million dollars worth of medical bills? Not impossible, Ale
supposed, depending on the length and severity of the illness

Megan moaned in her sleep, thrashed about a bit, the
calmed again. Loyalty, he'd wager, was a big part of he
makeup. She would do the right thing, disregarding her ow
needs. While commendable, look where it had gotten her.

Maybe when she felt better, he could get her to talk abou
her past. Carefully. Because one confidence demanded an
other, and he wasn't especially anxious to talk about his.

Rising, he stepped to the bed and pulled the covers up t
her shoulders. As he did, her eyes slowly opened. She blinke
as if disoriented, then he watched her gaze fly to the clock
Next, she glanced out the window, apparently checking to se
if it was night or day.

Nine at night! That couldn't be right, Megan thought
alarmed. Her clock must be wrong. She'd fallen asleep afte

Dr. Lane had left, around five. She'd only wanted to get rid of her headache.

"Four hours? No, I couldn't have napped for four hours." She threw back the covers and made an effort to sit up even though a spasm of pain shot up her entire right leg. "Ryan! Where's Ryan?"

"He's fine. Been in here twice to see you, but you slept on." He reached over to the nightstand for the aspirin and glass of juice. "Here. Take these."

Her mind fuzzy, Megan scowled. "What are those?"

"Simple aspirin, like the ones you've already had. You can read the imprint on each tablet." He shook his head, looking disappointed. "You really are a suspicious one."

It was easier to take the pills than to argue. Afterward, though she longed to lie back down, she ran a hand through her damp hair and swung her good left leg over the side of the bed. The headache, thank goodness, was gone, but her right ankle throbbed like the devil. Still, she had to see to her son.

"Where do you think you're going?"

"I have to help Ryan with his homework, make sure he takes his shower and...did he eat?"

"Let's see. Yes, he ate. Two bowls of Grace's spaghetti, salad and bread. Not the crusts. A glass of milk, two cookies. He did his homework—two pages of math—and I checked it. He's had his shower and he's in his favorite pajamas sound asleep for well over an hour. Anything else?"

Megan blinked. "You did all that?"

"Grace and I together. We've bonded. You'll be pleased to know we're great chums." Which wasn't exactly the truth, since Grace still regarded him darkly through suspicious eyes. But he was making progress.

She had trouble grasping all that. "That's nice," she muttered, looking down and suddenly realizing she was wearing only a thin gown. She reached for the blanket, awkwardly arranging it over herself. "I'll be fine by morning. I heal very quickly, always have."

"I don't think so. The doctor said three or four days off that foot and I have a tendency to believe his diagnosis over yours."

"Oh, damn," Megan complained, running a hand through her disheveled hair. "This is a bad time for this to happen." Was there ever a good time? She looked at Alex, a worried expression on her face. "Is Ryan really okay?" Poor little kid had been so scared for her.

"He's fine. Better than fine. He got an A-minus on his spelling test. Missed that word *impossible*. Let's see, what else? Billy Somebody-or-other threw up in class and got to go home in a taxi because his mother's expecting a baby any day and can't drive. I finished weeding the flower garden after dinner and you can hit me when you feel up to it." He paused, scratched his chin. "I guess that's about all the news worth knowing for tonight. Are you hungry?"

"No." Megan shifted her sore leg. If anything, it felt worse. Three, maybe four more days of this. She felt like screaming in frustration.

"Want the heating pad again? Or maybe an ice bag."

"I don't want you waiting on me." Suddenly, the lateness of the hour registered. "Come to think of it, what are you doing here at this time of night? Where's Grace? I want Grace to come up here." She saw he wasn't moving, decided to stop being so demanding and difficult. "Please."

"She'll be up as soon as she gets back from delivering your baked goods." He held up a hand to stop the protest he knew would be forthcoming. "Her idea, not mine. Says she didn't have a hot date tonight anyway. She's a damn fine-looking woman, you know?"

Even in her foggy state, Megan managed to feel a jolt of jealousy. A little one. Then she was disgusted with herself. She felt so rotten she didn't care if the two of them ran off and eloped. "Ryan can't go to sleep without his Tasmanian pillow. He gets real upset if he—"

"Already in his bed. We talked about the Taz. I kind of like him, too."

Megan couldn't picture it, a grown man, one who looked as appealing as Alex Shephard, admiring the Tasmanian devil.

"You sure you don't want a bowl of soup or something? That ice bag?" When she just shook her head, Alex decided she needed rest more than anything, so he stood. "If there's nothing else you need, I'll go now. Sleep well." He started for the door.

A wave of guilt washed over Megan. "Alex?" She'd been difficult, obnoxious and ungrateful and he'd been so nice.

He turned back, his face questioning.

"Thanks. I...I appreciate everything."

He gave her his slow, sexy smile. "We aim to please." He'd caught the disease, Alex realized. He was talking in the plural.

Chapter 6

"This is terrible," Megan complained. "I've never been sidelined like this before."

"You are now, hon, and you've got the crankiness to prove it." With her usual efficient movements, Grace whipped off Megan's damp bedclothes, piled them by the door and shook out a fresh fitted sheet.

Seated in the rocker vacated by Alex a short time ago, Megan leaned her head back. She felt slightly better after brushing her teeth, but she was still annoyed at her predicament. "I'd love a shower."

"Tomorrow morning, maybe. You couldn't stand up long enough on one leg tonight." Grace eased pale peach pillow slips into place, then fluffed the pillows before putting them back on the bed. "Did you finish your tray?" She'd brought up a chicken salad sandwich and tea after her run into town to the Cornerstone.

"Most of it." Her appetite seemed to have fled along with her sense of humor.

"Got to keep up your strength." She flipped the blanket onto the bed, tucked in hospital corners.

Dutifully, because it was hard to refuse someone who was mothering you, Megan drank the rest of her tea. "I think I scared Ryan when I fell. He sat next to me on the bed, his eyes so huge."

Finished, Grace sat down on the edge of the bed. "He's afraid you'll die, like Neal did," she told her friend. "You might know he'd think that."

"Yes, I do know. That's why I told him to give me a big hug, to show him I was on the mend. He felt better hearing the doctor say it was nothing serious."

"Your hug's what he needed. Though I must say, Alex has done a masterful job of keeping the boy occupied. Batting practice, catching practice. Homework. Even ate at the kitchen table with us, joking with Ryan whenever his little face clouded up. And he's driving him to school in that snazzy convertible in the morning." She shook her head. "What do you make of that man?"

Despite the heat of the tea, Megan shivered. "I wish I knew. He's a cross between a guardian angel and a very large pain in the butt." Bracing her hands on the chair, she hopped on one foot to the bed. "I think I'd better lie down. I don't know why I'm so shaky."

"Aftershock probably." Grace moved to assist her, then drew up the covers. "Too soon for more aspirin, but I'll be in with it later. Or maybe Alex will be. He'll probably arm wrestle me for the privilege. He has this thing for you."

Megan almost laughed. "Undoubtedly because I'm so gorgeous with this stringy hair and scowling face."

"He asked me some questions about you earlier." The answers she'd given had weighed heavily on Grace's mind. "I told him you'd filed for divorce from Neal."

Megan snuggled into her pillow. "That wasn't exactly a secret. What kind of questions?"

"He wanted to know if you're in financial trouble with this place."

Megan frowned. "Why would he want to know that?"

"Beats me." Grace fussed with the covers unnecessarily. "Says he likes to help people."

"You know, it's hard for me to believe that this man who, by his own admission, was never happier than when he was climbing mountains or scuba diving in some remote ocean or on safari in a faraway jungle is now happiest in this small town simply helping people out. What's wrong with this picture?"

"Maybe that was then and this is now. He said he had a really serious illness last year. Almost died. It changed him."

Megan sighed. "Do you suppose he had an epiphany? Because we both know how reliable the word of a man who says he's changed is, don't we?"

Grace, too, remembered Neal and his empty promises, to say nothing of her two exes. "Yes, we sure do." She gathered up the crumpled linen. "Is there anything else I can get you?"

"No, thank you, Grace. You're a treasure. I'll be fine tomorrow. I'll be downstairs to get breakfast and get Ryan off to school."

"We'll see. Meantime, I'm leaving my bedroom door open. If you need anything, just yell."

"Mmm." Annoyed with the world in general, Megan lay back. Maybe tomorrow by some miracle she'd be greatly improved. And maybe pigs could fly!

"I hate being confined." Sitting up in bed, Megan chewed disconsolately on a piece of toast. She'd thought about hobbling downstairs on one foot or taking the steps on her bottom, but sitting around watching Grace do the work she should be doing would only make her feel worse.

"So you've said," Alex answered.

"I thought I'd be able to get around better by this morning." She'd offered to sit at the kitchen table and peel vegetables, but Grace had nixed the idea, saying she didn't need Megan in her way. Later, she'd brought up a basket of mending and smilingly mentioned that Megan at last had time for that dreaded chore. Megan had glared at her, but she'd taken the basket.

"Sprains and pulled muscles have to run their course." He shook two aspirin out of the bottle on her nightstand and handed her the glass of juice he'd brought up.

Megan took them, not that they helped much, but maybe she'd feel even worse without something for the pain. But aspirin didn't take away her major concerns. "How're my guests doing?"

"All taken care of. Grace and I are handling things. I made western omelettes this morning. They went over big. Would you like me to make you one?"

"Toast is fine, thanks. Why didn't Ryan come in to see me this morning?" Most of all, she missed her little boy.

"He told me he stuck his head in earlier, but you were sleeping and Grace had warned him not to wake you."

The problem was, Megan thought, that she tossed and turned and moaned with pain half the night, then had fallen deeply asleep toward morning.

"Anyhow, don't worry about Ryan. He got off to school on time." He didn't mention that he'd driven the boy or that when they were passing the bus stop, Ryan's friend, Bobby, all but begged for a ride. So Alex had belted both boys into the passenger seat and continued on.

She found a smile. "Did he enjoy the ride in your convertible?"

"Apparently, the walls have ears." Aware of her frustration over not being in the mainstream, recognizing it from the long days of his own confinement, he sat down in the rocker. "I know just how you feel. I hate being laid up, too."

He looked so tanned and healthy. "You don't look as if you ever are."

"I've had my share of down days." Quite a few, actually.

Megan remembered he'd referred to recovering from an illness in the garden that first night and Grace had said he'd told her it had been a serious one. "What sort of illness did you have?" It seemed like a terribly personal thing to ask, but then, what could be more intimate than a man carrying her up to her sickbed?

"Major surgery," he answered, feeling like a coward at the vague explanation. "I'm fully recovered now." This wasn't the time to go into his transplant story, Alex felt. "The worst thing about being laid up is being dependent on others for so many things."

"Amen to that. I don't like to be told I can't do something."

Relieved that she had no more questions about him, he laughed. "I've noticed that about you."

She had to smile at that. "I'm a lousy patient, I know. I'm sorry if I gave you a hard time." This might be the perfect moment to say a few things she'd been avoiding. "Listen, I don't want you to feel obligated to visit me like this. I mean, just because you kissed me doesn't change anything between us, really."

"You kissed me back. Heartily. Lengthily."

Megan wished she could stop the blush she felt warming her cheeks. "All right, so it was a two-way street. The whole thing took me by surprise. Suddenly, we were there, up close and...and it had been a long time since..." She cleared her throat. "At any rate, I shouldn't have behaved like that. I'm not usually so...so..."

"Responsive? Passionate? Abandoned?"

Good Lord, why had she begun this conversation? "No, I'm not any of those things." If only he could check with Neal, he'd know that her husband had had to look elsewhere for passion. "I was acting out of character, caught off guard."

Alex rose, moved to sit on the edge of her bed. "Don't bother trying to convince me you're not all of those things. Because I know. I've kissed you and I know."

He spoke with such maddening assurance that she wanted to smack him. Perhaps if she tried another explanation. "Look, I've been widowed almost a year and I've had a few men try to...to..."

"Get you into bed?"

"Uh, yes. But that's all they want. Not me, not my son, not a future, just the bedroom scene. They try to get to me through Ryan. They press and push. I'm not interested in those games. I'm not interested, period. Not in you or in any man. I want you to know that."

"Uh-huh." He took her hand, found it warm and dry and slightly shaky. "I want to take you to bed, Megan, to test that theory, and for other reasons. But I won't press. I *never* press."

Why would he when women were undoubtedly lining up to warm his bed? Megan thought.

"I won't even ask you, not until you let me know you want me as much as I want you."

Determined blue eyes met sea green. "That day will never come," she said quietly.

Getting to his feet, Alex leaned back down and planted a brief kiss on her forehead before removing her tray. "Never say never, Megan. I've got to change clothes for an appointment in town. Grace said to tell you to take a nap and she'll be up around lunchtime." He walked out, leaving her with a few things to think over.

Alex stood in front of the full-length mirror in his room and examined his image. Blue shirt, gray slacks, loafers, no tie. Businesslike, but not stuffy. Residents of small towns in California, he'd discovered some time ago, seemed suspicious of people dressed too formally. Even lawyers and bankers. Still, a jacket would be in order, he decided as he took his navy sport coat out of the closet.

Whistling, he left his room. At the top of the stairs, he paused, listening. He could hear the shower running in Megan's room. Yet he knew that Grace had left after breakfast to do the marketing. Had Megan crawled out of bed and hobbled into the shower, risking further injury to that ankle? Had he ever run across a more stubborn woman? Alex asked himself as he took the stairs up to the third floor, two at a time.

* * *

It had seemed like a good idea a few minutes ago, Megan reflected as she leaned against the tiled wall of her shower. She'd hopped on one foot into the bathroom, turned on the jets, stripped off her gown and stepped under the spray. But she'd barely soaped herself before she began to feel light-headed. Probably because she hadn't had much solid food in two days, she decided as she rinsed off.

Just a few minutes more, she thought, standing with most of her weight on her left leg and straightening to allow the hot water to wet her hair. One-handed, she dribbled on shampoo, then rubbed it in. The steam was clouding her vision, making her dizzy. Bracing an elbow against the wall, she stuck her head under, rinsing out the shampoo. That's when her good leg started to shake.

Hurriedly, she grabbed the shower door handle and leaned into the door with her eyes closed for several moments. Grace was going to be upset that she hadn't waited. But the poor soul already had so much to do that it seemed unfair to ask her to nursemaid a grown woman. At last, she took a chance and gingerly hopped out. It was too far to reach over to shut off the water, so she let it be.

Holding on to the wall, Megan made it across the small room and shakily wrapped herself in a thick towel before sitting down on the closed lid of the toilet. Her trembling leg was undoubtedly a nerve reaction. She closed her eyes and tried to take slow, calming breaths. But a sound from the other side of the door drew her attention.

"Megan, are you all right?" The voice was muffled over the noise of the shower, but she knew it belonged to Alex.

"Please," she answered, "get Grace for me." A whisper was all that came out, upsetting her further.

"Megan? Can you hear me?" Alex's imagination had her in a crumpled heap on the floor in a dead faint. "I'm coming in," he shouted.

"No!" Megan squeaked. But it was too late. The door flew open.

He thought she resembled a drowned waif with her wet

hair hanging down and a panicky look on her pale face as she clutched an oversize towel around her slim shoulders. He flipped the switch for the overhead fan, then reached in and shut off the shower. Looking down at her as the steam slowly swirled out of the room, he shook his head. "You just couldn't wait, could you?"

Megan drew in a deep breath. "Never mind the lecture. Please ask Grace to come up."

"Sorry, she's in town running errands. You're stuck with me." He saw her shoulders droop and hoped she wouldn't cry. Grabbing a second towel, he began drying her hair. "How is it you and I always wind up together in steamy bathrooms?" he asked, trying to lighten the mood. But she didn't smile. Finished, he stepped back and noticed the gown she'd had on earlier lying on her clothes hamper. "I'll get you some clean clothes."

Humiliating was what this was, Megan thought now that she was fairly certain she wouldn't fall or faint. "Don't bother. Just hand in my robe, the green one from my closet. I'll get dressed later." No way did she want him going through her drawers, handling her underclothes.

Cocking his head, Alex thought he knew what she was thinking. "Don't be shy, Megan. I've seen women's underthings before. You'll feel better getting dressed." With that, he left the bathroom, not noticing Megan's scowl aimed at his back.

Alex opened the first drawer of her dresser. Soft, silky panties on one side, so small he wondered why she bothered wearing them at all. He chose a pale peach pair, then let his hand wander to the bras. How could women stand wearing these things? he wondered, choosing a matching peach bra.

Shorts would probably be better than slacks, he decided, since she'd probably put on the air cast that went up past her ankle. In the third drawer, he found a white pair on top and grabbed them. No tops in any of the other drawers, so he walked over to the closet.

Blouses, T-shirts, slacks, skirts, a few dresses. He scanned the lot and finally chose a loose pink T-shirt because it had an imprint on it that made him smile. When Cranky, Feed Chocolate. Maybe he should get her a box today.

Walking back into the bathroom, he saw that she held a comb she'd used on her wet hair and was sitting there glowering at him. Ignoring her bad mood, he smiled. "Here you go. Need some help?"

With no small effort, Megan erased her frown. He was, she supposed, just trying to be helpful. "Thanks. I'll take it from here."

He was hesitant, the mental picture of her lying on a cold bathroom floor still vivid. "What if you fall again?"

"I won't." She stared at him, trying to look in control, not an easy thing to do in a steamy bathroom wearing only a towel.

"You can keep your back turned. I'll just stand here in case you need me."

Megan gritted her teeth. *"I can manage."* And he thought she was stubborn.

"Okay, but I'll be right outside."

"You needn't wait," she told him through the closed door. "I'm fine now." She listened for his footsteps leaving, but she couldn't tell if he had. Carefully, she stood and unwrapped herself, then slowly got dressed, wondering just what Alex had been thinking while he'd picked out her clothes.

Gripping the sink, she stood up and wiped the steam from the medicine-cabinet mirror, then brushed her teeth. Only a bit unsteady now, at least she felt almost human again. Cautiously, she opened the door a crack and didn't see him. Maybe he'd listened to her for a change and left. Drawing in a grateful breath, she held on to the door and then the wall as she made her way to the bed.

"Better now?" his deep voice asked from across the room.

Startled, Megan quickly sat down in the rocker, grimacing as a pain shot up her right leg.

"Are you all right?" Alex was all concern.

Ignoring the ache, she tried a smile. "Yes. It appears you've rescued me again. Thank you."

He walked over and sat on the edge of the bed. "You should have waited."

"I know, but I felt so clammy." She had been frightened there for a minute in the shower when her vision had started blurring, but she felt a lot better now. "I haven't been confined to my room like this since I was a teenager with a bad case of flu. I'd forgotten how helpless it makes you feel."

Alex seized the opening to talk about her background. "I'll bet you were a beautiful teenager."

Threading her fingers through her hair to dry it, she made a face. "Beautiful? No, quite ordinary-looking, actually, compared to my sisters. Karen's got gorgeous blond hair and she's tall and sooo thin."

Alex had caught a long glimpse of Megan's shape last night beneath the thin material of the gown she'd had on. Curves in all the right places, enough to make his palms sweat. "What's so great about thin? I like a woman to have a few hills and valleys."

Megan ignored that, knowing a man wouldn't understand. "But my youngest sister, Jeannie, is the real beauty in the family. She should be a model. Even when we were young, my dad used to say that Karen and Jeannie got the looks and I got the brains."

What a warm and loving thing for a father to tell his daughter, Alex thought. Megan had to be better off with that jerk out of her life. Surely she hadn't believed that crap?

Alex leaned forward, intent on making her see herself the way he saw her. "Your dad was mistaken. I haven't seen your sisters, but they'd have to be dynamite to top you. You've got the kind of hair that makes a man's hands itch to reach out and touch it. Your skin is so soft, absolutely incredible. And your eyes, the bluest eyes I've ever seen, like the ocean on a perfect summer day. As for your body, from what I've seen, you could make strong men beg if you wanted to. Instead, you wear clothes several sizes larger than necessary, pull your fantastic hair back with a rubber band and probably haven't worn anything other than lipstick since your high school prom.''

Stunned, Megan answered with the first thing that came into her befuddled mind. "I didn't go to my high school prom. That's when I had the flu." And Neal had taken someone else because he'd already bought the tickets and rented his tux.

Alex wasn't so easily sidetracked. "Why do you downplay your looks, Megan?" He'd been wondering that ever since he'd first seen her.

"I don't, really. I'm not a great beauty, despite what you've just said, so I don't see much point in pretending. I know what I am. I'm a small-town innkeeper, a mother, a Cub Scout leader, a daughter, a—"

"A woman," Alex interrupted softly. "First and foremost, you're a woman. Have you forgotten?"

Blinking rapidly, Megan bit down on her lower lip. Yes, she had, and she fervently wished he hadn't come along to reawaken all those useless urges. "That's irrelevant. I—"

"No. It's all that *is* relevant." It was getting late in the day and Alex had an important errand in mind. He rose and picked up his jacket where he'd tossed it onto a stool, needing something to do with his hands that wanted nothing more than to reach out and pull her into his arms, to show her without words what he meant. "You're a very lovely woman, Megan. Don't ever forget that."

For the second time in the same day, Megan watched him walk away, left with his cryptic comments to consider.

Obviously surprised to see Alex again so soon, Lawrence Williams nonetheless was pleased. As chief loan officer for First National, it would be a real feather in his cap to be instrumental in funding a development project for Shephard Construction. Since Alex's first visit, Williams had had the San Diego firm checked out thoroughly and found their rating to be A-1. Hopefully, this alliance would be the first of many.

Smiling, Williams waved Alex to a chair across from his desk as he sat down. "I assume your feasibility study came back favorable and you're ready to proceed."

Sitting back, Alex crossed his legs. "Actually, the report's not back yet. I'm here about another matter."

"Of course. How may I help you?" Running through the possibilities mentally, Williams hoped that Shephard Construction wanted to switch their business account to his bank.

Alex had thought long and hard about this situation and had made up his mind after his last conversation with Grace. When he'd asked her if Megan was in financial difficulties, Grace had been vague and suddenly testy, unwilling to meet his eyes. Her body language and defensive comments had led him to believe he'd guessed right.

That's when his conscience had kicked in. Because of him, Megan's husband was gone, cutting the family income at least in half. Whatever Megan had done with the insurance money, it had undoubtedly gone to pay bills. And she still owed more. Because of him.

If she found out what he was about to do, she'd undoubtedly be angry. Alex intended to see to it that she never found out. She might wonder about the identity of her benefactor, but she wouldn't know for sure. And his conscience would be assuaged, at least a little.

Alex cleared his throat. "Last week, you alluded to the fact that the mortgage payments on the Delaney property might be in arrears. As a family friend, I'm interested in helping Megan Delaney during this rough time. To accomplish that, I need to know the outstanding amount so that I can bring her account up to date."

Williams raised one shaggy brow. "How very kind of you." It was none of his business who paid, as long as someone did. "I'll be right back." He left the room.

Alex removed his checkbook from his inside jacket pocket and set it on the banker's desk. Money had never been a problem for him, but lately, staying at Delaney's, he'd seen firsthand as he never quite had before how difficult not having enough could be. Megan was obviously struggling, working long hours, trying her best. He had to do something to ease her burdens.

Aside from his generous salary and yearly bonuses from Shephard Construction, Alex had inherited a sizable amount when his mother had died, which his father had invested for him until he'd come of age and taken over his own portfolio. Despite large expenditures for his luxury condo, his sailboat, his car, Alex had plenty of money and need never work another day, if that was what he wanted.

But he enjoyed his work, the challenges, watching homes or commercial buildings go up, seeing something solid where before there'd been only vacant land. One day, he'd take over from his father as sole heir.

No, money wasn't a problem. But being generous with it might be, if Megan got wind of his plans. If she wouldn't easily accept help to repair a doorknob, he could only imagine how she'd feel about receiving this sort of assistance. Hopefully, he could keep his name out of the transaction. Aside from the mortgages, Alex had decided he'd have to set up something for Ryan's education. Since he'd robbed the boy of his father, the least he could do would be to fund his schooling.

Maybe then he could put the matter to rest.

Carrying a manila folder, Williams walked back in and closed the door before handing a piece of paper to Alex, then wordlessly resuming his seat.

Alex studied the figure. "This is the equivalent of what, two or three missed payments on the first mortgage?"

"Three, yes."

"What about the second mortgage?"

"That's up-to-date." He referred to his notes in the file. "The payments are much smaller, only $310 a month on the second."

"And what is the balance on the second mortgage?" If she had that amount extra each month, perhaps she could hire a handyman.

Williams found the figure in his folder and told Alex, then sat back, waiting.

Alex did some quick calculating on the slip of paper, then opened his checkbook. In short order, he finished writing the check, but before handing it over, he looked at the middle-aged banker, hoping he could trust him. "This will bring the first mortgage up to date and satisfy the second. There is only one stipulation I ask of you. This whole transaction must be completely confidential."

Williams sat forward, folding his hands over the Delaney file. "And what are we to say to Mrs. Delaney when she asks who paid off the entire second mortgage and brought her first one up-to-date?"

"That's up to you. I'm sure you can come up with something, just as I'm equally sure this isn't the first time someone not on the original note has made payments. Parents often do it to help out their children. Some employers have been known to assist a valuable employee who's in a bind." Alex handed over the check, pocketed his checkbook and rose. "Whatever you tell Mrs. Delaney, my name must not be mentioned, nor do I want it to appear on any of the paperwork. Agreed?"

"Yes, certainly. Would you like a receipt?"

"My canceled check will do." He reached out to shake the banker's hand. "I'll call you when that other report's in." Leaving the First National Bank building, Alex felt as if a portion of the guilty burden he'd been carrying around ever since he'd learned of his father's clandestine maneuverings regarding his transplant had lightened.

As to Ryan, the boy was only eight. There was plenty of time to set up an educational endowment for him. He'd take care of that when he got back to San Diego.

San Diego, Alex thought, walking back to his car. Home. He'd been gone over a week and his father had made grumbling noises when he'd called the office this morning. *When are you coming back? Why are you staying there so long?*

He had no answers that would satisfy Ron Shephard or even himself.

Because the real reason he'd come to Twin Oaks—to make sure Neal Delaney's widow and child were at least financially in good shape—hadn't quite been satisfied yet. Did she owe even more? And, if so, to whom? How solid was the inn, the roof, the furnace? How could he walk away right now with Megan laid up and even more vulnerable? If nothing else, he had to see her through this injury. Grace couldn't run the place all alone, take care of Megan and watch Ryan, as well.

Besides, Ryan had a game tomorrow night. He'd promised to take him.

As he reached his Porsche where he'd parked it on the street, Alex happened to glance into the window of a shop he'd visited once before. Several model cars were displayed, including a sharp Austin Healy convertible. He stood staring at the box for several seconds, then made up his mind and went inside.

Ryan would love it.

The three of them were having a serious discussion at the dinner table in the kitchen. Ryan had the floor. "I don't know why I can't have a kitten. I'd take care of it and make sure it didn't bother anybody. Kids should have pets, don't you think?" he asked, sending a plea in Alex's direction.

Alex gathered from the long-suffering look on Grace's face that this was an old argument. "Whenever possible, sure. always wanted a dog, but I couldn't have one, either."

"You grew up in a house that had guests all the time, too?" Ryan wanted to know.

"No, but remember I told you I had asthma? And also, my mother was allergic to animals. Being around them made it hard for her to breathe." Then after his mother died and Maddy came to live with them, she had only one irreversible rule: She wouldn't take care of any house pets, even if Alex could have tolerated one by then. Alex remembered how crushed he and Patrick had been. "I know it's hard, Ryan, but maybe one day, things will change."

The boy set down his chicken leg, looking woebegone. "Yeah, that's what Mom says. But I want one now. Bobby's family has *two* pets. A dog *and* a cat."

"Yes, but does Bobby's mom bake fresh cookies every day?" Grace wanted to know as she cleared away his plate, then set the cookie jar on the table.

"I guess not," Ryan conceded, taking a chocolaty bite.

"And," Alex joined in, "does Bobby get a present even when it's not his birthday just because he's a terrific kid?" He reached for the paper bag he'd set under his chair earlier and placed it in front of Ryan. Some would say he was spoiling the boy. But not Alex. The kid had no father, a mother temporarily out of commission and he lived with a houseful of strangers. He deserved a treat now and then.

"Wow, for me?" The kittens and dogs forgotten, Ryan scrambled up on his knees.

"Well, I don't think it's for me," Grace said, sitting back down after clearing. Instead of watching Ryan, she kept her eyes on Alex as the child ripped open the package. The man was as excited as the boy, she decided.

"Hey, look! A convertible almost like yours, Alex."

"Not quite. It's a '65 Austin Healy. Think you can put it together?"

"You bet." He jumped down from the chair and leaned into Alex, giving him a spontaneous hug.

The small body smelling of chocolate nestled against him evoked a response in Alex he hadn't been expecting. Mitch's kids had been taught to shake hands, not embrace. The open, unrehearsed sincerity of the boy jolted him. He was thoroughly unprepared to like much less honestly enjoy the hug. Yet there it was.

Not realizing something momentous had happened, Ryan chewed his cookie while he studied the model car's box. "Maybe we could start it tonight."

Grace glanced up at the kitchen clock. "Not tonight. It's

time for your shower. Oh, wait. What about your homework?" She'd been so busy with the baking that she'd wanted to finish early plus making dinner that she'd forgotten his schoolwork.

"It's all done. Alex helped me." He started for the stairs. "Can I show Mom my car?"

"Sure." Grace had taken Megan's dinner tray up earlier and found her reading a novel after having finished the entire basket of mending. Her unexpected injury had a couple of benefits, Grace decided. Megan was getting rested and the mending was finished. Another was that she had an opportunity to probe a little into the mystery that was Alex Shephard.

"Okay." Footsteps pounding, he trudged up.

Grace seized her chance. "You're good with the boy, Alex, but you're spoiling him something terrible." She had to tell it like she saw it. "How are we going to handle him after you leave?"

After you leave. Funny, Alex didn't want to think about that just now. The land deal wasn't firmed up yet and he still had things to resolve about the Delaneys. Perhaps Grace could supply a few answers.

"Kids should be spoiled. They're not kids very long. Besides, I'm going to be around for a while yet." He carried glasses to the dishwasher and began loading them, wondering how best to get some information from Megan's closest friend. Finally, he decided just to come out with it. "Grace," he began, turning to her, "I'm curious about something. Didn't Neal Delaney carry any life insurance?" He already knew the answer to that one, but he wanted to hear what she had to say. No one was closer to Megan than Grace.

Shoving a hairpin into her thick hair, Grace snorted. "Oh, yeah, he sure did. Over a quarter of a million bucks."

So far, so good. "If that's so, where'd the money go? I mean with that much in hand, why would Megan be in financial difficulties not even a year later?"

"Good question." Grace ran hot water into the frying pan.

her movements choppy, angry. "If only Neal were here, we could ask him."

Alex wrinkled his brow. "What do you mean?"

Wiping her hands on a dish towel, she swung about. Bitterness oozed from every word. "I mean the creep had borrowed on every policy to the max, even the one his parents had bought and paid for when he was just a child. There was only enough money to pay off the loan shark."

Alex's face registered shocked surprise. "Loan shark?"

"You heard right. A slimeball from L.A. that Neal borrowed from to finance his high living. Scared Megan half to death when she found out. She was terrified that the man would somehow harm Ryan. Oh, you don't want to get me going on all the things that that man did. The list is longer than a dead snake."

Perhaps Megan wouldn't like Alex knowing such personal stuff, Grace thought, but why not? If it was up to Grace, she'd take out a billboard and let the world know what a heel Neal Delaney had been. Megan wanted to shield Ryan, so the boy wouldn't know the truth about his father. Grace didn't agree. The truth had an uncanny way of getting out, and Ryan had already asked some sticky questions. It was a shame to shatter the illusions of childhood, but wasn't it worse to fill his head full of lies?

So that was it, Alex thought. He'd begun to suspect that Neal had been the spendthrift, but he hadn't been certain. Still, could he have spent that much? "A quarter of a million is a lot of money."

"Well, the amount of the cash value of the policies wasn't as much as Megan would have received if Neal hadn't borrowed against them before he died, naturally. He got maybe half the total face value. Still a good chunk, probably a hundred twenty or thirty thousand. What did he do with all that money? Spent it on crazy things he had no business buying. A fancy boat, a spiffy sports car. Ran with a fast crowd—gamblers, drinkers, hangers-on. Everyone loves a guy who always picks up the check. And all the while, Megan's here trying to make ends meet and trying to keep Ryan from knowing what his father was really like.''

She hadn't wanted the truth to get out to protect Ryan. That figured. "I guess she sold his expensive toys after he died. Did she get anything for them at least?"

"Not a cent. He'd made exactly two payments on that boat, so Megan just signed it over to the lender. The sports car was in the process of being repossessed when Neal died." Turning back to the sink, she scrubbed viciously at the pan. "You don't want to get me started on Neal Delaney unless you've got all night."

Actually, he did have all night. But he had to wonder why Grace was so willingly telling him this now when earlier she'd been so reticent. "Did you finally decide you can trust me?" he asked, walking over and picking up the dish towel.

She shrugged. "Partly. The other part is I kind of got the feeling with all the questions you've been asking about Megan that you had this notion that she's hiding something." She looked up at him. "She is. The truth, which is that Neal hurt her in every way it's possible for a man to hurt a woman. He deceived her royally and I'm not sure she'll ever get over it. I thought I'd tell you the truth before you put two and two together and came up with five. The financial mess Megan's in right now is all due to Neal."

"Why'd she stay married to him so long?"

Grace sighed. "She had nowhere else to go. Her mother's barely getting by herself, her two sisters are unmarried and still living at home, sometimes working, sometimes not. So Megan toughed it out. That's why I don't want you thinking bad things about her because she's the sweetest, the kindest, the most honest—"

It was then that they heard a loud crash coming from the direction of the top floor.

Chapter 7

By the time Alex reached the second floor, he could hear the frightened wail of a young boy. Two steps at a time, his long legs scaled the stairs, not stopping until he was halfway down the third-floor hall. There was Ryan pinned under a rolling television stand, the TV on its side on the wood floor and Megan in her skimpy nightie standing on one foot, trying to right the cart to free him.

"Here, let me," he said, moving in as Grace arrived, stepping in to steady Megan. "Ryan, you all right?" Alex asked.

"I think so," a wobbly voice replied.

"Oh, God, Ryan," Megan whispered, moving aside to give Alex room.

Grace squeezed her friend's arm. "He's all right, so don't you worry."

Alex saw that the cord from the portable television set had gotten tangled in the wheels of the stand, causing it to topple. "Hold on," he told the frightened boy. Grunting, he picked up the TV and shifted it to a clear spot, then pulled the two-tiered stand off Ryan.

He quickly scrambled up and ran into his mother's arms. "I'm sorry, Mom."

Now that he was safe, she relaxed, hugging him to her as she leaned against the wall. "Are you hurt? Let me see." Easing back from him, she checked him over, pulling up the pant legs of his Tasmanian devil pajamas, then the sleeves. "You might have a bruise on your elbow later from when you hit the floor." She framed his tear-streaked face in both her hands. "Whatever were you doing?"

Ryan sniffled loudly. "I thought you looked lonely, so I was taking my TV into your room so you could watch it." He turned away, looking toward Alex who'd placed the set back on the stand. "Did I break it?"

"I don't think so," Alex told him. "I think one of the wheels on the cart is bent, but that's simple enough to fix." He eyed the small fry. "Next time you get the urge to move furniture, sport, maybe you should call me, eh?"

Glad no one was yelling at him, gladder still that his TV wasn't broken, Ryan nodded. "Okay," he agreed in a small voice.

"It was a lovely thought, sweetie," Megan said now that her heartbeat had normalized, "but let's leave the TV in your room. I'm not really in the mood to watch anything tonight."

"But when I peeked in, you looked so lonesome."

Megan smiled at his soft little heart. "I am, a little. Why don't you come in and talk to me for a little while before lights-out, okay? You're much better than TV."

Swiping at his cheeks, embarrassed that he'd been scared enough to cry in front of Alex, Ryan nodded and allowed her to lead him into her bedroom with Grace's assistance.

"Would you mind putting that back in Ryan's room, Alex?" she asked over her shoulder.

He looked up from the cord he'd been winding, a look of exaggerated shock on his face. "What's this, Ms. Delaney? You're actually asking for help with something? You must have developed a fever."

"You're quite the comedian," she said, but she smiled.

After several minutes, Grace returned, releasing a relieved sigh. "That boy just put a dozen new gray hairs on my poor little head."

"You'd be gorgeous bald, Grace, and you know it," Alex told her as he wheeled the stand and set into Ryan's room. Maneuvering it into the empty spot beneath the Michael Jordan poster he'd hung for Ryan, he bent to plug it in. Then, because he knew Ryan would want to know, he turned it on for a test run. Sure enough, the picture came on, the colors nice and bright and the sound fine. "A good, sturdy set," he told Grace, shutting it off.

"It's not even a year old. Megan sold Neal's gold watch and bought this for Ryan shortly after the funeral. The only other television's down in the community room and most of our guests don't turn on children's shows. She felt he needed something in his room."

"I agree." He shook his head in wonder. "Imagine, he thought she looked lonely."

Grace studied him up close for a long minute.

He caught her and frowned. "What?"

"You're falling for the two of them, aren't you, Mr. Magic Man? And I'd bet my best cubic zirconia that you surely hadn't planned on that happening."

"Who, me?" Alex shook his head emphatically. "No, ma'am. Like you, I've already struck out in the marriage game. I travel single-o and I like it that way."

"Uh-huh," she said, walking out of Ryan's room. "If I was a betting woman, I'd sure bet the farm on this one." And what's more, Grace wasn't absolutely convinced she approved.

Stretching his long legs, Alex walked up the hill behind the Delaney house, climbing slowly, his eyes on the ground. The grass was scraggly here, peppered with stones both smooth and sharp nestled among the wildflowers. Manzanita grew wild along one side and there were patches of poison oak. He recognized wild lupine looking silvery in the spotty moonlight, and even creosote. Hardly noticing, he strolled on.

Finally, he reached the edge of the cliff and gingerly sat down on the ledge made by a large flat rock. It was quiet except for the furtive scramblings of a few furry creatures. No birdsongs tonight, not even a cricket serenade. If he listened carefully, he could hear ocean waves in the distance rolling into shore with a rush, then being sucked back out to sea. He caught the scent of salt in the night air.

He'd come out here because he needed some distance. He felt a little like a fish who'd been struggling on the line for a long while, thinking he was winning the battle only to be slowly reeled in after all. Down there at that house, for days now, he'd been pulled in emotionally. For all his travels, his many adventures, he'd never experienced anything like it.

He'd set out on a mission—to make sure what remained of the Delaney family was handling things well, financially and otherwise. Not altogether altruistically, but to ease his conscience. And he'd found more than he'd bargained for.

He'd found a woman who'd had a difficult childhood, a disappointing marriage, and who was still having a rough go of it. Yet she never complained. She operated a business that drew repeat customers because of her generous nature and a marvelous flair for cooking and because she made them all feel welcome and at home. Let's not forget that she kissed like every man's dream. A woman a man so inclined could easily love.

Then there was the boy. Eager to learn, anxious to please, with a mischievous grin and a laugh that could warm the coldest of hearts. The boy who looked at him with trust and admiration, with worship in his deep blue eyes, who made him feel ten feet tall. No one had ever looked at Alex like that before. The kind of boy who had him wondering if he could live up to the kid's expectations. A boy a man could learn to love without half trying.

But he kept coming back to one thing. He wasn't in the market. Not for a woman or a boy or the family they represented. Oh, he might be inclined to linger a while, coax the woman into bed, be a stand-in father to the kid until he had a handle on the guy things every boy needed to know. He'd enjoy them, write a few checks to further ease his conscience, then go back to his carefree, uncomplicated single life. He was good at being single. A man should do what he's good at.

Alex swallowed around a bitter lump in his throat at the mental assessment he'd just made of himself. Not very pretty. Not really a stand-up guy. Not a hell of a lot better than the about-to-be ex-husband who'd died.

How was it that after less than two weeks here, he viewed his life before this trip with a somewhat jaundiced eye? What was wrong here? What had changed? He didn't want what Megan and Ryan might offer him because he was happy with his life the way it had been before his illness, before the surgery. He didn't want a family, a commitment to one woman for the rest of his life, a child, possibly more. Hadn't he already divorced one woman who'd wanted to have that kind of life with him? He'd run fast and furiously from Cynthia because he'd told himself he needed to be free.

Look at his mother, struck down in her thirties by a fatal illness, missing out on so much. And Patrick, so young, having experienced so little. Alex had learned from their deaths that life was awfully damn short and that, although work was important, you'd better have some fun because no one knew what was around that next corner. There was so much he hadn't tried yet, done yet. How could he pursue an adventurous lifestyle tied to a family?

But wait. Alex shifted, stretching out his legs. Whatever made him think Megan would want him anyway? *He deceived her royally and I'm not sure she'll ever get over it.* That's what Grace had told him about Neal's relationship with Megan. She'd been hurt, betrayed, disappointed. What would she say when she learned, as surely she must, that his being here was also a deception?

Just when she was beginning to trust a little, how could he

destroy her a second time? Yet, if he was to stay much longer, how could he not tell her? He'd only wanted to help, yet he'd made a mess of things.

Slowly, he got to his feet. He hadn't wanted to hurt anyone, yet maybe he already had. With a heavy heart, Alex started back.

"Okay now, I'll hold the nail and you hammer it in. Watch that you don't hit your fingers. Or mine, for that matter." Alex shoved the corner board into place, then positioned the nail. "Now."

His face a study in concentration, tongue in the corner of his mouth, Ryan lifted the hammer with both hands and brought it down. Only he missed the nail by about an inch. "Phooey!"

"Try again," Alex advised, exhibiting more patience than he'd thought he had. Ever since Ryan had come home from school, they'd been working on the tree-house floor in the grass of the backyard for nearly two hours and they were nearly finished. *The fun is in the doing, not just in the finished product,* he reminded himself. The purpose was to teach Ryan some guy things. Again, he positioned the nail.

Ryan swiveled the baseball hat on his head until the bill was in the back, then raised the hammer again. To his surprise and enormous pleasure, he hit the head dead center. He flashed a grin to Alex. "I did it!"

"You sure did. Now keep going. We've got to bury that nail." Alex made sure the nail had caught before removing his hand.

The boy pounded three more times, then gave a final smack for good measure. The nail was firmly in place. "Hey, this is fun."

Alex had done the preliminary nailing, showing Ryan how, then finally turning that chore over to him. "I knew you'd like it. We need to put another one at the other end to make sure the board holds." Shifting, he positioned another nail. "Go to it."

Ryan raised the hammer.

"What on earth are you two doing?" Megan asked, coming onto the scene as she stepped out the back door.

Startled, Ryan dropped the hammer. The business end landed on Alex's hand. He yelped in pain. "Ow!"

"Sorry," Ryan said, bending over to see what damage he'd done.

Alex scowled at Megan. "What are you doing walking?"

Wearing her air cast, Megan hobbled over to them, taking care on the uneven grass. "I can't spend the rest of my days with my foot elevated. I'm fine. What, may I ask, are you two building?"

"A tree house," Ryan explained, a wide smile on his face.

"I see." It was Megan's turn to scowl, and she aimed it at Alex. "I thought we had an understanding that you and I would talk things over before they were brought up to the *c-h-i-l-d?*"

Sitting on the grass, Alex's smile was sheepish. "I didn't want to bother you when you weren't feeling up to par. We were going to tell you as soon as we finished the floor."

"I know what word you spelled, Mom," Ryan said, pleased to have caught on. "Child. What child?"

With her free hand, Megan swiveled his hat around. "You, silly. You're the child, I'm the mom." She turned her blue eyes to Alex. "The one who approves all of the child's projects."

Obviously, she was feeling better since she was back to feisty, Alex thought. She'd lost that pained look. She was wearing a long T-shirt that came almost to the edge of her shorts. At the sight of those incredible legs, Alex had trouble keeping his mind on the current project and their conversation.

Pointedly, he glanced at the small pile of lumber pieces, then up at her. "All right, we can break it up and quit if you like."

"Ah, Mom, no!" Ryan was heartbroken. "We were going

to move it up into that bald spot in the tree over there.'' He pointed at the chosen location. "Please, can we?"

The onus was on her, yet how could she shatter the boy's dream now that they'd begun? Narrowing her eyes, she saw that Alex was aware of her dilemma. Megan studied the old tree, wondering if it would hold both the weight of the wooden structure and her son. Something else to worry about. "How are you going to get up and down?"

"Alex is going to help me build climbing steps up." Ryan shuffled his feet in nervous excitement.

"I realize you're in construction," she told Alex, "but is this thing going to be sturdy enough?"

"Absolutely. Shephard Construction guarantees every job." He grinned boyishly.

"All right, I guess I'm outnumbered yet again." Her tone seemed to imply that she was running out of patience with his backhanded maneuverings.

"I'll test the steps and building with my own weight, then we'll know it'll hold his and a friend's. All right?" He knew how skeptical women were about such things.

"I guess so." Shuffling to a tree stump, she sat down to watch.

It took Ryan and Alex another fifteen minutes to get the last board in place. Alex stepped back, his head cocked, mentally critiquing the finished product. But to Ryan, it was a work of art.

"Isn't it swell, Mom?"

"Mmm." Squinting, Megan again eyed the tree. "That spot's up awfully high, Alex. Couldn't you anchor it a bit lower?"

Hands on his hips, he turned to her, a look of amused patience on his face. "Are we being a tad overprotective again, Mom?"

"Maybe, but if he falls—"

"He won't. Eight-year-old boys are agile. By the time we're finished, you'll feel better. There'll be handholds along the steps, natural ones from the tree branches.'' He gazed down at Ryan affectionately. "He'll be fine."

"Yeah, Mom, I'll be fine."

A conspiracy, that's what it was. That male-bonding thing. Only what would happen when Alex went on his way? Would Ryan still be thrilled with his tree house? Or was she just borrowing trouble?

Megan checked her watch. "Time to go in and do your homework, Ryan."

"Can't we put the floor up in the tree now, Alex?"

"Tomorrow's another day, sport." He bent to return the hammer and nails to the somewhat rusty tool chest he'd found in the backyard shed. "Homework comes first."

"Okay. Thanks, Alex. I...I love it." Embarrassed at his own emotions, Ryan skipped off and went inside.

That was the second time the kid had really gotten to him, Alex thought. The first time had been his spontaneous hug when he'd given him the Austin Healy model.

"You really like him, don't you?" Megan asked, her voice soft. She'd been watching the two together, first through the kitchen window, then closer up in the yard as they hammered away. She'd been worried about allowing her son to get close to a man who'd soon be leaving. Yet maybe Grace was right. Maybe some exposure to men was better than none. And she'd have to rely on Ryan to handle the goodbye scenes somehow.

"Yeah, I really do. He's a tornado, a whirlwind, a dynamo. I'm nuts about him."

A tornado, Megan thought. Wasn't that what she'd labeled Alex—whirling in, taking over, devastating the calm she'd worked so hard to achieve?

Alex flipped the lid closed on the tool chest and sat back down, bracing his forearms on his raised knees. "Does that surprise you?"

"I guess, in a way."

"Me, too. I've never spent much time with kids. Ryan's terrific, but I think you already know that. You've done a great job raising him.'' Unspoken were the words *without much help from his father*.

"Thanks. You mentioned you'd been married for less than a year. No children, I take it?"

Alex shook his head. "Cynthia wanted kids." He left it at that as his eyes got stuck on the indentation in her chin. He remembered how he'd kissed it that day in the shower, how he'd kissed her. And he badly wanted to do it again. Seated close, her scent wrapped around him, adding to the ache.

"Apparently, then, you didn't. Is that why the marriage broke up?"

"Partly. I was twenty-two, too immature for marriage, much less fatherhood." And too busy having fun to want to settle down. "Children are a big responsibility."

"You can say that again. Once you have one, your whole life changes forever. In a good way, that is." She watched the leafy shadows of the big tree limbs drift across his face. He was such a dichotomy—strong yet tender, bossy yet softhearted. "From watching you with Ryan, I'd say you'd have made a terrific father."

Alex plucked a blade of grass and stuck it in the corner of his mouth. "I don't think so, certainly not then. When Cynthia became adamant about having a baby, I asked for a divorce. I didn't want to wind up resenting her and any children we might have for my missing out on the things in life I wanted to do that I couldn't have done tied down to a family. She'd changed from a fun companion to wanting a house, picking out china patterns, decorating a nursery. And never wanting to go anywhere anymore. It's a big world out there. I couldn't imagine staying in only a small corner of it all my life."

"And I can't imagine wanting to keep searching for greener grass all my life."

He sent her a sharp look. "Is that what you think I'm doing?"

Megan shrugged. "I don't know. Are you?"

"No." He wasn't used to explaining himself, his motives,

his philosophy. But he wanted her to understand. "I just want to see all I can, to experience all life has to offer, to do everything I can before...before the Grim Reaper calls my name."

Megan frowned. "Do you have some reason to suspect you might die young?"

"No. I've felt like this ever since my mother died at age thirty-two, which is the age I am now. All she'd known her whole life was working alongside my father. My younger brother was a workaholic, like both our parents. He died at twenty-seven in a stupid boating accident. He'd never even traveled farther than San Francisco. The only pleasure he allowed himself was his sailboat. Ironic that he died in a fall from it."

"My husband was the opposite of your brother, his philosophy more like yours. He wanted to go places and do things, too. Only what I didn't know was that he had a hereditary liver disease that usually skips a generation and is almost always fatal without a transplant. Perhaps if I'd have known sooner...well, at least I might have understood why he did some of the things he did." She'd spent many an hour seeking an explanation for Neal's behavior and had finally settled on that.

This was a new twist to Alex. "You mean he knew way back when that he'd die young?"

"I didn't find out till afterward, but five years before his death, the doctors had warned him that if he didn't stop drinking, he'd be inviting liver damage. He didn't stop. Neal had trouble facing reality. He told no one and instead stepped up his destructive way of life. He drank way too much and didn't take good care of himself. By the time he finally acknowledged that the disease had a stranglehold on him, he was a very sick man." She sighed heavily. "The disease is genetic, but if a victim is aware of all aspects, so much can be done to slow or even halt its progress. Neal was his own worst enemy."

Alex immediately thought of Ryan. "You said the disease skips a generation?"

"Yes, but I'm taking no chances. I've had Ryan to a specialist already and he's being closely monitored. Once he's old enough, we'll have to tell him so he can be aware and take good care of himself. And, of course, his children could be affected."

"Maybe by the time Ryan has children, they'll find a cure."

"I pray they do." Megan rose somewhat stiffly. "I'd better see to his dinner."

Alex also stood. "Is it because of Neal's self-destructive behavior that you've sworn off men?"

"It's certainly a contributing factor. I'm just better off alone with my son. Relationships lead to complications. I need to lead a simple life."

"Don't you miss having a man in your life? Not just in the bedroom, but in other ways?" He honestly wanted to know.

In the bedroom? Hardly. But she could scarcely explain her true feelings to Alex. "I'll manage. Celibacy's not so difficult once you get the hang of it." She tried a smile to lighten her words.

"No." Alex stepped closer, ran a finger along one silken cheek and watched her eyes darken against her will. "You're too passionate a woman to decide to be celibate. I know. I've kissed you, remember?"

If only she could forget, Megan thought, flushing to the roots of her dark hair. Carefully, she sidestepped him. "I've really got to go. Little League night, you know."

"Yeah, right." Alex stood watching her make her way to the door. Her hand on the knob, she paused, turning back.

"You're coming to Ryan's game, aren't you?" she asked. "I think he's counting on your being there. Unless you have other plans, of course." Ryan had reminded her that Alex had promised at least half a dozen times already. Although she might be uncomfortable in his presence, especially after this last conversation, she didn't want her son disappointed.

She couldn't drive yet with that foot, he knew. But that aside, he *wanted* to go. "No other plans." He watched her smile in that hesitant way she had.

Well, Shephard, Alex told himself as he followed Megan inside, you've got it bad when watching a kid's softball game in a dusty field seated on hard bleachers alongside a sweet-smelling woman is exactly how you want to spend a warm spring evening.

Alex turned on the powerful engine of the Porsche and headed toward Delaney's B and B. His two morning meetings had gone about as well as he'd expected.

The feasibility study had arrived in the overnight mail and been very favorable. He'd taken it to Williams and gone over his figures with the banker. Then he'd met with the Parsons family. As before, the two daughters were all for the purchase, pleased with Shephard Construction's offer. But the son had balked again, saying he was certain they could get more.

However, Alex thought as he turned onto the hillside road, again, one daughter had re-stated that they still hadn't had even one other serious inquiry and their father's nursing home bills were mounting. Watching the three of them, he was certain the son was stonewalling. But he had no intention of raising the bid to satisfy the man's greed.

Very calmly, as was his habit, Alex had told them they had seven days to come to a decision, after which he'd withdraw his offer. That, he felt, was more than generous. Then he'd walked away.

Driving back with the sun high in the sky, he felt good. Of course, some other firm could show up and outbid him, but he doubted that. Most often, when land parcels came on the market, if they weren't snatched up within the first few weeks, the chances of the offer increasing was minimal, all other things being equal. So the son who was holding out was likely in for a rude awakening. And Alex knew that both sisters were ready to sign on the dotted line. They'd probably give him a call even before the seven-day deadline.

Humming along with an old Beatles tune on the radio, he turned into Delaney's lot and almost screeched to a stop. The car parked nearest to the door was unmistakable. A long gray custom Lincoln with vanity plates reading "Shephard." His father's pride and joy.

Parking the Porsche, Alex wondered what had brought Ron Shephard all this way. True, he hadn't been checking in daily, but then he seldom did when he was away on acquisition trips. Had his father sensed something amiss in their last phone conversation? Or, and this was the most likely, was he worried about Alex's health and needed to see for himself how his son was doing?

Inside the foyer, Alex noticed that no one was around. About to walk through the dining room into the kitchen where he could usually find either Grace or Megan around noon, he stopped when he heard voices coming from the lounge. His father's deep tones and Megan's soft answer. Squaring his shoulders, he strolled in.

Ron Shephard was seated in a cane-back chair next to a round table, where a bright red tray held a pitcher of iced tea, glasses, sugar and lemon. Standing near him, braced on a cane, was Megan, wearing white slacks and a blue top the same shade as her eyes. The same eyes that registered a wariness as they met his.

"There he is," Megan said, her smile a little self-conscious.

Ron rose, his smile reserved. "Hello, son. Surprised you, I see. I was in the neighborhood, so I thought I'd stop in and see how things are going with the Parsons property."

In the neighborhood, my Aunt Tillie, Alex thought. Shephard Construction had no other business up this way. Twin Oaks was a good two-hour drive from San Diego, not even in the same county. He put on what he hoped passed for a welcoming smile. "Dad, good to see you." Stepping closer, he shook hands with his father.

"Can I pour you a glass of tea, Alex?" Megan asked, amazed at the resemblance between the two men. Although the father's hair was more sandy than blond, his tanned face, the broad shoulders and impressive height were like mirror images of Alex with twenty-five years or so added. "Or would you two like lunch? Grace could put together a chicken salad in no time."

"No, thank you, my dear," Ron said, smiling down at her. "I won't be staying long."

She raised questioning brows at Alex.

"I'll pour my tea, thanks." He glanced down at her foot and saw she was wearing sandals without the air cast. "How's the foot?" To his father, he said, "Megan sprained her ankle badly a few days ago."

"Much better. I'll leave you two to visit."

"Why don't you join us for a few minutes?" Alex suggested. At best he'd be postponing his father's inevitable questions, but he decided he wanted Ron's impression of Megan for reasons he couldn't explain even to himself.

"Oh, thanks, but I've got things to do." She smiled at Ron. "Nice to meet you, Mr. Shephard." She let her eyes drift over Alex's face for the briefest of moments before leaving, hardly relying on the cane at all.

Alex sat down on the couch across from his father and fixed his tea. "So why are you really here, Dad?"

Reseating himself, Ron Shephard had known his son would see through his excuse. He didn't much care. Alex had been gone too long with only vague phone calls. He'd decided to see for himself just what was keeping him in this small town. After watching the eye contact between his son and the young woman who'd just left, Ron thought he'd found the reason. But first things first.

"How are you feeling, son? No adverse reactions?"

"None whatsoever. Is my health the reason you're here?"

"The better question is, why are you here for several weeks on a land purchase that could easily have been tied up in two days tops, then finalized by phone and mail?"

Alex tasted his tea, then set down the glass and sat back. "Things are moving rather slowly. People in this small town don't hurry. I just came from a meeting with the bank. The feasibility study you sent me was very favorable, as you know. The financing's all set. But my second meeting with the Parsons family didn't result in signed paperwork. Yet. The two sisters are ready to roll, but the son's holding out. I've given them a week to accept our offer or I'll withdraw it."

Ron's lips twitched. "So, you have been working."

Alex tried to look surprised. "What else did you think I was doing up here?"

Pointedly, Ron sent a look in the direction Megan Delaney had just disappeared. "She's very lovely."

Alex shifted in his seat, cleared his throat. There was no point in denying the obvious. "Yes, she is."

His hands relaxed on the arms of the chair, Ron studied his son. Alex looked healthy enough, his tan even deeper, so he had to be spending some time outdoors. But there was something about him that was different. He didn't meet his father's eyes for very long, as if distracted or nervous. Or deliberately evasive.

"I talked with Mitch. Finally got him to open up. You hired a private investigator, I understand."

Alex sighed. He'd specifically instructed Mitch to say nothing to his father. But Alex knew only too well how persuasive Ron could be.

His father guessed what he was thinking. "Don't blame Mitch. I forced his hand." Again, Ron glanced toward the arch leading to the foyer and lowered his voice. "What were you thinking?"

"Listen, Dad, you did what you thought best in securing my transplant and didn't seek my advice. I also had something I had to do. It's as simple as that."

Ron knew his son was as stubborn as he was, a fact that made dealing with him difficult. "Did you tell her? Does she know the real reason you're here?"

Alex frowned. "The reason I'm here is to purchase land

for our company. Anything else is...is my personal business."

"Alex, you have nothing to atone for, nothing to feel guilty about. Neal Delaney would have died during surgery. If the man was that ill, he probably would have died on the operating table."

"Probably?"

"That's good enough for me."

"Not for me." Growing angry, Alex rose, walked to the window and stood looking out. "He wouldn't have been on the list if his chances of survival weren't good."

After a long minute, Ron strolled over, wishing he had a better argument. "So what is it you hope to accomplish by coming here, by befriending his widow?"

"I don't honestly know. I only know I had to do something. He left her with no money. She has a son, eight years old. She works twelve hours a day running this place, then bakes for two more and sells the stuff in town. It's not fair."

Ron placed a hand on Alex's shoulder. "Life's not fair, son. It wasn't fair that your mother died. Nor Patrick."

"I know." Alex lowered his gaze to the row of African violets on the low sill, all six in bloom. Megan had a way with plants and flowers and food and kids. And she'd managed to enchant a certain man who'd never been so confused in his life.

Ron wore a worried frown. "Are you attracted to this woman, Alex? And if so, is it for the right reasons? Pity is a rotten basis for a relationship."

Alex moved away, his anger resurfacing. "I don't pity her. I just feel she's had a lot of bad breaks. And the boy, too." He decided not to mention that he felt a need to try to make up for Megan and her son's hardships, sure his father wouldn't understand.

Ron decided to take another tack. "I also came to see you because I have a project I'd like you to oversee."

Suspicious at the abrupt change, Alex looked up. "What would that be?"

"You might recall there's this property in England that my grandfather left me." Relaxing somewhat, Ron shoved his hands into his pants pockets, trying to sound casual. He didn't especially want his son to travel so far away, but a short trip might get his mind off this guilt foolishness. "It's been years since I've inspected it. I'd like you to fly over, check it out, see what we can do with it. Maybe sell as is, or make improvements and then put it up. See what the current zoning is and the market value. That sort of thing. Possibly even build on it. Who knows?"

Alex smiled. He couldn't help it. The man was so patently obvious. "Dad, that land's been yours for fifty years or more. I'm sure it can wait. It's not going to work, sending me off on some obscure junket. I'm not going anywhere until this situation is settled to my satisfaction."

Ron wasn't licked yet. "What about the next America's Cup race? Aren't you planning to get your boat in shape for that? When you went into the hospital, you vowed you'd be healthy enough to enter the next one."

Alex nodded, remembering. "I did say that. Things change, Dad. Priorities shift. Maybe next year." Funny, what little appeal that race held for him right now. He clapped his father on the back as he edged him toward the exit. "Be patient with me. I've got to work this out my way."

In the foyer at the door, Ron turned to his son. "All right, but one thing you must do. You owe it to Megan Delaney to tell her the truth, to explain the real reason you're here." And maybe she'd have the good sense to send him away.

"I will." He embraced his father somewhat awkwardly, then watched him don sunglasses, walk to his Lincoln and get in. His expression thoughtful, Alex stood in the doorway as the big car with the tinted windows drove off.

In the dining room folding napkins, Megan looked up. It had been impossible to avoid overhearing them at the door. What had Ron Shephard meant when he'd said that Alex owed it to her to tell her the truth? What was the real reason Alex was here, if not to conduct his business?

What was Alex hiding?

Chapter 8

Megan stepped out into the twilight of the backyard, intent on taking down the last load of linens from the clothesline. The dryer had finally given up the ghost.

Dinner was finished, dishes and baking done, her son safely in his bed. One more chore before she could get off her feet and put them up. Her right foot still gave her twinges of pain.

Walking carefully, she reached up to unfasten a top sheet, inhaling the clean fragrance of laundry dried out in the open air. The dryer was faster certainly and less work, but nothing smelled like things straight off the line. However, she'd have foregone the pleasure if only the work-worn old machine had held up a bit longer.

Folding the sheet and placing it in the basket, she sighed. Always something. Grace had wanted her to call Eddie Jenkins, but Megan decided to face facts. She was only throwing good money after bad, constantly repairing a dryer that was destined for the discard pile. How to find the money for a new one was the problem.

Credit was another, Megan thought as she tossed clothes-

pins into a canvas bag that hung by a wire on the line. If only
Neal hadn't ruined their credit by buying so much, then ignoring the monthly payments, she might have been able to
charge a new dryer. As it was, no place would take a chance
on her past credit history, even though she'd paid off Neal's
most pressing debts. In time maybe, but not yet.

Nevertheless, Megan knew she couldn't get by for long
without a dryer. Reaching for the next sheet, she found herself
frowning, something she did all too often lately. Who
wouldn't frown faced with her problems? Her foot still ached,
though not nearly as badly as before. Naturally, it would heal
faster if she remained off it. But she couldn't let Grace shoulder so much of the work.

While drying the many sheets, towels and table linens outdoors was an option, it clearly was too time-consuming and
required more ironing. She'd simply have to give in and use
some of the money she'd been saving to bring her mortgage
payments up to date and buy a new dryer tomorrow. Maybe
if she stopped in and had another chat with Mr. Williams at
the bank, she could buy some time.

Lord, how she hated to keep asking for favors, for exten-
sions, for loans. When would she ever get caught up? Maybe
she should just sell Delaney's Bed & Breakfast, take a small
apartment for herself and Ryan and get a job where she
earned a paycheck every Friday. What a relief it would be
not to have to worry constantly.

She placed another sheet in the basket and moved to the
second line for the remaining towels. The problem there was
that the inn needed work before anyone would want to buy
it. And she had no money for repairs, either. And how could
she get rid of the only home Ryan had ever known? She'd
fought with Neal about purchasing the old house until he'd
given in because she didn't want their son to grow up in the
same vagabond existence she'd had, moving often, one jump
ahead of bill collectors. Yet despite her best efforts, she was
in basically the same boat that had nearly sunk her mother.
Round and round her thoughts went, circling like a trapped

mouse in a maze. There had to be a way out of this mess she'd made of her life, but what was it?

She still owed a substantial amount of money, she was worried that she would have to let her son down, and her emotions were in a jumble because of Alex Shephard. Mysterious, enigmatic, evasive Alex, with his keen sense of humor, that killer smile and a sixth sense about children. And a mouth that made her throat go dry and her knees weaken.

He'd been oddly scarce this evening, most probably in his room, for his car was out front. Even when he wasn't in her line of vision, she was painfully aware of his presence.

Wanting a man like that, even fantasizing about him, was an unexpected annoyance. Maybe in her teens, she'd felt like this, Megan admitted. But certainly not since, and not very exuberantly then. Years ago, she'd come to grips with the fact that she'd gone after Neal Delaney more out of a desperate desire to get out of her mother's unhappy household than a wild desire for him as a man. Too late she'd learned to regret that foolish ambition.

But Alex was another story. Just last night, she'd awakened in a sweat, tangled in the sheets, finding herself struggling with the remnants of a dream where he'd been holding her, kissing her, making love with her. As dreams are wont to do, their union was perfect, of course. That was truly a fantasy she would surely regret if she ever gave in to it.

Pausing, Megan straightened up from the basket, her hand involuntarily touching the small scar beneath her bangs near her hairline. Odd how all this time later, she still vividly remembered that night when—

"Penny for your thoughts," Alex said, standing on the edge of the patio.

Startled, Megan jumped, so wrapped up in her dismal thoughts that she hadn't heard the back door open. She rearranged her features before turning to see him standing in a splash of moonlight. Darkness had moved in quickly. "I'm afraid you'd get change tonight."

Casually, he strolled toward her. "Can't be that bad, can

it?'' He glanced over at the last few towels as she reached up to remove them, having heard about the problem from Grace in the kitchen minutes ago. "Is it the death of your dryer that's got you frowning?"

That was only the last straw, but she'd let him think what he would. "Pretty good reason, wouldn't you say?"

Tomorrow, he'd see about a dryer for her. He wouldn't tell her, just order it. "I guess so."

Determined to stop her melancholy meanderings, Megan changed the subject. "You certainly resemble your father."

"So everyone says." He scooted the clothespin bag closer to her. "He's a good father, even if he worries too much."

"That's a parent's prerogative, to worry about their children."

"Did Neal worry a great deal about Ryan?"

"Neal worried about Neal." Now why had she let that slip out? Megan wondered as she dropped the last folded towel into the basket. "I'm sorry. I'm a little tired and I don't want to talk about Neal tonight."

"Why, Megan? Because he not only didn't take care of his health, but he didn't take very good care of his family, running up debts, almost bankrupting you?" In the patchy moonlight, he saw her eyes go wide, then suddenly turn sad.

"Yes, that's exactly why." She was tired of fencing, of alibiing, of pretending. Guiltily, she glanced toward Ryan's upstairs bedroom window, worried that he might somehow overhear. Guilt, a constant companion. "Forget I said that. I shouldn't be telling you such personal things."

Alex stepped closer, so close she couldn't avoid looking at him. "It's too late for that. I already know."

Her silvery blue eyes studied his face. "Grace. I should have guessed."

"Don't be angry with her. I kept after her. I had to know." His hands settled at her waist.

Megan felt the heat of his touch through her clothes. "Why?"

The humiliation of the debts was bad enough, but Grace

had hinted at Neal's unfaithfulness, as well. That had to have hurt even more. Alex wanted to let her know that her husband's roving eye wasn't her fault, because he had a feeling she blamed herself. The injured party generally did.

"Neal was a fool to look elsewhere when he had a treasure like you right here in his home."

So he knew that, too, or perhaps had guessed. Still, she had a small measure of pride left. "Don't say that. You don't know what happened between us. Neal needed more than I could give him." Like constant bolstering, daily praise to prop up his low self-esteem and tons of affection to build up his deflated ego. Seeing to his many needs had worn her ragged.

Alex felt a spurt of anger start simmering. "And just what was it that you weren't able to give him?"

Averting her eyes, Megan shrugged. "Oh, you know."

"No, I don't know." He slid his hands along her forearms, so close to her now that they were toe to toe, so near he could smell the delicate fragrance of her shampoo as a light breeze shifted a lock of her hair. "Tell me."

She might as well tell him and then maybe he'd back off, go home and stop messing up her head. Taking a deep breath, she met his gaze. "All the things a man needs from a woman—respect, understanding, admiration, affection, unconditional love. You can let go of me because I have nothing to offer you, either."

"Did he give *you* all those things? Marriage is a two-way street, I've heard."

"A man doesn't stray if he's happy at home. Apparently, Neal didn't care enough for me to want to stay."

He hated hearing her defeated tone. "That's odd because I've wanted you almost from the first moment I saw you." He reached to skim his thumb lazily along her bottom lip, heard her sharp intake of breath. "I want you even more now. And you feel the same."

Megan did her best to ignore the thrill of anticipation that skittered along her spine. "No," she lied. "You're seeing what you want to see, not what is really there."

He trailed a hand up her back, his fingers stopping to massage her vulnerable nape. "Tsk, tsk, Megan. You can lie to me, but you shouldn't lie to yourself." As if to emphasize his words, he drew her closer.

"You're trying to convince me that I want you, but it's not working." How had her hands wound up against his chest, nervously fidgeting, clutching his shirt?

"Isn't it?" Against his own, he felt her heart thud, then skip a beat. He almost smiled before he planted a light kiss on the corner of her mouth. Involuntarily, she turned toward the kiss.

Megan shuddered, realizing she was fighting a losing battle here. But she couldn't back down. "I thought I told you I'm not a physical person. I won't go to bed with you just to prove that."

Alex's eyes narrowed and his hands on her shoulders tightened. "Is that all you think I want? Because if it was, we'd have been wrestling in the sheets long before this, and you damn well know it." He banked the quick surge of rage at the ex-husband who'd made her doubt herself so much that she'd deny herself the pleasure of her own sensuality.

"If not that, then what is it you want from me?" Sensing his exasperation, knowing she'd inadvertently caused it, gave her the courage to speak up, to be honest. "I'm no match for you in this department, Alex. I can't swim with the sharks. I'm a small-town girl, and I've been with only one man in my entire life. Don't toy with me. I don't know how to handle it."

All anger drained from him. He believed her. "I'm not toying with you."

She shook her head, feeling lost. "I don't know what you want from me."

His hands slid into her hair, his fingers gripping her head and moving it closer to his. "This." His mouth captured hers as he dragged her against him. He couldn't seem able to convince her with words, so he had to use other means. His lips dominated, his hands roamed, his hips ground into hers, his meaning clear. His actions spoke volumes, their message unmistakable: He wanted her.

A frighteningly helpless passion exploded inside Megan as she clung to him, her hands clutching the fabric of his shirt at his back now, holding on to stay upright. She could taste his frustration mingling with her own. She could feel the heat that leaped between the two of them and spread like a wildfire raging out of control.

Shamelessly, she let his aroused body inflame her, her needs moving to a new plateau. How was it that this man could make her feel things she'd scarcely let herself dream of before, feelings that would match her restless dreams, when her husband hadn't been able to awaken this same kind of desire in her? Could she have been blaming herself when all along Neal had been the lousy lover?

But there was no time to think about the past, no time to ponder, only time to feel. Alex's hands snaked beneath her loose top and moved around front, touching bare flesh, and this time she let him. When his fingers closed over her breasts, she felt her knees buckle and would have fallen if his strong arms hadn't held her pressed tightly to his heated body.

Always, Alex had thought of himself as a tender, gentle lover, considerate and slow, never rushing to fulfill his own needs. Yet it had been so very long, and these past few weeks, always close to Megan yet not close enough, had taken their toll. And now, with Megan here in his arms, her mouth wild and frantic on his, demanding more the way he'd dreamed she would, he could only struggle to keep up.

He could feel her straining against him, this woman who would try to deny she wanted him. Beneath his palm, his fingers encircling her soft breasts, her heart did a staccato beat. He slanted his mouth over hers and heard her moan his name while her taste drove him crazy. He could have her now, he knew, right this minute. He could drag her under the big old tree silently waiting to hold the tree house he had yet to finish. Or he could carry her up to his room and take all night to learn every inch of her.

And then what? a small, rational voice inside his head asked.

Because if he followed through, if he took her now even as willing as she was, there would be nothing left between them in the morning. Not friendship or a relationship, not even respect.

Abruptly, he eased his hold on her and took a step back. He gazed into dark blue eyes still hazy with passion and a hint of confusion. *I don't know what you want from me,* she'd told him. Small wonder. He didn't know himself.

Cursing uncharacteristically under his breath, he turned from her, gulping air. He needed some breathing room, some time and space. "I've got to go," he said, his voice thick.

"Yes, so do I."

Alex ran a shaky hand through his hair. "No, I mean I've got to go back. To San Diego. My father needs me at the office." The lie rolled off his tongue easily. He ground his teeth, wondering when he'd lost all manner of conscience. But he couldn't keep doing this to her. It was too unfair.

She wouldn't cry, Megan told herself. Not now, not yet. "Oh, I see. All right." With trembling hands, she straightened her clothes, smoothed her hair.

Like a man coming off a binge, he took two heavy steps toward the door. "In the morning."

"Yes, okay. I'll have your bill ready." With dry eyes, she watched him go inside, heard the back door click shut. Strolling to the big tree, she leaned against it and gazed up at a half-moon playing hide-and-seek with the clouds.

There'd be plenty of time to cry later, plenty of time to face yet another hard fact—that despite what had just happened between them, Alex, like Neal, didn't care enough to stay.

At six in the morning when Megan came downstairs, she found two envelopes on the kitchen table. In one, there were ten hundred-dollar bills and a note scribbled on the back of his business card asking her to send him a bill if he'd shorted her. The other envelope was addressed to Ryan.

Walking to the front door, she drew in a bracing breath before swinging it open. Alex's Porsche wasn't in the parking lot.

Mixed signals. He'd been sending her mixed signals, Alex admitted to himself as he sat at his desk at Shephard Construction, no more able to concentrate on the work in front of him than he had in Twin Oaks. Because of Megan Delaney.

He'd been back three days and nothing seemed to help. He swiveled in his chair, then rose and walked to the bank of windows. The same sailboats he'd noticed yesterday and the day before were out on the water below, skimming along, the people aboard enjoying the warm May morning. The day after his return, he'd taken the *Black Sheep* out for a trial run with Mitch. He'd been determined to have a good time, to forget about everything pertaining to the past couple of weeks, to recapture his carefree way of life.

Only it hadn't worked. He'd held the rudder in his hands, felt the welcome salt spray, turned his face up to a bright California sun. It had been a perfect day for sailing. Mitch had brought along a cooler filled with chicken sandwiches and beer. The same sort of setup they'd enjoyed on many a lazy afternoon in the past.

Yet Alex had been distracted, his mind so occupied with other thoughts that twice Mitch had had to poke him to get his attention. Finally, when they'd reached Catalina Island, they'd thrown a blanket on the sand and Alex had poured out his story.

It wasn't a pretty one. But then, deception never was.

"Why didn't you tell her?" Mitch had asked. "I mean, in all that time, surely you had an opportunity."

"I don't know," he'd answered.

"So now that you've gotten her bills paid up and even

stopped to order a dryer for her, you feel better? You don't need to go back?''

"I didn't say that," he'd answered enigmatically.

Mitch had scrunched up his beer can and tossed it into the trash receptacle, then zeroed in. "Sounds to me like you're hooked, buddy."

"What do you mean?" he'd demanded to know.

"You know, as in hook, line and sinker. As in over the top. As in in love with the woman."

Alex had nearly spilled his own beer hearing that. "You're crazy. I'm attracted, that's all. That's *it*. She's a beautiful woman, and I'm a normal guy. Who wouldn't want her? And I'll even admit that the boy's terrific. But love? Hey, man, you know that scene's not for me." He was certain he'd sounded convincing.

Until he'd looked at his friend.

"Uh-huh," Mitch had said, eyes narrowed, mouth curled in disbelief. "Well, that's good. Because love can't be based on a deception."

Alex watched the boat with the bright yellow sail nearly topple over in a strong breeze, then finally right itself. After lunch and their disturbing conversation, they'd sailed back to the marina. Mitch had droned on about things at the office and several anecdotes about his family. Alex had half listened, all the while mulling over Mitch's earlier words.

Love can't be based on a deception. Of course not. Even if love wasn't a consideration, friendship couldn't be based on a lie, either. So what was his relationship with Megan Delaney?

I don't know what you want from me, she'd said. The way he'd pulled her into the kiss had surely told her that a physical relationship was what he wanted. Yet he'd acted insulted when she'd accused him of wanting only that. He had in fact defended himself vigorously.

How could she know what he wanted when he sent her all those mixed signals? Thrusting his hands deep into the pockets of his slacks, Alex frowned as he gazed out the window.

Instead of the calm ocean scene, he saw Megan's face, those sky blue eyes, that hesitant smile, that wonderful dimple in her chin. He pictured the way she looked when she gazed into her son's face and the stunned passion reflected in her eyes after he kissed her.

The thing was, Alex thought as he strolled back to his desk, he wasn't an ambivalent person. From an early age, he'd known what he wanted to do, to be. True, he'd been sidelined by Cynthia, making a young man's error in believing that she felt as he did, that life was meant to be lived full tilt. No one had been more shocked than him when she'd done a one-eighty and opted for a vine-covered cottage complete with family dog and two-point-five children. He'd chosen to move on rather than compromise.

From that day on, he'd made sure in all his relationships that permanence wasn't what he was headed towards. If the women in his life could handle that—and there'd been plenty who could—he would see them from time to time. If not, he'd had nothing to do with them. Truth and honesty, that's how he'd played it.

Until Megan.

From the beginning, he'd lied to her. Sitting down in his chair, Alex leaned back. He'd arrived at her home under false pretenses, at least partly. It didn't matter that his motive was an honest concern for her welfare and that of her son. He'd been no better than her husband. *He deceived her royally* was what Grace had said about Neal's behavior toward his wife. Motives be hanged. Alex, too, had deceived her royally.

So just say, for a minute, for the sake of argument, that perhaps she had somehow gotten under his skin. That he cared more for her than any woman he'd ever known. He supposed he could admit to that, to himself only, of course. Then what made him think, when he confessed his dark secret to her, as confess he must, that she'd have anything to do with him ever again? If he knew anything about Megan, he knew she'd despise duplicity.

So there you are, he told himself. Even if love was a factor—which it was not—the lady herself would stop the progress of their tenuous relationship before it ever really got off the ground once she heard his story. And that would be that. No use pondering what couldn't be.

Leaning forward, Alex picked up his pen and reached for a stack of mail his secretary had opened for him earlier. He'd wait out the rest of the time limit he'd given the Parsons. If their answer was favorable, he'd finish the transaction by mail and phone. If it wasn't, he'd forget all about Twin Oaks and everyone in it.

Except that he'd have to tell Megan about the list, the transplant operation, the switch. Confession was good for the soul, or so they said. Perhaps it would be kinder to do it by mail. Or was it that he couldn't stand the thought of the usual warm welcome in her eyes turning to frosty rejection or worse when she learned the truth? He'd still set up the educational trust fund for Ryan, of course. He'd have the bank notify Megan of that and stay personally uninvolved. For the sake of her son, she couldn't refuse him that much.

Yes, that's how he'd handle things, Alex decided. The last thing in this world he needed was a doe-eyed woman with roots firmly entrenched in a small town and her charmingly mischievous son to divert him from his personal goals. Finally, he was back on track.

Coward! a small voice inside his head screamed.

"Oh, shut up!" Alex said aloud, then bent to his paperwork.

Megan knocked once on Ryan's bedroom door, then opened it. Her son was sitting on his bed with the Austin Healy model car beside him, Alex's printed note in his hand. Obviously, he'd been reading it yet again, trying to understand. His young face was a study in sadness.

She walked over and sat down, slipping her arm around him. She was certain his heart hurt almost as much as hers. Uncertain what to say, she waited for him to speak first.

"I just don't understand why he couldn't have waited to

talk to me in person before he left," Ryan got out finally, his voice wobbly. "He said he'd go on our field trip and chaperone and everything. It's next week. What if he's not back by then, Mom?"

Struggling with her own emotions, Megan chose her words carefully. "His note said something really important came up and he had to leave. Sometimes business problems have to be taken care of and chaperoning of field trips has to be canceled." Lord, how many times had she had to make similar explanations to this boy for Neal's many absences? More than she cared to count, and here she was, doing it again.

"Yeah, I guess." Abject misery sat on his small shoulders as he hugged his Tasmanian devil pillow to his chest. "He did say he'd probably be back. Probably doesn't mean for sure, right?"

"No, it doesn't." Perhaps she'd brought this unhappiness on her son by allowing him to get close to Alex Shephard. And herself, as well. But how could she have prevented it? He'd come storming into their lives like a runaway train. After the briefest resistance, they'd accepted him with open arms, even skeptical Grace. And Megan, who'd stopped believing, stopped hoping and dreaming, had begun to think maybe this time something good, something solid, would take place. And now they were left with the broken pieces of their hearts and shattered dreams. Hadn't she learned long ago that wishing alone didn't make it so? "I'm sorry, Ryan."

Blinking against tears, Ryan looked up at his mother. "You liked him, too, didn't you, Mom?"

She never lied to her son, not unless the truth would hurt him badly. "Yes," she whispered, drawing his warm little body close to hers, "I liked him, too."

A look of determination settled on his young face. "He's going to come back. I just know he will."

"Glad to meet you, Liz," Alex said, shaking hands with the tall blond woman. He turned to Mitch's wife, Jan. "I'll bet you're glad to have your sister visiting for a while." He'd completely forgotten that Jan had a sister. He wouldn't have accepted Mitch's dinner invitation had he remembered. He'd fallen into yet another matchmaking trap, one his best friend was deviously clever at setting.

"Would you like a glass of wine, Alex?" Jan asked. "Dinner won't be ready for another half an hour."

"Sure, that'd be fine." He followed Jan as she led the way out to their brick patio. Mitch enjoyed barbecuing and the coals were already glowing. Cushioned rattan furniture was informally arranged at one end of the roofed terrace where the soft light of overhead lanterns cast a yellow glow on the outdoor scene. Alex almost smiled at the way Jan maneuvered him to the only two-seater, then waved her sister over to join him. Not too obvious.

While Jan busied herself pouring wine and Mitch went inside for the platter of meat, Liz Trent smiled at Alex. "I understand you work closely with Mitch. Funny that we've never met before, I've been living in Boston. Just moved to California last week."

"How do you like our state so far?" Alex asked, more to make polite conversation than because he really wanted to know. Liz was lovely, with warm brown eyes and a body a man wouldn't easily forget. But he hated being thrust into these situations and had warned Mitch about this many times. Apparently, their little talk on Catalina had caused his friend to give it one more shot.

Liz crossed her long legs. "It's wonderful. So much sun and sand and water. Do you like to sail, Alex?"

So she'd been briefed on his interests. Mitch, it seemed, had no shame. "I can take it or leave it," he answered, feeling contrary.

Returning with the meat platter and overhearing the conversation, Mitch glared at him. "Don't let him kid you. Alex is planning to prime his sailboat to compete in the America's Cup race."

"Oh, that sounds so exciting," Liz purred.

Alex sipped his wine and wished the evening would end quickly.

"Grace, I want you to look at this," Megan said, sitting down at the kitchen table and handing over a letter attached to another sheet of paper. "It just came in the mail."

"What is it?" Grace asked, taking both in hand. Quickly, she read the brief official letter, then flipped the page over and studied the second sheet. "Your promissory note on the second mortgage has been satisfied, it seems." Raising both brows, she glanced across the table where she'd been working on the books. "Did you come into an inheritance you forgot to mention to me?"

"Hardly." Megan reached for the letter, read it again. "I don't get it. There must be some error."

"Like there was on the dryer that arrived day before yesterday marked paid in full?" Grace's skepticism was being sorely tried.

"I'm going to call Mr. Williams. Something's not right here."

Grace watched her leave the kitchen on her way to the front desk. Her friend had one thing straight at least. Something truly wasn't right here. Megan walked around the inn with dark shadows under her eyes, her temper frayed and her sense of humor almost totally absent. Ryan came racing into the parking lot after school every day, hope clearly stamped on his eager little face, only to be dashed when he saw no blue Porsche convertible parked there. They both looked as if they'd just lost their best friend.

And maybe they had. Neither had been this sad when they'd buried Neal, not that Grace blamed them for that. She'd warned that man with the devilish smile and the vagabond spirit not to hurt the two people in this world who mattered most to Grace, but he'd managed to do it anyhow. Even she had begun to believe, had dropped her guard.

But, true to form, he'd left them all in the lurch, sneaking out before dawn like a thief in the night.

"Well," Megan said, returning to sit down again, "I don't quite know what to think. Mr. Williams says that the second mortgage has been paid off in full and our primary mortgage brought current, all by someone he won't name." She glanced into the laundry room at the dryer that was industrial-size and top of the line. "Three guesses who's done this, and the first two don't count."

"I thought so," Grace commented, knowing exactly who Megan had in mind.

"How dare he!" Megan was too agitated to sit still, so she paced the kitchen. "Thinks he can whip out his checkbook and fix everything."

Grace looked up over her reading glasses. "What is there to fix?"

The way he'd left her that night, weak with wanting, heart breaking as he walked away, not even looking back once, maybe. But how could she explain that to Grace? "Oh, I don't know."

"Conscience, do you think?"

Megan frowned. "Conscience over what?" Men didn't have consciences about walking away from women. Her father had left without a backward glance. Neal had strolled off whenever he felt the urge, leaving when she'd been pregnant, home with a newborn or scrubbing floors. None of it had mattered. "Do you really think his conscience is bothering him because he stayed too long at the fair and let us all begin to like and trust him? So he writes a check for thousands because of that?"

"I imagine he can afford it."

"That's not the point, Grace."

"Maybe he did it because he cares about you. And Ryan."

That she didn't believe. A man who cared for a woman didn't walk away. Eyes on the letter again, Megan shook her head. "I can't accept this. The dryer was one thing. But twenty-seven thousand plus three back payments? No."

"It's done, Megan. The bank's not going to give back the money. They don't care who pays as long as they get theirs."

"Well, I care. I'm going to write Mr. Alex Shephard and tell him I'll set up a payment schedule with him to pay back every cent." That decision made, she rose. "I'm not ever going to be beholden to another man, not as long as I draw breath." With that, she turned away. But at the doorway, she stopped, her head downcast, one arm braced along the frame. For a long moment, she was silent. When she spoke again, it was in barely a whisper. "How'd I get to this place in time, Grace? Again." Slowly, she left the room.

Alone, Grace sighed as she turned to stare out the window, wishing she had a crystal ball.

"Thanks for calling, Ms. Parsons," Alex said into the phone. "I'm glad the three of you have decided to accept our offer. I'll contact Mr. Williams at the bank and have him finalize the paperwork." He listened to her express her appreciation, as well. "You're very welcome. I'll be in touch."

Alex hung up the phone and was staring at it when his father strolled into his office. Ron never knocked.

"Must be bad news the way you're frowning," Ron commented, dropping his lanky frame into the chair across from Alex's desk.

"No, actually, it's good news. The Parsons children have accepted our offer on the land in Twin Oaks at our original price."

"Good, good." Ron steepled his fingers, watching his son carefully. There was something bothering the boy. Alex hadn't been the same since returning from that little town. And Ron had a feeling he knew exactly what that something was. Or rather someone. "Are you planning to go back to set it all in motion?"

"I don't think so. The rest can be done by mail and phone." Alex picked up his pen and made a notation on the Parsons file.

"What about the girl?"

"What girl?"

"Don't play dumb with me, Alex. The one at the bed-and-breakfast. Megan Delaney. What's happening with her?"

Alex's eyes slid to the letter he'd received that morning lying next to his desk blotter. A very formal letter stating that Ms. Megan Delaney would be paying him a sum of three hundred dollars a month at a fair interest rate until the debt he satisfied with the bank was paid off. Not a personal word anywhere in the two short paragraphs. "She has nothing to do with the Parsons transaction."

Impatiently, Ron sat forward. "I know that. But you've got that woman on your mind, and there's no use denying it. Did you and she...I mean, are the two of you...damn it, Alex. Are you involved with her?" Ron hoped not, had been willing to send his son to England or Timbuktu, anywhere else to forestall such a thing happening, but seeing him this distracted and obviously unhappy, he had to do something. Even Mitch thought so.

Ordinarily, Alex would have gotten angry at his father for delving into his personal life so boldly. After all, he was thirty-two years old, certainly past the age of needing parental permission for the things he did. But oddly enough, he just felt numb. "Depends on what you mean by involved."

"Do you need me to spell it out for you? Are you sleeping with her? That I could understand. She's a fine-looking woman. But it's more than that, I suspect." He drew in a breath, held it a moment before expelling it noisily. "Are you in love with her?"

For the first time since he'd entered his office, Alex met his father's eyes. "I don't know."

Exactly what Ron had been afraid of. His objections centered around the fact that this had all happened too quickly. A man should get to know a woman, court her a while. They should come from the same background, the way he and his wife had. A man shouldn't impulsively marry because his hormones were raging, like Alex had done with Cynthia. The bottom line was that he didn't want his son hurt.

But no man could protect a grown son from everything.

Ron pushed himself to his feet. "Then maybe you should find out."

Alex sat staring at his father's back as he walked out, his strides reflecting his displeasure with his only son. Yes, Alex thought, maybe it was time he did find out.

Chapter 9

Alex had known from an early age that timing was important. As a young boy, he'd soon discovered that catching his father as soon as he walked in from the office and asking permission to do something usually earned him a refusal. But if he waited until his father had had time to unwind and relax, he'd be all smiles and willing to grant most anything. That lesson also served him well in business in later years.

Which was why he'd carefully plotted out the time of his return to Twin Oaks the following day. Too early in the morning would mean that Megan would be busy serving breakfast to her guests. Right after and she'd be cleaning rooms and changing beds alongside Grace. Just before lunch would be good since that was when Megan wandered the hillside picking wildflowers for the tables or worked in her garden while Grace usually ran errands.

When he pulled his Porsche into Delaney's parking lot, only three cars were there, one of them Megan's old Mustang. Stepping out, he stretched, admitting he was a shade nervous. Although he'd timed his arrival carefully, what he hadn't done was prepare what he wanted to say to her. Perhaps playing it by ear would be best, gauging her mood first.

After all, he'd been gone exactly a week without a call or a note of any kind. His reception was bound to be guarded or downright chilly.

The public rooms were deserted except for Mrs. Kettering dozing in an armchair in the lounge with the television on. He found Grace in the kitchen, seated at the table strewn with papers, her fingers flying over the keys of an adding machine. She looked up as he walked in through the swinging doors, surprise registering on her expressive face before a look of concern moved into place.

Grace removed her half glasses. "So, you've come back. More business in the area?" She was aware her voice wasn't particularly welcoming and even revealed a note of skepticism.

Alex pocketed his keys. "You have every right to be annoyed with me for leaving the way I did."

"Go on."

Grace wasn't quite his father's age, but old enough to make him feel as if he was being called on the carpet. She was also as protective of Megan as Ron was of him. "Let's just say I had some thinking to do. Is Megan around?"

"And that's all you're going to tell me?"

"The rest of the explanation is for Megan's ears only. Where is she?"

Grace drew in a thoughtful breath. What good would it do to delay the inevitable since he'd find her eventually? Besides, despite the fact that she disapproved of Alex's abrupt departure, she had to admit his timely payment of some of Megan's overpowering bills had kept the wolf at bay for now. How could she fault a man like that, one who'd also been good to Ryan?

Unless, of course, his return came with a lot of strings attached. That, only time would tell.

She stalled for just a minute. "I assume you know you've hurt her after I warned you not to."

"Yes, and I'm sorry."

"The boy, too."

Despite his note, he'd guessed that Ryan wouldn't understand. "I'll make it up to him." The mention of getting hurt reminded Alex of something that had been nagging at him. He could probably get a straight answer quicker from Grace. "I need to know something. The scar on Megan's temple looks to be fairly recent. Can you tell me how she got that?"

Grace's lips thinned as she debated about telling him the truth. While it was true he'd left in a big hurry, he'd also come back. That scored a lot of points with her. She removed her glasses and sat back. "They were arguing in the kitchen. Neal had already moved out, but he had the nerve to come to Megan and ask for money to pay back his loan shark. She lost it, told him to leave and never come back. She had a check in her pocket from a guest who'd checked out earlier. He lunged at her, trying to get it. She fell and hit her head on the kitchen counter, right over there."

Alex didn't even realize his hands had balled into fists.

"And do you know what that coward did when he saw the blood? He ran away. I found her there, bleeding and dazed, took her into the clinic. Six stitches it took. The bastard!"

He couldn't have phrased it better himself. "And still she took him back in when he got sick?"

Grace nodded disapprovingly. "Took him in and nursed him. I'd have slammed the door in his lying face."

"Thanks for telling me." Alex forced himself to relax. "Where is she?"

Grace allowed herself a weary sigh. "She's outside picking flowers up on the hill."

Alex leaned down and kissed her on the forehead, then hurried out the side door.

Grace stood and walked to the window, curious as to what kind of reception Mr. Alex Shephard would get from Megan. Her friend had tried to hide her feelings during the past seven days, but Grace had noticed the haunted eyes and the restlessness that hinted of sleepless nights. Would Megan send him packing or welcome him with open arms? Grace wasn't sure.

Peering out, she spotted Megan halfway up the hill, just starting down, both hands full of flowers. She watched as Alex started the climb. It didn't appear as if he called out because her eyes were downcast as she carefully watched her footing around the rocks.

Grace knew the moment Megan became aware of him. She stopped, obviously stunned. Then she saw Alex start to run the rest of the way up the hill. She could just make out Megan's wide smile as she dropped the flowers and ran to meet him. In seconds, they met in a fierce embrace, then Alex picked her off her feet and swung her around. Grace could hear distant, delighted laughter drift through the screen door. Then she saw Megan's arms wind around his neck as Alex stopped turning. So close together, not even a shadow could intrude, they kissed.

Eyes suddenly damp, Grace stepped away from the window. Some moments were too private to be witnessed. She prayed that Alex hadn't returned to lift Megan's hopes only to dash them again later.

It was back, Megan thought, the rich male taste she'd been dreaming of nightly. The hard, masculine hands that held her close to his pounding heart, the ones she'd been longing for since the last night she'd been in his embrace. The sweet euphoria that chased away all rational thought. It was back. *He* was back.

She'd pictured his return, imagined it, craved it. She'd mentally rehearsed what she'd say and do. All of that paled in light of the real thing. All of her anger at the way he'd left, her ache over his stealthy departure, her pain at not hearing from him for seven long days and nights—all of it forgotten in this glorious moment. None of it mattered, not really. He was back.

She trembled in his arms, humbling him. Alex gentled his hold, yet kept her very close. The familiar scent of her wound around him, the wild taste of her exploded on his tongue, and the soft, womanly feel of her straining against him aroused a throbbing need he could no longer ignore.

He'd tried to stay away, tried to tell himself she was just an interlude, a pleasant memory. But the memory only sharpened with each day away from her and the need for her only grew and the desire he'd tried to bank only increased. He'd never felt like this for any other woman. Not for Cynthia whom he'd married. Not for any of the women who'd wandered through his life, eager to please and be pleased.

Megan wasn't like that. She was hesitant, initially shy, then almost reluctantly reaching out to touch, to taste. She wouldn't pursue, wouldn't call him back, wouldn't phone. She wanted, yet was afraid of her wanting. She vacillated, sometimes pushing him away, then drawing him close. Despite years of marriage, she seemed almost untouched.

Letting her slide down his body, Alex ended the kiss, but eased his head back from her only slightly, staring into her sky blue eyes. "I'm sorry if I hurt you by leaving like that," he said, his voice thick with emotion, with desire.

"Shh," she whispered. "You're here now. That's all that matters." She might regret this later, Megan knew. Probably would. But for this moment in time, she didn't care. All her life, she'd walked a straight line, done the right thing. There came a time when a woman had to follow her heart.

"I've missed you. I couldn't stop thinking of you." He spoke only the truth, truth he'd only recently admitted to himself.

"Oh, Alex." She buried her face in his neck, inhaling his special fragrance, content to stand there like that for the rest of time.

For a wild moment, he imagined taking her there on the hilltop, following her down to lie with her amid the wildflowers she'd gathered, with the scent of the sea teasing them and the gentle summer breezes caressing them. It was a fantasy he'd dreamed of many a sleepless night. But the reality was that Grace was a short distance away and one or more of Delaney's guests could return and wander out any moment.

He wanted privacy, to be alone with her, to spend hours learning her.

Bending, he slipped a hand beneath her knees and picked her up into his arms. She gave no resistance, instead laying her head on his shoulder as he turned and started down the hill. The time had come and they both knew it.

Alex avoided even looking at the side door, unwilling to meet Grace's judgmental gaze, going around to the back door and up the stairs. Not knowing if his old room was occupied, he continued on up to the third floor until he reached Megan's room. Inside, he bumped the door closed with his hip, then paused to turn the lock before carrying her over to her cozy double bed.

Megan's heart was thudding so hard she was certain he could feel it. Her desire had brought her this far, but now, faced with the inevitable, some of her anxiety returned. As her feet touched the floor, she finally met his eyes.

"It's new, this bed," she told him, needing him to know, despite her fears, how special this moment was for her. "It's the only thing I replaced after Neal moved out."

The sweetness of her confession, her need to tell him that he wouldn't be using the bed she'd shared with her husband, touched him. "Thank you for telling me." He kissed her then, a soft, lazy kiss, drawing out the pleasure by holding back. Then he grew impatient again and followed with a hard kiss that nearly sapped all her strength.

But before things got out of hand, Megan felt the need to say more. Her hand on his chest, she eased back. "Wait. We need to talk, please."

Talking was the last thing he wanted or needed, but he had no intention of rushing her, knowing greed would end things before they'd begun. "About the night I left..." he began.

"No, not that. We can talk about that later." Megan ran a shaky hand through her wind-tossed hair and sat down on the rose-colored quilt covering her bed. "I want to warn you that I might disappoint you."

That again, Alex thought. Her fears. What in hell had Neal

Delaney planted in her head to make her believe she was
disappointing? Still, he couldn't just dismiss her feelings, for
he could see they were very real to her.

Alex sat down next to her, took her hand. "Listen, Megan,
not every woman whose husband strays has a problem. Did
Neal say you did?" He needed to know just what she'd been
told.

"No, not in so many words. It's just a feeling I have. Why
else would he have needed other women?"

Alex searched for a way to explain. "Some men have affairs to prove to themselves that they can get any woman they
want. It's an ego thing." They'd fought, Grace had told him,
over bills, the jobs he'd lost, the loan shark. "If the two of
you were quarreling a lot, his self-image was probably not so
hot. What better way to feel you're special than to find some
willing woman? Maybe he even wanted you to find out, to
show you he was attractive to others."

Megan thought that over. Neal *had* seemed to flaunt his
women, not caring who saw him with them.

Alex watched her carefully as she considered his words.
"The fault wasn't yours. It was his. I know that for a fact
because I've kissed a fair share of women and there's no way
you're the problem, Megan." She was quiet such a long while
that he wondered what she was thinking, feeling. He had to
get through to her. "That you could even think any of that
was your fault staggers me. Don't you see what a coward he
was, shoving you, hurting you and then running away, rather
than face what he'd done? How could you believe anything
a man like that said?"

Shame had her coloring, then raising her eyes to his.
"Grace told you that, too?"

"Don't be angry. I badgered her and I'm glad I did."
Hands on her shoulders, he stood and drew her up with him.
"None of what happened was your fault, Megan. Let me
prove it to you."

"What if I'm right and..." She gasped as he pulled her

close against his hard body and dipped his head to trace her ear with his clever tongue. "Alex, I—"

"Do I excite you, Megan?" he asked, his lips shifting to her temple, then gently grazing the small pink scar.

A shiver raced up her spine as he moved his attention to the sensitive skin along her throat. "You know you do."

"Then why can't you believe how you excite me?" He opened his eyes and watched the sunlight dance in through the slatted blinds at her window, light and shadow on her beautiful ebony hair. He thrust his long fingers into its thickness and tipped back her head, watching her eyes grow dreamy. "Believe me when I say you've brought me to my knees like no other woman's ever done. You've got me twisted into knots, I want you so much. I didn't sleep last night for thinking of you, and a lot of other nights, as well. I drove here today like a madman, so anxious to see you, worried you wouldn't want me."

That he should even consider that baffled her. "Oh, but I do. I want you so much. It's just that I'll die if I disappoint you."

"Stop worrying." Alex framed her lovely face with his big hands, then kissed her slowly, hoping he wouldn't mess this up by rushing her, praying he could hang on to his own tenuous control. She needed slow loving, gentling, infinite care, and he honestly feared he might not be up to the task, his own needs crying for release.

She was wearing a full red skirt and a white blouse with a red tie at the scooped neck. His mouth made love to hers while his hands moved to undo the tie. Working slowly, he finally felt the knot give, but as he began to slip the blouse from her shoulders, he felt her stiffen.

"It's all right, Megan," he murmured into her mouth, then occupied her with another kiss. His hands caressed her smooth arms, then her shoulders, soothing, stroking. His tongue traced her lips from corner to corner, then back again before moving inside and engaging hers in a gentle duel. He swallowed her soft gasp, knowing she was finally distracted, then shifted his hands to her back to unbutton her skirt. It slipped to the floor with a soft swish while her fingers closed over his forearms as if attempting to control his actions.

Almost lazily, he kissed her closed eyelids, then returned to her mouth. The kiss was soft, seductive and mind-numbing. He felt her shudder right before her knees buckled slightly. It was his cue to ease her onto the bed.

His mouth again on hers, his one hand slipped off her sandals as he toed off his own shoes. She wore no slip, just silken panties. Too soon to wander there, he told himself, and moved his hand up to caress her shoulders. He felt her tongue grow bolder and fence with his, heard her labored breathing and knew she was becoming more involved, overcoming her initial hesitancy.

Alex was aware how vulnerable she'd feel if he exposed too much of her while he remained fully clothed. So while he rained kisses over her face, he unbuttoned and unzipped his jeans and shoved them off. He had a few anxieties of his own. Moment of truth, he thought as he sat away from her and whipped his shirt off over his head, tossing it aside. Waiting, watchful, he saw her eyes go to the very long scar that crisscrossed his abdomen.

Her breathing unsteady, Megan forced the mists to clear as she studied the scar. It had to be a foot and a half long, bisecting the blond hair that trailed from his chest down into his briefs. She remembered he said he'd had surgery last year. He appeared to be waiting for her reaction. Silently, she rose on one elbow and pressed her lips to the center, much as he'd kissed the scar on her temple.

"Ah, Megan," Alex sighed, then kissed the top of her dark head. Before she sank back, he grabbed the hem of her blouse and pulled it off, watching her cloud of hair settle around her lovely face. She was so beautiful and, finally, so trusting as she lay looking up at him.

He bent to her, kissing first one breast then the other through the thin silk of her bra. Automatically, her fingers dug into his hair, pressing him closer. He drew on her deeply and felt her hands clutch, heard a soft moan escape from her. She hardly noticed when he unfastened the bra and dropped it to the floor. Her skin was satiny smooth, her bones delicate, her frame slender. His hands skimmed along her rib cage, then moved lower to caress the soft skin of her inner thighs.

Megan was too steeped in pleasure to be afraid, to be concerned that she wasn't doing her part. She heard his heavy breathing, felt his strong heart beating beneath the fingers she splayed over his chest, and knew he was as excited as she was. If only she could be all he wanted, needed.

His patience astonished her. Almost lazily, his mouth played with hers while those long fingers traveled over every inch of her. When he slid her panties down her legs, she was too involved to protest. Her own hands wandered over his smooth, hard back, the strong, tense muscles. She could see how aroused he was, yet still his hands lingered, his mouth explored unhurriedly.

She was used to fast and impatient, to rough and ready, to a passionless coupling that had left her feeling unfulfilled and ashamed. She'd blamed herself, thinking she'd been too tame, too inexperienced, too inhibited by her mother's strict teachings about how a lady should behave. After Neal had gone, she'd been secretly relieved, glad there'd be no more pressure to perform for so little satisfaction. Then she'd set aside all feelings of passion and desire, deciding they were for others, but not her.

Until Alex.

Now she'd been lulled and coaxed into an intimacy she'd never dreamed possible. Her body would no longer be still, moving of its own accord as his hands caressed every secret place, to be replaced by his lips and tongue as Megan struggled with new and glorious sensations. She was helpless to stop the sudden, dizzying climb, to do anything but react with a low sound from deep in her throat as the first peak hit.

Alex watched the stunned surprise on her lovely face as she turned toward him. Then, with just another light touch, he sent her soaring again, wanting to show her what her own body was capable of. This time, her cry of release was muffled as she buried her face in his shoulder.

Before she was fully recovered, he slipped off his briefs. Reaching for his jeans, he dug out his wallet, then the foil packet, and took the time to protect them both. Then he leaned over and gazed into eyes hazy with passion and satisfaction. He saw her smile like the Cheshire cat as her arms reached out for him.

Shifting, he entered her and paused, giving her time to adjust to the feel of him. Straining for control, his own completion long overdue, he finally began to move. But this time, he could linger no longer. The ride was fast and furious, his arms holding her close, her hands clenched at his back. Even so, he felt her shudder mere seconds before he let himself go.

His final thought was that she'd definitely been worth the wait.

She lay sprawled over him, the side of her face pressed to his chest, listening to his heartbeat settle. Her own, Megan was certain, wouldn't calm for days. Perhaps weeks.

Alex raised a hand to brush her hair from her face so he could see her eyes. "So then, as you were saying, you're undoubtedly going to disappoint me?"

That sobered her and she propped herself up on both elbows. "This is going to sound like some scene out of a really bad movie, but was that really all right for you?"

He couldn't help it. He laughed. At her chagrined look, he stopped. "I'm sorry, but that's so funny as to be unbelievable. Did you think I faked it? Women can, I hear, but men? Not on your life, lady." Still, he realized what she wanted to know. Not was that all right, but was *I* all right. Alex cupped her chin, gazing into her worried eyes. "Megan, you have no idea of your incredible appeal. It was far more than *all right*. It was over the top, off the charts, a home run."

She frowned. "You wouldn't just be saying what you think I want to hear?"

"Absolutely not. Now it's my turn. How about you?" He

doubted that he had to ask. The flush on her face was still evident. But men liked to hear the words, too.

Megan touched his face with just her fingertips, in joy, in wonder. "I honestly never knew it could be like that." She blushed, remembering. "So powerful, so…so wonderful."

His smile was pleased and just a bit smug. "Told you."

"I guess you did." She rolled off him and lay back, feeling a contentment she couldn't put into words. Turning her head, she noticed his scar again and reached to touch the light ridge. "This must have been a very serious surgery. What did you have done?"

Here goes nothing, Alex thought, his eyes on the ceiling. "A liver transplant."

Megan's interest was aroused. "Really? That's what Neal was waiting for when he died. I think I already mentioned it. Did you have a disease, too?"

Alex nodded. "I borrowed a guy's razor and got hepatitis C. I never dreamed it would be that easy to catch a potentially fatal disease." He hesitated, then went on. "I have a new liver now—and no trace of disease. So you're safe."

"Oh, I know that. It's just…you and Neal having such a similar problem. What an odd coincidence." He rolled toward her, needing to keep it light, to distract her. And he knew just how. "The world's full of coincidences. And speaking of that—" he trailed a fingertip around the peak of one breast and watched it change, swelling to his touch "—it would seem you haven't had quite enough yet. By another odd coincidence, neither have I."

Megan felt the sensual pull, but reality was settling in. She glanced at the bedside clock. "It's two already. Ryan will be home soon and—"

And his mouth covered hers with a long, soul-shattering kiss. By the time it ended, her arms were wrapped around him and her lips reluctant to lose contact. "Not for another hour. Plenty of time." He went back to work.

Grace checked in the new occupants of the second-floor French provincial room and showed them to their suite, then paused at the foot of the stairs leading up to the third floor. She hadn't heard a sound from up there in over two hours. Apparently, Megan and Alex were getting along just fine. She didn't know whether to cheer or start worrying again.

Down in the kitchen, she poured herself a glass of iced tea before sitting down to read the morning paper, the one she seldom got to till evening. But it was a relatively quiet day. Except perhaps up in Megan's room.

Well, it was about time. Megan was too young to spend every waking minute working and every night alone in her bed. If only Alex was trustworthy.

She sipped tea and skimmed the paper, turning pages until she spotted an article that caught her attention. The words "Shephard Construction" jumped out at her. Leaning closer, she read the whole piece, then sat back thoughtfully.

Shephard Construction, Alex's company down in San Diego, had just received a grant of $1.2 million to do some work for the government on a navy project. That was a lot of bucks. She'd had no idea his firm was so large, so prosperous.

Which had to mean Alex was wealthy. She knew that Alex's mother and brother were both dead, meaning he was his father's only heir. So one day, possibly soon, this lucrative company would be all his. Which had Grace wondering even more why a man of such means, obviously well educated and well traveled, would show such interest in a small-town girl like Megan.

Not that Megan was a girl. She most decidedly was a woman, and a beautiful one at that. But she also was small town. She'd barely finished high school before marrying, and although she was intelligent, she hadn't attended any fancy finishing schools or colleges. If this relationship of theirs was to continue and possibly become permanent, how would Megan fit in with Alex's friends and relatives?

She remembered Alex telling her that his father had worked his way up, that even his mother had worked in the company, and that Ron had had his sons start at the bottom. So the Shephards hadn't inherited their wealth. But they'd undoubtedly had quite a bit of money for a lot of years. And money changed people.

Maybe she was jumping to conclusions, Grace decided. Still, it wouldn't hurt to check out a few things. At the very least, she should find out so she could inform Megan. After all, forewarned was forearmed. She was sure her friend had thought of Alex as coming from some small family company, not some multimillion-dollar firm. Even though he'd paid off her second mortgage, they still hadn't realized he was in the big time. That was a clue that should have warned them.

Grace glanced again at the picture showing Ron Shephard shaking hands with a government official. Yes, this was definitely the big time. She remembered the day Ron had stopped in at Delaney's. He'd seemed even more confident and self-assured than his son. That alone was intimidating.

Rising, she went in search of the phone book. A call to Dun & Bradstreet should tell her all she needed to know.

"I can't let Ryan find us up here in bed together," Megan said in an effort to persuade Alex to let her up. He was curled around her spoon fashion, his big hands covering her breasts still tingling from their second lovemaking.

Lovemaking. What a beautiful word. She couldn't stop smiling.

"Of course you can't." Alex nuzzled into her neck. "I locked the door, remember?"

"I need to get up and take a shower."

"Mmm-hmm. In a few minutes."

"I shudder to think what Grace is going to say."

"Do you answer to Grace?"

"No, but I've never had to deal with anything like this, walking downstairs after several hours spent on a sunny afternoon in my room behind locked doors with a man. She's going to know." She made as if to rise.

"Wait. Don't leave yet. I want to hold you for a few

minutes longer, just hold you." Replete, relaxed, he was honest and vulnerable. "My mother used to hold me when I was little, and I'd fall asleep listening to her heart beat. So nice."

Megan's heart turned over. As quietly as that, love was born. She brushed back his hair and wrapped her arms around him. "I'm right here. You rest."

A full twenty minutes later, Alex untangled himself and stretched. "Mmm, that was a great nap."

She hadn't slept, had just held him, watched him. Again worried about the lateness of the hour, Megan swung her legs over the side of the bed, surprised to find she ached in places she hadn't known could ache. But it was a good aching.

Alex leaned over and pulled her back down. "Maybe, before we leave this room, we should clear the air. About my fast getaway last week." He shifted so he could see her face. "Do you know why I left in such a hurry?"

"Because you realized things were moving too fast and you needed time to think."

Amazed she knew him so well, he let his face show it. "That's what I told myself, too. But it was more than that. I realized something far more important."

Megan's heart fluttered, but she kept her features even. "And what was that?"

"That I'm falling in love with you. And frankly, that thought scared me to death."

She raised trembling fingers to touch his face, his strong, handsome face. "I feel the same and I'm just as scared."

"What are we going to do about it?"

She managed a shrug. "I'm open to suggestions."

"How about we take it one day at a time for now?"

"That works for me." And would give her a little breathing room, time to sort out all that had taken place today in the way of changes in her life. "Is the way you feel the reason why you paid off my second mortgage and brought me up-to-date on my first? Mr. Williams didn't tell me, but I figured it out. Why'd you do it? Because you felt sorry for me?"

"No!" Alex's scowl was fierce as he sat up. And tinged with just a shade of guilt, because he *had* felt sorry for her. At first. "I did it because I'm so damn proud of what you're doing here keeping the inn going. And more importantly, the terrific job you're doing raising Ryan. When I found out from Grace how Neal had left you with a mountain of debts, I just had to do something. Don't be angry. I can afford it. All I wanted to do was make life a little easier for you and Ryan." There was more, but he thought he'd said enough for one day.

"I'm not angry, although you know how I hate someone else paying my way. Did you get my note at your office?"

Alex grinned. "You mean your formal promissory note to repay every cent? Yes, I did. And I promptly tore it up." Bending down to her, he kissed the tip of her nose. "Don't you see? I don't want your money. Not now, not ever. I just want to ease some of your financial burdens." His eyes on hers, his hand trailed down the silken line of her throat and settled on her breast, causing her to draw in a quick breath. "And maybe a little lascivious compensation from time to time."

"Mr. Shephard, you want to *buy* my favors?"

Sobering, Alex shook his head. "Honey, there's not enough money in the world to pay what you're worth." With that, he touched his mouth to hers.

Chapter 10

The morning after was more like the afternoon after since it was nearly three when Megan made it downstairs. She noticed that Grace had apparently gathered up the flowers she'd dropped, arranged them in vases and set the tables for morning. She'd also run her errands and was in the foyer talking with Mrs. Kettering.

"Hello, ladies," Megan said in greeting, keeping her eyes on the senior citizen rather than subjecting herself to her friend's shrewd gaze. "Anything happening?"

"You tell us," Mrs. K answered, peering up at Megan through her thick granny glasses. "I noticed that nice young man's convertible is in the parking lot. Does that mean he's back with us for a while? I sure hope so. He's a charmer."

Yes, isn't he just? Megan thought, praying her face didn't reveal her feelings. "Yes, he's back."

"Good, because I'm stuck. Just one more word and I'll have it licked." She held up her folded newspaper. "Crossword puzzle. I need a five-letter word for *nose*. He's a whiz at 'em, you know. Gets the hard ones every time, even the *New York Times*.''

"Really?" Alex had helped Mrs. K with crossword puzzles? Apparently, there was a great deal she didn't know about him, Megan realized. "He should be down shortly." Finally, she turned to face her friend. "Anyone been looking for me?"

Grace was trying without much success to keep a straight face. "No, it's been quiet. You picked a good afternoon to take a...nap." Despite her best efforts, a knowing smile appeared.

Flushing slightly, Megan cleared her throat.

"Napping? Are you ill, my dear?" Mrs. K wanted to know. "Because you look really healthy. Your color's wonderful."

Coughing into her fist, Grace turned aside.

"I'm just fine, Mrs. K. If you want to go back into the lounge, I'll send Alex in as soon as he's available." She'd left him still in her room using her shower after she'd finished hers. Left him most reluctantly. But he couldn't spend the nights there. Ryan would be right next door.

As the old woman walked off, her tennis shoes making a squishing sound on the tile, Megan turned back to Grace. "I believe the Southwestern suite's empty. Let's book Alex in there, okay?"

Grace moved to the registration desk and opened the daily book. "Whatever you say."

Now that they were alone, Megan wanted Grace's opinion. Not that it would be her guiding force, but her friend rarely looked at things through rose-colored glasses. A mature evaluation couldn't hurt. "You don't approve?" she asked, walking over to where Grace was entering Alex's name.

Finishing, Grace looked up. "I didn't say that. I know how crazy you are about him." Which was why she felt she ought to share the information she'd learned earlier. "I just don't want to see you get hurt again."

"Oh, Grace, neither do I. But I wonder, are there ever any safeguards against getting hurt?" Megan had thought a lot about that during the week of Alex's absence. She'd wondered what she should do or say if he came back. And the moment she'd seen him running toward her on the hillside, she'd let her heart make the decision for her. "I can stay in my nice, safe life and probably avoid problems, or I can reach out and take what's offered and hope for the best. Which would you do?"

Grace smiled. "No contest, honey. You *know* which one I'd choose. Aren't I always telling you not to hide out in this old house?" Still, she couldn't help worrying. "But there is something I think you should know."

At that moment, the sound of running footsteps could be heard along with a whooping shout. Turning, Megan watched her son barreling toward her through the door and into the foyer, a wide grin on his face.

"Where is he?" Ryan wanted to know. "I saw Alex's car out front."

"Right here, sport," Alex said, walking toward them from the back stairs. He grabbed Ryan and swung him into a bear hug, more or less the way he had swung Megan into his arms earlier. "I missed you."

"Me, too. I *told* Mom you'd come back. I knew you would 'cause you promised to chaperone my field trip. It's tomorrow."

Alex set the boy down and tousled his hair. "I remember. End-of-school treat. A trip to Water World."

"You don't know what you're in for, Alex, chaperoning twenty-six eight-year-olds to a water fest all day," Megan commented. "Are you sure you're up to it?"

"Sure he is!" Ryan insisted.

"You bet I am," Alex agreed. Bursting with happiness, Ryan stepped close and leaned into him for a spontaneous hug. Over the top of his dark, curly head, Alex looked at Megan and saw her eyes soften. His arm circling the boy's small frame tightened and he blinked rapidly, realizing he was utterly lost to these two.

How the hell had this happened?

Noticing, Megan stepped in. "Go upstairs and change clothes, Ryan."

"Okay, Mom." In his happy state, he was agreeable. "I'm going to be in the fourth grade next year," he said, looking up at Alex. "No more homework till then."

"The fourth grade. Well, I guess you're probably ready for some heavy reading. I picked up something you might like. Ever hear of *Goosebumps?*"

"*Goosebumps?* You got me *Goosebumps?* Oh, wow! I read one from the school library. They're great. Really scary."

"I've never read one," Alex confessed. "Maybe after awhile you can read it to me. Go change and I'll see you later." Alex watched the boy run off, trailing his book bag after him. "What a dynamo!"

"You don't really have to go tomorrow," Megan began.

"Are you kidding? I promised him. Besides, I think it'll be kind of fun. Are you going?"

"Yes."

His eyes warmed, but he didn't touch her since Grace was nearby, leaning on the registration desk, watching. "Then I know it'll be fun."

Megan felt her cheeks heat again. Was this how it was going to be from now on? She was totally unused to being so flustered. "Listen, Mrs. K's in there," she said, pointing to the lounge. "She says she could use your help with a crossword puzzle."

"Is she stuck again? Okay, thanks." He strolled off.

Slowly, she turned toward Grace, knowing her friend would have some comment.

She did. "I hope you know what you're doing, honey."

Megan let out a trembling sigh. "I hope so, too. By the way, what was it you wanted to tell me earlier?"

"Oh, yes." Grace glanced toward the lounge. "Let's go into the kitchen."

Curiosity had Megan frowning by the time she and Grace

sat down at the kitchen table. "You're being very mysterious."

From her skirt pocket, Grace took the folded article she'd cut out of the paper. "Read this." She watched Megan's face as she scanned the report on Shephard Construction's million-dollar-plus contract with the government.

Megan looked puzzled. "I'm not sure what you're getting at."

"I took the liberty of checking Alex's company out with Dun & Bradstreet." At Megan's surprised scowl, she waved a hand. "Now don't get angry. I thought we should know. Are you ready for this? He's loaded."

Megan's scowl deepened. "Loaded?"

"Shephard Construction is worth millions. As in *beaucoup* millions. And Alex is his father's only heir."

"Oh. I see." Megan sat back, somewhat stunned. She'd known he had money, that his company was profitable. But millions? "You're sure?"

Grace nodded.

The realization sank in slowly. "So you're wondering what a multimillionaire is doing here in Twin Oaks with us plain folk, right?"

"I'm not putting you down, Megan. You're a beautiful, intelligent woman with a lot to offer. But I think it's important to know what you're up against."

"Yes, so do I." She stared at the picture of Alex's father looking confident, formidable, unapproachable. Though Ron Shephard had been nice enough the afternoon he'd shown up, she'd thought him a little stiff. What would someone like that think of his son—his *only* son and obvious heir—becoming involved with a small-town innkeeper? He'd have plenty to say, she imagined. Folding up the article, she handed it back to Grace. "Thanks. You've given me something to think about."

"I didn't want to burst your bubble, but..."

Megan waved a dismissive hand. "It's all right. I hate being the last to know something that could affect my life."

She heard Ryan's loud footsteps coming downstairs. "We'll talk later."

She got up, wondering why every time she started feeling good about something, a zinger came whirling in from left field.

"Ryan, you can't eat cookies straight out of the oven. You'll burn your mouth." Megan set the cookie sheet on a wire rack to cool.

"But, Mom, we're starving. Right, Alex?"

"Yeah, Mom." Alex sat back in the kitchen chair. But his mind wasn't really on cookies as he studied the model they'd just finished. "Ryan, I made a mistake, didn't I? I shouldn't have bought the snap-together version. I should have stuck with the model cars we can glue together."

"No, no, really. It's great."

Alex leaned down, touched a finger to the boy's chin so he'd look up. Eyes as blue as his mother's stared at him, just a shade evasive. "You're being polite and saying what you think I want to hear. I can tell that you like the other kind better. But if you don't tell a person how you feel, they'll keep on making the same mistake over and over. Know what I mean?"

Ryan nodded. "I didn't want to hurt your feelings. I love the Porsche because it's just like your car. But...but it's more fun gluing the parts together."

"Okay. Thank you for telling me. Next model, it'll be the glue kind."

"You're not mad?" The little face still looked worried.

"Absolutely not. People can't read minds. You have to share your feelings even if they might not be what the other guy wants to hear. How else will we learn about each other? If you'd have gone on faking it, I might have bought another thirty snap-together models and you'd hate them all. And I wouldn't know why. See what I mean?"

"I think so."

"Be up-front and do it in a nice way, and you won't hurt

the other guy's feelings. He'll respect you for being honest. Understand?'' Or did he overexplain it? This counseling of kids wasn't as easy as it appeared on the surface. Kids took things so literally, Alex had come to realize.

"Yeah, I do."

Listening, Megan wondered how talking with Ryan came so easily to Alex when he'd never been around children much. His advice was good, on target, teaching her son to think for himself, something that wouldn't have occurred to Neal. She took over a plate of cooled cookies and set it on the table. "Can I interest anyone in a glass of milk?"

Two male voices sang out with a resounding yes. She poured, then sat down and took a cookie for herself.

It had been quite a day, Megan thought, half-listening to Alex and Ryan discuss the merits of chocolate chip cookies versus peanut butter. She'd felt a bit blue this morning, picking flowers on the hillside, wishing she could turn back the clock to the first day Alex had arrived and do things differently.

Then, like a wish fulfilled, he'd returned, and she'd spent the most glorious afternoon of her life. Just looking at him warmed her. Remembering the way he made her feel, the way he touched her, kissed her, made love with her, had her skin humming and her senses quivering. And he'd said he was falling in love with her.

She wasn't certain she believed him. Perhaps he *thought* that now, but was it a lasting emotion or a fleeting one? As for herself, she was head over heels, absolutely, wildly in love with him. But she'd been too much of a realist for too long to actually count on something coming of this wonderful union. Maybe it would, but the chances were greater that he'd get bored with her and the life she represented and go off to look for greener pastures.

Especially since she'd learned that he was heir to a huge fortune. What could she in all honesty offer a man like that? She wasn't well-read, hadn't had the time or energy to do more than glance at the newspaper in years. She'd had no opportunity to travel, not like Alex who'd been everywhere. She knew little about art or opera, about fine wines or aperitifs, about haute couture or haute cuisine, about tennis or bridge—the things she'd read the very rich were well versed in. How could she get along with his family, converse with his friends, impress his business associates?

If this relationship was to develop any further, what would they have in common outside of the bedroom? The very question was depressing.

"Mom, what's wrong? You look sad." In imitation of his mother, Ryan, too, looked suddenly sad.

Brightening for her son's sake, Megan put on a smile. "I'm fine. So, how're the cookies?"

"Great. I only had two *little* ones. Can I have one more?"

"Only if you promise to brush your teeth twice as long."

Giving her a chocolaty smile, Ryan reached for another cookie.

Megan shifted her gaze to Alex and saw that his eyes were shadowed. Was he having second thoughts, too? Was he regretting his impulsive rush into her waiting arms? Was he wishing he'd never mentioned that fearful four-letter word, *love?* Or was there something more he hadn't told her, some secret from his past still troubling him, the something his father had insisted he tell her? If so, when would he trust her enough to confide in her totally?

"My turn to offer a penny for your thoughts," she told him.

His smile came easily, erasing the shadows. "They're X-rated."

The heightened color spread quickly as she glanced at Ryan, who fortunately was too busy chewing to notice. "Maybe later, then," she answered, rising. "I've got to get these baked goods wrapped for Emily."

Alex stood, as well. "I'll help you. Matter of fact, we can take them over tonight if you like." Walking over to where she was reaching for the plastic wrap from a high cupboard, he bent his head and kissed her ear before whispering into it,

"And stop somewhere to neck in the car. How long since you've done that, Ms. Delaney?"

"You are a bad influence," she murmured. Scooting from beneath his arm, she turned back to her son. "Time for your shower, Ryan. Tomorrow's going to be a big day."

He downed the last of his milk. "After tonight, I won't have to go to bed so early, will I, Mom? I mean, for the summer?"

"We'll see." She wiped the table with her dishcloth and gathered up the empty glasses. "Wash your hair, too."

"Aw, Mom." His footsteps dragged.

"You heard me. I'll be up to check shortly."

Alex picked up the towel and began drying the pans she'd recently washed after baking. "You're a tough lady."

"Have to be." She started packaging the cookies into one-dozen lots.

Alex tossed aside the towel, went to her and took her in his arms. When she looked up at him, he noticed that her eyes seemed worried. "What did make you sad a minute ago?"

She shrugged. "Not sad, just thoughtful. A lot has changed for me today. It takes some getting used to."

"For me, too."

"Yes, of course. I want to take this slowly, Alex. I don't want any of us to get hurt. And especially not Ryan."

"We will. Don't worry so much." Only he, too, was worried. How was Megan going to handle the story he had yet to tell her, the one about the transplant-recipient list? And how was he going to find the right words? "Everything'll be fine."

"Will it?"

He tipped his head to the side. "Let's not overthink things, Megan. Let's enjoy the ride." His mouth teased the corners of her lips, then settled into a deep, breathtaking kiss.

When he touched her, when he kissed her, all worrisome thoughts fled from her mind. But even as she let him take her deeper, Megan knew that at the end of every ride, reality waited.

Megan paused to yawn behind her hand, then returned to her registration book. "That's Glenn Richards and Louie Mendell," she repeated to the two men standing in her foyer. "For one night only, is that right?"

"Right you are, honey." Glenn, the taller one with curly auburn hair, a lock falling boyishly onto his wide forehead, leaned on the top ledge of the desk, his flirtatious brown eyes skimming over Megan. "Nice place you got here."

"Thank you." She took a step back, uncomfortable with the stranger's closeness. "Will you be paying by credit card or check?"

"Here's my gold card," Louie said, tossing it onto the desk. He had a shorter, stocky build and sandy hair. He flashed deep dimples at her. "Any chance we can get something to drink around here?"

"We have iced tea available in the lounge all day." Megan ran his card through and waited for approval.

"I think he meant something stronger," Glenn added.

"I'm afraid not." Megan copied the approval number onto the slip, then took Glenn's card in hand.

"Both of these rooms have king-size beds?" Louie asked.

"Yes, they do." Finished with the authorizations, she handed each man their copies. "We don't have air-conditioning, but there's a nice breeze at night if you open the window. There's a complimentary newspaper there on the ledge and breakfast is served from seven to nine. Any questions?"

"What do you do for excitement around here?" Glenn wanted to know.

"Not much," Megan answered, the same question she'd been asked by traveling salesmen looking for fun many times over. "There's a restaurant in town called the Cornerstone that has very good food. But for alcohol or other excitement, you'd have to drive farther. Twin Oaks is fairly quiet."

"You can say that again. Good thing we brought a bottle."
Louie picked up his bag. "Would you have any mix available?"

"Just water," Megan told him.

"We'll go for a drive and look around," Glenn said.

"If you'll follow me, I'll show you to your rooms."

Glenn sent her a broad wink. "Yes, ma'am."

Upstairs, after she opened both doors, Louie stepped in front of Megan, checking out her ring finger none too discreetly. "What's a pretty woman like you doing buried in a burg like this?"

She was not amused. "I like this burg." She handed them their keys. "Enjoy your stay." Sidestepping him neatly, she went back down.

"I don't think you impressed the lady," Glenn told his friend.

"Give me time," Louie answered.

In the kitchen, Megan yawned again, not giving her latest guests another thought. She was used to one-nighters who'd seen her billboard and wanted the coziness of an inn along with all the amenities a first-class hotel offered at lower prices. She'd likely never see these two again after morning.

Another yawn had her closing her eyes momentarily. Spending yesterday on Ryan's field trip had put her way behind in her work, even with Grace helping out. But it had been fun. She and Alex had wandered the small park area, keeping an eye on their young charges, along with the other six chaperones. They'd kept the conversation light, laughed a lot and gotten splashed by a couple of exuberant kids, including young master Ryan Delaney.

After stopping for burgers and shakes, they'd come home exhausted but happy. She'd had to do her baking after getting Ryan to bed, even though Alex had all but begged her to skip it. It had been past midnight when she'd finally fallen into her own bed. Although Alex had broadly hinted that he wouldn't mind if she'd stop in his room for a while, Megan had declined the invitation. Not only was she too tired, but the very thought of sneaking out of a man's room before dawn, shoes in hand, had turned her off mightily.

And, of course, she'd been up at six as usual, preparing breakfast, serving, cleaning up. No rest for the wicked, she thought, even though she'd been considerably less than wicked.

Alex, too, had been up early and off to several meetings with the Parsons group and bankers right after breakfast. He'd told her he wasn't sure when he'd be back. That was fine with her. She wasn't very good company as sleepy as she was. Maybe if she hurried to do her baking now, she could sneak off to bed earlier tonight.

Or have the late evening free to spend with Alex.

Getting out her pans, Megan smiled. Odd to be thinking about being with a man again. Maybe they could go for a ride, provided Grace would hang around in case Ryan needed something. Necking in the car, as Alex had suggested last night, even sounded like fun. Or they could have dinner somewhere other than a pizza joint or a hamburger stand. She could be waited on instead of doing the serving. Now there was an appealing thought.

She heard heavy footsteps on the stairs and decided the two men she'd just checked in were probably going out in search of excitement. Had to be them because the two other paying guests were on all-day tours, Mrs. K was in her room and Alex was still out. Even Ryan was gone, visiting at his best friend Bobby's house two doors up the winding road. Ear cocked as she took out sugar and flour, she heard their rather loud voices as they paused to inspect the lounge, then returned to the foyer. She also heard the roar of a powerful engine and recognized the sound of Alex's car. Megan felt a rush of pleasure knowing she'd see him in minutes.

But instead, she heard excited male voices greeting one another like old friends. Curious, she quietly stepped into the dining room, listening.

"Alex Shephard, you old dog," Louie Mendell said. "I can't believe we've run into you."

"Me, either," Glenn Richards added. "Where the hell you been, man? We haven't seen you in probably a year or more."

Alex's voice was lower, less enthusiastic. "I've been around. Good to see you, Glenn, Louie. What are you doing around these parts?"

Louie made a face. "Business trip. We're calling on stores all the way to Sacramento. Daddy's threatened to cut off the money flow if I don't earn my keep. Says I spend more time playing than working."

"And he's right." Glenn laughed heartily. He could afford to since he lived off a generous trust fund left to him by his grandmother. But Louie's father owned a string of auto-parts stores up and down the West Coast and held on to the family money with a stingy fist.

"Life's tough at times," Alex commented dryly, well aware that his old buddies hadn't worked too many days of their lives.

"What are you doing here?" Glenn asked. "Got a little sweetie stashed away far from home?"

"No. Business trip, like you."

"Hey, Alex, remember two years ago when we took the *Black Sheep* down the Baja coast fishing?" Louie chuckled. "Hell, we didn't get much fishing in, but we sure downed a few, didn't we?"

"Yeah, I remember." Those had been the good old days, Alex reflected, when he'd thought his good health would last forever.

"You sure had a great time with that gorgeous blonde with those long, long legs," Glenn recalled. "What was her name again? Bubbles? Or was it Bambi?"

"It was Bianca," Alex corrected.

"Man, she was sure a hot one." Louie wiggled the fingers of one hand as if they'd been singed, then laughed. "When we going out again? I could sure use a little blond diversion. My old man's tightening the choke hold and I'm not a happy camper. You still have that sailboat?"

"Sure do. Mitch and I were out on it just last week." And all he'd done was wish Megan had been with him, Alex recalled.

"How's old Mitch doing?" Glenn asked. "He's such a stick-in-the mud, getting married like that, having kids. He still as dull as dirt?"

"Actually, he's very happy. He's got a great family."

Louie squinted up at Alex. "That so? Better him than me. No broad's going to tie me down. Right, partner?" He punched Glenn lightly on the shoulder.

"You got that right." Glenn eyed his old college friend. "You did the right thing divorcing, Alex. Why settle for one when the sea's full of 'em, eh?" He nodded toward his Lexus with his chin. "Want to come along and tip a few, reminisce about the old days? This place doesn't have anything but *iced tea*. What kind of a man drinks that garbage?"

In the dining room, Megan thought she'd heard quite enough. Quietly, she backed into the kitchen.

She hadn't liked the two men she'd checked in earlier. Hadn't liked their roaming eyes and their bordering-on-rude remarks. But then, she'd seen and heard worse. To discover that they were old friends of Alex's—old drinking and carousing buddies—disappointed her. They reminded her too much of Neal and his pals. She hadn't imagined that Alex, too, might be like that.

With a sigh, Megan set to work on her baking.

In the parking lot, Alex shook his head. "Can't make it this time. I'm working on a land purchase in town. I just came back for some papers," he lied.

Glenn wasn't buying his excuse. "Look, it's already late afternoon. Can't you change your plans?"

Actually, he could, but he didn't want to. He'd finished up at the bank and gone in search of a nice quiet restaurant away from the madding crowd that one of the Parsons sisters had recommended. He'd found the Hideaway, scoped it out and made a reservation for eight tonight. Then he'd hurried back to the inn to persuade Megan to go out with him.

The last thing Alex wanted to do was to go drinking with two guys from his past, friends who seemed oddly out of sync with what he wanted to do. "No can do. Since you're staying here, too, maybe we can get together tomorrow."

"We're leaving in the morning," Louie said, annoyed. "Damn, Alex, we haven't talked in months. Can't you spare old friends a couple of hours? Call and reschedule."

Glenn shored up the argument. "We were close once, Alex. You and me, Louie and Patrick. What happened?"

Alex wasn't sure what had happened. Even as short a time as a year ago, under similar circumstances, he'd have gone with them without hesitation. But things had changed. *He* had changed.

Still, both Louie and Glenn were a part of his past. A part he'd have to put to rest perhaps. Maybe he needed to explain himself.

Alex checked his watch. "All right, but just one drink."

"Great!" Louie dug out his keys. "You know of a place around here?"

Following them to the Lexus, Alex nodded. "There's a tavern about three miles off the highway. I haven't been inside, but it looks decent."

"Who said we want decent?" Louie asked with a laugh.

"I'll drive and you guys follow." He wasn't taking a chance on being without wheels if his old drinking buddies decided to make a night of it.

"Like old times, eh, Alex?" Glenn asked, opening the car door.

"Yeah," Alex answered thoughtfully. "Like old times."

Megan heard a car engine leap to life, then the squeal of tires. She waited to hear Alex's footsteps coming into the kitchen. After several minutes of silence, she wiped her hands on a towel and walked to the front to look out. Both cars were gone and Alex was nowhere to be seen. He'd gone with his old friends.

And why wouldn't he? she asked herself, going back to

the kitchen. He couldn't resist the pull of the good old boys. Neal had been coaxed out by his so-called friends easily and often until he'd run out of money. Only Alex would probably never run out of money. She had no idea if his two friends had big bank accounts, but not to worry. Alex was flush.

Megan blinked back tears. How could she have let herself believe, even for a short time, that he'd prefer her over the world he'd come from? Unlimited money, fast boats and flashy cars, women willing and able, and the time to indulge oneself. Who was she to compete with that?

The disappointment was that she'd thought he was different. From Neal, from those two lunkheads with the greedy eyes. She'd wanted desperately for him to refuse their offer and turn instead to her.

How foolish, how stupid, how naive!

It was time she grew up, Megan thought, swiping at a tear that trailed down one cheek. She was who she was and Alex was light-years different from her. And never the twain shall meet.

Alex was angry. Furious, actually. He'd been sitting in the lounge for over an hour in the dark, fuming.

Where in hell was Megan?

He'd returned from his short reunion with his old friends around five o'clock, having grown tired of listening to exaggerated tales of their endless conquests. Maybe if he'd been drinking along with them, he'd have been more receptive. But since his surgery, since having to take fourteen pills a day, he'd steered clear of alcohol. He hadn't told them about his transplant, his need to take it easy, so they'd tried repeatedly to coax him away from iced tea, but Alex had stuck to his guns.

An awakening, that's what tonight had been. He'd listened to his old buddies and tried to take part.

"Remember that weekend in Madagascar?"

"Hey, how about the time we took over a whole car on the Orient Express?"

"Alex, do you ever hear from that babe in London, the one who sang in that smoky little club and couldn't keep her hands off you?"

Memories surfaced and were reflected in the faces of his friends, and there he saw himself. And what he saw didn't please him.

Alex had grown bored all too quickly with their growing hilarity as they'd ordered round after round. Under intense questioning, he'd finally confessed that he'd met someone special, that he was in love. They hadn't believed him, had knowingly remarked that he'd outgrow it. That hadn't set well with Alex.

When he'd announced he was leaving, he'd suggested they go, too. Driving under the influence in California could cost you your license in a heartbeat. But neither Glenn nor Louie seemed worried and waved him off.

Had he been that foolishly stubborn back in his early years? Alex asked himself. But then, he'd never been a heavy drinker like many of his friends. True, he'd been adventurous and ready to try new things, go new places, but alcohol hadn't been high on his list of requirements. Some of the dangerous stunts he'd done had given him a natural high that no drink could match.

Even that appeal had somehow disappeared, replaced by a soft-eyed woman and her gap-toothed son who'd quietly, stealthily and permanently moved into his heart. And his mind.

But when he'd hurried back to Delaney's, quickly parked the Porsche and dashed inside, Grace had told him that Megan wasn't there. She'd left Ryan with Grace and gone to her mother's. Some family emergency, Grace said.

That had been nearly five hours ago.

He'd worked on the tree house with Ryan, eaten dinner with Ryan and Grace and listened to Ryan read two chapters of *Goosebumps* to him before bedtime. Ryan had insisted Alex tuck him in instead of Grace, which had brought a frown to the woman's face, but she'd allowed it. Then he'd settled down to wait for Megan.

He was still waiting.

Grace had been reluctant to say much about Megan's family, only that Megan was the one her mother and two sisters turned to whenever there was a problem. There must be one hell of a problem for her to be gone so long, he thought.

Alex flicked on the television, channel surfed a bit, but nothing held his interest. He was too annoyed to fall asleep. And a bit worried. The country roads around Twin Oaks were winding and twisting, dark and dangerous. Maybe he should ask Grace for Megan's mother's phone number and call over there. Just to offer his services if needed. Nah. He could just imagine how Megan would react to that, as independent as she was. Propping his feet on the footstool, Alex settled back and closed his eyes.

It was some time later when he heard a car turn into the parking lot. There was no mistaking Megan's wheezing old Mustang. Alex sat up and waited for her to come inside.

And waited. When several minutes had gone by and the front door hadn't opened, a puzzled Alex got up and walked outside. Megan's car was in its usual spot, but she was nowhere to be seen. Frowning, he went around to the side, looking every which way. There was a nearly full moon in an inky sky tonight, lighting the way even after he'd walked past the lampposts in the parking lot.

He was on the garden path when he spotted her climbing up the hill, her slim figure silhouetted in the pale moonlight. She was probably on the way to her favorite spot, Alex decided, and hurried to follow. Something was going on in her head, maybe more than a family crisis, and he was determined to find out what it was.

He moved slowly, quietly, not wanting to spook her, for he imagined she thought herself alone. When he cleared the ridge, he saw she'd climbed onto a six-foot-high boulder and was sitting with her shoulders slumped, her head down. It was a moment before he realized she was weeping.

"Megan," he whispered, and hurried to her.

Her head swiveled around and she quickly swiped at her cheeks. "What…what are you doing up here?"

"I could ask you the same thing." She looked even paler in the silvery moonlight, her eyes haunted. "What's wrong? Is it your mother?"

Of course, he'd have learned where she'd gone from Grace. "No, she's fine."

Standing alongside the boulder, he reached up and helped her down. "One of your sisters, then? Is someone hurt?"

"My youngest sister, Jeannie. She's pregnant and wants to marry the guy. Mom doesn't want her to." Megan dug for a tissue in the pocket of her slacks, wiped her face.

"Is that why you're crying?"

"No." She didn't want to tell him why, that he was the reason. She was so tired after listening to her mother rant and rave for hours, both her sisters crying. She had no easy answers to offer, steeped in her own problems, her own worries.

After the euphoria of yesterday, today she'd learned that Alex wasn't what she'd thought. He was a playboy like Neal, only with money. Even if there had been a future for them, her discovery today dashed all hopes. She couldn't go through all that again.

"Then what is it? Tell me." He tipped up her chin, forced her eyes still swimming with tears to meet his. *"Tell me."*

Her defenses down, feeling exposed and vulnerable, Megan closed her eyes. "I can't!"

"Yes, you can. Tell me, Megan. There's nothing you can't tell me." What could be so terrible, so frightening?

All right, she would. And then it would really be over for all time. She met his intense gaze, her heart in her throat. "It's you. You went with those men. That's the life you want, drinking with your buddies, boat rides, lots of willing women. Just like Neal. I…I thought you were different, but now…"

Hands on her shoulders, he shook her gently. "No! That's not true. I don't drink at all anymore, Megan. I went with Glenn and Louie to explain to them that I've outgrown all that. It's true, I used to be pretty wild. But not anymore. I used to want to go out all the time, but now, I want to be with you. Only you.''

She wanted to believe him. Lord, how she wanted to believe him. ''But you left, you didn't come back, and I—''

''I did, but you were already gone. I made reservations for us to have dinner together, just the two of us, at a place called the Hideaway. Smell my breath, Megan. I drank iced tea. They laughed at me, but I didn't care. I told them I was in love and no longer interested in playing the field. They didn't understand and I feel sorry for them.'' He studied her face, but still she held back. ''Tell me that you believe me.''

''I want to. But…but, Alex, you're rich. You have so much money and I…I owe everyone. You've been everywhere, traveled, gone to the opera, the ballet, Europe. I'm a simple woman.''

Was his money what all this was about? ''I'm a simple man, too, even though I've traveled. I hate opera and I've never been to the ballet. We can go to Europe anytime you say, or anywhere else.''

''No, you're just saying that now. But later on, you'll tire of me. We…we're not compatible.''

''Not compatible?'' Anger rose in him, white-hot and fierce. ''I'll show you compatible.'' He yanked her to him and crushed her mouth with his. The kiss was hard, unyielding, nothing like the others they'd shared. He plundered, ravished, his strong hands touching her possessively.

Megan was pummeled by sensations that threatened to overwhelm her. She tasted frustration and desperation in his kiss. She felt him back her up to the huge boulder behind her, then he lowered his head to her breast, drawing deeply, savagely on her. The wild heat spread downward until she was writhing and twisting under his relentless onslaught.

Alex was beyond slow loving, beyond gentle. He needed to convince her and maybe himself. He wanted to brand her, make her his, to let her know. Needing to taste her flesh, he ripped the blouse down the front, felt the buttons scatter, and then he feasted. He heard her cry out, her breath coming in short, ragged spurts, but he recognized not fear, not pain, but shocked pleasure.

His fingers fumbled to open his jeans, then shoved her slacks down and off her trembling legs. Her chest was heaving now and her hands gripped his shoulders. His blood swam hot and tormented as he struggled to free himself. His fingers found her and he heard her cry out, a strangled sound.

Megan felt his hard, rough hands travel over her, sending shivers of sensations throughout her sensitive system. She'd never known this kind of passion, never been wanted like this, never craved this dark, fierce mating. Until now. Boldly, she reached for him and heard his fierce intake of breath, felt him buck as her fingers curled around him.

He was on the verge of exploding, Alex knew. But this was Megan, the woman he loved more than his own life, the one he desired more than his next breath. He looked at her in the moonlight, a question in his eyes.

The expression on her damp face was utterly female. "I want you inside me, *now.*"

With one fierce thrust, he was inside her, anchoring her legs around his body, feeling her heels dig in. Alex closed his eyes on the sheer pleasure of it, the raw beauty of it. He was exactly where he belonged. Never had he felt so certain.

He began to move then, wildly, ruthlessly. In a frenzy of need, he pounded into her, her body braced against the solid rock at her back. Her breathing was as ragged as his own as she climbed with him. Blood thundered in his veins like the savage sea in the distance. Her release came quickly, fueled by her emotions, driven by an urgency that totally controlled her. When she shuddered and her head dropped to his shoulder, he let himself follow.

He held her there, leaning into her, barely able to keep them both upright as the afterwaves trembled through him. He clung, letting his breathing settle, hoping he hadn't been too rough.

Megan felt fiercely alive, her body glowing. She was outdoors in the moonlight, her blouse ripped open and her slacks and underwear scattered on the ground somewhere, nearly naked in the arms of a man who'd made love to her in a way she'd scarcely imagined, much less experienced. She should be angry, outraged. Instead, she was gloriously happy.

For she'd watched his face, looked into his eyes, heard the sensual sounds he'd made at the moment when he'd emptied himself into her. Now she knew for certain just how well and completely she could satisfy a man. Neal's infidelities hadn't been her fault as she'd feared all along.

Gently now that his anger had dissipated, Alex drew back slightly and let her regain her footing. "I'm sorry if I—"

Megan pressed two fingers to his lips. "No, don't apologize. I'm the one who should. I'm sorry I doubted you. I guess my insecurities run deeper than even I thought."

"I have a few myself. But not about you. I love you, Megan. I want you to know that, to believe it. Anything else we can work out."

Drawing him close again, Megan prayed he was right.

Chapter 11

Midmorning of the next day, Alex was in the lounge rear-ranging papers in his briefcase when he heard the unmistakable sounds of two young voices yelling. Neither sounded happy. Knowing that both Grace and Megan were upstairs readying the vacated rooms for new guests, he walked out the front door.

Ryan's closest friend, Bobby, was leaving by the driveway and Ryan was shuffling dejectedly toward the inn. And quite a sight he was. His sneakers were untied as usual, his jean shorts were hanging low and his striped T-shirt was dirty and torn on one sleeve. He was fighting tears, his face was smudged, and a nasty red bruise under one eye was beginning to swell. He also had a bloody nose.

Alex waited for the boy to reach him.

Ryan stopped two feet from Alex. "Hi."

"Hi yourself. Had a little scuffle, did you?"

Sniffling noisily, Ryan nodded. "I got into a fight with Bobby." He swiped at his nose, stared at the blood on his fingers.

"I thought he was your best friend." Alex handed him his handkerchief.

"Not no more." Ryan blotted his nose with the handkerchief.

"I see." Alex crouched down so they were face-to-face. "What was the fight about?"

"He said bad things about my dad."

Uh-oh. Walk carefully here, Alex warned himself. "What kind of bad things?"

"He said my dad spent all our money and that's why Mom has to work so hard. His mom told him. And he...he said my dad had girlfriends. Lots of girlfriends." Mopping his nose, Ryan squinted as he looked at Alex. "Married dads aren't supposed to have girlfriends, are they?"

When in doubt, go with the truth. "No, they're not."

Ryan kicked at a pebble with a scruffy sneaker. "I guess Bobby was right, then. My dad was bad."

"Not exactly. Your dad did some bad things, but he wasn't a bad man. There's a difference, Ryan."

The boy looked up hopefully. "You think so?"

"I'm sure of it."

"Alex, do you love my mom?"

Nearly reeling from the abrupt change of subject, Alex cleared his throat. "What makes you ask?"

"I saw you kiss her neck the other day in the kitchen. None of our other guests kiss her neck."

Alex sincerely hoped not as he swallowed a smile.

"Well, do you?"

Alex gave him a sheepish smile. "I guess you caught me. Yes, I do love her. How do you feel about that?"

Screwing up his face, Ryan thought for a minute. "Are you going to take her away from me?"

Alex's reaction was immediate. "Whoa, never! What made you think that? If we ever leave here, you'll come with us."

"Honest? You mean it?"

He'd forgotten how often Ryan had been told things, promised things that had never turned out to be so. The legacy of his father and something Alex would have to overcome. "Honest. And another thing, Ryan. I won't ever promise you something unless I'm really going to do it. Okay?"

The boy studied him silently. "I guess it's okay, then." He glanced at his torn sleeve. "Mom's gonna kill me. My shirt got ripped."

Straightening, Alex slipped an arm around the slim shoulders. "Let's see if I can't help you out with that." Together, they walked around back.

From the upstairs window where she'd been cleaning the room one of Alex's old friends had vacated, Megan stepped back. She'd opened the window when she'd heard Ryan and Bobby shouting and had been about to yell down and ask what happened when she'd seen Alex stroll out. Curious as to how he'd handle the situation, she'd unabashedly eavesdropped. And was glad she did.

"He handled that like a pro, didn't he?" Grace asked, entering the room from next door.

"Oh, you heard, too?" Megan shook her head. "I'm amazed."

"A born father, I'd say, wouldn't you?" Grace winked and went back to hauling soiled bed linens down the stairs.

Megan sat on the edge of the bed she'd just finished making up. A born father. Alex had been wonderful with Ryan from the start. He had to know that she and Ryan came as a package deal. *I'm nuts about that boy,* he'd once told her.

And last night, on the hillside, he'd said more. *I love you, Megan. Anything else we can work out.* Could it really be happening, that he loved both her and her son? But what about all his money and all her debts and their entire future? Could all that be worked out? If you loved someone enough, did all the thousand other little details of your lives just fall into place to everyone's satisfaction? Could it possibly be that simple?

Sighing, Megan got up, patted the bed a last time, looked around the room to be sure she hadn't forgotten anything, then moved on to the room Alex occupied.

He was neat, she'd give him that. Neater than either she or Ryan. His clothes were all hung carefully in the closet, his underwear and socks in tidy piles in the drawers, the few items on the dresser top lined up just so, including a large assortment of pill bottles. Except for the bed.

His bed hadn't been slept in because he'd spent the night in hers. A nervous night for Megan since she'd worried that either Ryan on one side or Grace on the other would hear them. But she hadn't wanted Alex to leave her after their rendezvous on the hillside. She'd been too mellow, too in love to part from him. Yet he'd left before anyone else in the house had awakened.

Apparently, he'd come to his room and spent time going through some business papers since the spread was scattered with them. Megan decided to put them into several neat piles for him, then clean the bathroom. While she was straightening the last pile, something on the top sheet of paper caught her eye.

Her husband's name. The letterhead gave the address of the hospital in San Diego. Looking more closely, she read the heading. Liver Recipient List. And in the number-one position was Neal Delaney. In second place was Alex Shephard.

What did this mean? Had both men been scheduled for surgery, but Neal had died before a liver had been located, so Alex, in the number-two position, had gotten the next liver? She didn't know the date of Alex's operation. But why would he have this list? When had he obtained it? Surely the hospital didn't hand these out to just anyone. And if he had this list when he first showed up in Twin Oaks, that had to mean he'd known about Neal's death. Why hadn't he ever mentioned that?

There was probably a very good explanation, Megan decided as she placed the stacks of papers on his bed. She'd ask Alex first chance she got. On that thought, she went into the bathroom with her cleaning supplies.

Alex was in a good mood. He'd gotten everyone to sign on the dotted line and the agreements were in his briefcase.

The financing was in the works, and as soon as that was completed, he'd send his first crew up to see about clearing the land.

Turning the Porsche into Delaney's parking lot, he decided to try for that cozy dinner for two again tonight. Only this time, he'd clear it with Megan first, make sure she was free, then call for reservations. Whistling, he got out and went inside.

As usual, he found her in the kitchen lining up her baking things. He'd already decided that one of the first changes he would make was to persuade her to give up her second job of supplying baked goods to the Cornerstone. There were other changes he'd been mulling over, but they required more thought and planning. Knowing how touchy Megan was, he'd have to go slowly, be diplomatic.

"Hi there," he said, moving to her. "How's it going?" He leaned in and kissed her neck. "Mmm, you taste good."

Megan had been deep in thought, but the moment he touched her, her heart fluttered. Would it always be so? she wondered. Turning, she went into his arms and rose on tiptoe to kiss him properly. In seconds, he had her all but purring. "Hello yourself. You look pleased. The deal went through, I take it."

"Yes, indeed." He locked his hands at her waist, leaned back. "I want to ask you a favor." He saw the quick worry leap into her eyes and wondered if she'd ever lose that.

"And that is?"

"Tell Emily to get her cookies and muffins elsewhere. I don't want you working so hard. If we're going to be a team, I don't want you exhausted every night."

A team? What exactly did that mean? "Oh, I don't think so. I can't just abandon her. She counts on me."

"She can count on someone else." He had plans for her, and for Ryan. Big plans. But he had to initiate changes slowly so he wouldn't overwhelm Megan. "There are other bakers, I'm sure."

He'd distracted her with his kiss, with his request. But before they went any further, Megan needed a few answers herself. "Listen, I need to ask you something, too."

Fortunately, the house was quiet. Grace had taken Ryan to the park and all of her guests had either checked out this morning or were gone for the day, except, of course, Mrs. K who was in the lounge. Megan wanted privacy for this discussion.

Slipping out of his hold, she reached for a sheet of paper she'd placed on top of the refrigerator. "I don't want you to think I was snooping in your room. This was lying in plain sight on your bed, along with a lot of other papers. I was straightening up when something familiar jumped out at me." She held the sheet out to him. "Neal's name is on here, right above yours. Can you explain this?"

Alex's heart stuttered. He'd waited too long, searched too hard for the best way to tell her. Now he'd have to just spit it out and he still wasn't prepared.

"Let's sit down," he said, leading her to the table and taking the chair next to her, buying a few minutes to organize his thoughts. "I realize I should have told you the whole story a long while ago. I'm sorry now that I didn't."

Growing worried, Megan frowned. "What whole story?"

"Let me fill you in." Alex shifted nervously in his chair. "You remember I told you that I had hepatitis C and that I had a liver transplant last year? Well, while I was in intensive care, I overheard two nurses discussing how my name had been moved to the top of the hospital's recipient list even though another man had been scheduled to receive the next available liver."

"How'd that happen?"

"My father's well-known in San Diego, on the governing board of the hospital and a generous donor. He called in a few favors." Alex held up a hand, forestalling her predictable reaction. "I know what you're thinking, that he threw his weight around in favor of his son. And you'd be right, but I'd like to explain why. I've mentioned before that Dad lost his wife, my mother, after only fourteen years of marriage. And just two years before the doctors told me I might die if I didn't get a new liver right away, my younger brother drowned. I was all Dad had left. I'm not excusing what he did, only explaining it. I also want you to know that I didn't know anything about the switch until after it was a done deed.''

Megan was quiet, thinking over what he'd said. ''You're saying that, according to the list, Neal was scheduled for the next available liver, but your father twisted a few arms and you got it instead. Is that right?''

''Yes, that's about it.''

''So when you showed up here, you already knew that this inn belonged to the man you replaced on the list and that I was his wife?'' She seemed confused, uneasy, but not angry. Not yet.

''Yes. I felt I needed to see how you and Ryan were doing.'' Nervous now, he ran a hand through his hair, wishing he'd gone through all this days ago, praying she'd understand at this late date.

''You knew about Ryan, too? How did you know where to find us?''

Alex swallowed hard. ''I hired a private investigator to find out all he could about you and Ryan.''

Now her brows shot up. ''Why? If this switch wasn't your fault, why did you want to know more about us?''

''Because I felt guilty. Though none of it was my doing, I couldn't help feeling guilty.'' He dared to reach for her hand and found it cool and unresponsive. ''I wanted to make sure you were both all right, financially and otherwise. I knew about Neal's insurance so I thought you'd be debt free. Then when I got here, I learned that he'd borrowed on the policies and spent it all. I felt I should help.''

Megan felt icy fingers close around her heart. He didn't love her after all, or Ryan, either. He felt sorry for them. She pulled back her hand, straightened her spine. ''So you came to us out of curiosity and remorse, a guilty conscience, to atone for the sins of your father?''

Miserable now, Alex leaned forward. ''It started out that way, I suppose. But in no time, I learned to honestly care for both of you.''

''Honestly? Nothing you did here was honest.'' She let her anger build. Anger was so much easier to handle than hurt. Rising, she walked to the window, staring out unseeingly. ''You don't care about us. You pitied us, the poor over-worked widow and the forlorn little boy who didn't have a daddy to teach him baseball.'' She turned sharply to face him, her eyes boring into his. ''How could you do that to us?''

Alex stood, went to her, but didn't touch her. ''Maybe I wasn't honest, Megan, but—''

''Maybe?''

His jaw clenched. ''All right, I wasn't honest about my reasons for coming here. But I didn't pity you. I never felt that. I've been honest about my feelings for both of you. I just wanted to help and—''

''So you bought us a dryer and paid off my second mort-gage, brought my first mortgage up-to-date. And you bedded the lonely little widow, even taught her a thing or two.'' Heat moved into her face, whether from anger or a sensual mem-ory, she wasn't certain. ''How you must have laughed up your sleeve at how eagerly I fell into your arms.''

''That's not how I felt at all. Not then, not now.'' He placed his hands on her upper arms, compelling her to listen. ''You've got to believe me, Megan. I fell in love with you. And you must know how crazy I am about Ryan. I want to make a home together with the two of you. I want us to get married, to be a family.''

Eyes swimming with a myriad of emotions, with unshed tears, Megan just stared at him. Disappointment, anger, shock, feelings of betrayal—all had her reeling. ''I wanted that, too, and that's what hurts the most. I *trusted* you and you betrayed that trust as surely as Neal did with his infidelities. A love based on deception can't last. You'd always look on Ryan and me as atonement, payback for getting the transplant Neal should have had.''

"I was afraid you'd blame me, and you do.'' Wearily, Alex dropped his hands, tasting defeat.

"Not for the organ switch. That wasn't your fault. But I blame you for building a relationship with me and with my son based on a lie. How could I ever trust you or believe you again?'' Tears flowing down her cheeks, she was trembling now, scarcely aware of them.

No, this couldn't be happening. "I never meant to hurt you, Megan. I wanted to tell you, I really did. I...I just couldn't find the words.''

Gripping the counter with one hand, Megan stepped back. "This is what your father wanted you to tell me the day he dropped in, isn't it? Yes, I overheard the two of you talking. Well, now I know. And now, you can go. Go back to your friends, the high-living, heavy-drinking good fellows you enjoy traveling the globe with. Take them out on your sailboat, pick up a bunch of women and have fun. Go find another playmate, like the blonde the three of you reminisced about yesterday. Good-time girls who won't make demands on you, who don't want love or commitment or those other mundane family things you've always run away from. Go find a woman who doesn't have a little boy who hands you his heart, which you so carelessly break. Go to them, go anywhere, but just go.'' Turning aside, she groped for a tissue.

"Don't do this, Megan.'' He wasn't a man who asked, who pleaded easily, but he was doing both now. "Don't throw away what we have. It isn't easy to come by.''

Through her tears, she stared out the window and noticed the lone rosebush she'd been nursing back to health. It was drooping again because she'd been too busy to water it daily. She was like that rosebush, alone and struggling to survive. She'd gotten along before Alex Shephard and she'd get along after he went back to his privileged life. She needed no man or woman feeling sorry for her or her son. She and Ryan would be fine.

Megan turned to look at him. "No, something real isn't easy to come by. Something fake often looks just as appealing on the outside, but when you peel back the layers, there's nothing there but duplicity."

"I never lied to you."

"Lying by omission is still lying." She rubbed a hand over her burning eyes. "But there's no use debating this anymore. We never would have worked out together. You're very rich, Alex, raised in a household of servants, probably more money at your beck and call than you can spend in one lifetime. Why, your father can even buy body parts for you." She saw him flinch at that, but she was too hurt to stop now. "I'm a simple person, living a simple life in a simple little town. Whatever made me think we could live together happily? The only place we're compatible is in bed, sad to say."

A muscle in Alex's jaw twitched from the tense way he was holding himself. She had a right to her anger, but she'd gone over the line and aroused his. "Don't cheapen what we shared in bed. And don't judge my father by that one deed. He's a fine man, hardworking, honorable. And I'd venture to say he came from pretty much the same background as you. His father walked out on his family, too, which made Dad determined to make good, pretty much the same as you feel." He gave a mirthless laugh. "I kind of feel the two of you would like one another."

"We'll never know, will we?"

Alex took two steps back and thrust his hands into his pants pockets because they itched to touch her, to hold her, to make her see somehow that this whole thing was a travesty. "I'll go, Megan, but don't think that things are over between us. I think we both need a cooling-off period, time to think things through."

"I've already thought things through." Her throat hurt and her chest was heavy and tight. She wanted him gone so she could mourn the loss of her future in private. "Please, just go."

"I'm not a quitter. I'm not giving up on us. I'll be back."

"No, please. Let's just make it a clean break." She glanced at the clock, saw that it was getting late. Grace would be coming back with Ryan soon. She wanted Alex gone before that. She wasn't sure yet what she'd tell Ryan, but it would be far easier after he'd left. "Please, Alex."

There was no point arguing with her right now, no way to reason with her in this frame of mind. He wasn't sure just how, but he'd find a way to win her back. "All right. I'll go. Please prepare my bill and I'll check out." With angry strides, he took the stairs two at a time to pack his bag.

Alex was writing a check at the registration desk, trying not to look at Megan standing there waiting, when he heard a car turn into the driveway. Glancing over his shoulder, he saw Grace and Ryan jump out chattering, then head for the door. He did look at Megan then and saw she wore a pained look.

So she hadn't wanted her son to see her throw him out, eh? Did she think he was so depraved that he'd say something to upset that boy? He ripped off the check and handed it to her.

Megan gave him his receipt without meeting his eyes. "Have a nice trip home." With that, she hurried from the room through the back hall leading to the kitchen before she burst into tears in front of everyone.

"Hi, Alex," Ryan called out, running over. Noticing the suitcase beside him, he looked up. "Where you going?"

Turning, Alex saw Grace watch Megan disappear, then swing her measuring gaze back to him. He slipped on his sunglasses and crouched down. "Got to go back to San Diego, sport. I've got a lot of work waiting for me at the office."

"Oh. When will you be back?" Innocent blue eyes searched Alex's face.

"I'm not sure." He ruffled the boy's thick hair. "You keep up your batting practice like I showed you, tossing the ball up and then swinging, okay? And read a chapter in *Goosebumps* every night."

"Okay, but Alex, don't you have any idea when you'll be back?" There was just the slightest tremor to the voice as Ryan picked up on the tension in the air.

In many ways, this was harder than leaving Megan, Alex thought. Megan was a grown woman, one he'd hurt, who needed time and space to consider her options. But Ryan was a little boy who'd already had one father check out on him, and now, here was a man he'd begun to depend on, saying he, too, was leaving. He had to choose his words very carefully.

"Ryan, remember earlier when I told you that I wouldn't promise something unless I really was going to do it?" He waited for the boy's solemn nod. "Well, I can't tell you exactly when I'll be back, but I will promise you this—I will see you again. That's the best I can do for now, okay?"

Alex hurled himself into Alex's arms, nearly knocking him over. "I don't want you to go. My next game's tomorrow night."

Behind his sunglasses, Alex blinked rapidly. "How about if I call you tomorrow after your game, see how it went?"

"It's not the same."

"I know." He hugged the solid little body, kissed the top of his head. "You be good, you hear?"

Releasing him, Ryan nodded, but he looked miserable.

Alex looked into Grace's dark eyes and found them cool and contemplative as she hustled Ryan inside. He picked up his suitcase, then remembered something. "I left my briefcase up in the room." He turned and moved to the stairs, wondering why life had to be so damn hard.

Ryan slammed through the swinging doors and found his mother at the table, just staring into space. He hardly noticed. "Mom, Alex is leaving. Do something."

Slowly, she turned to look into the anxious eyes of her son. "What do you want me to do, Ryan? He has to go."

"No, no, he doesn't." He nearly stuttered getting out the words. "He'll listen to you. He loves you. He told me so. Go ask him to stay with us, Mom. Please?"

Pressing her lips together, Megan shook her head. "I can't, Ryan. Let him go. We'll be fine." She reached to gather him close.

But he slipped away from her, his face turning angry. "No, I don't want to let him go. Why won't you go ask him? What did you do to make him leave?"

Megan had never heard such an angry outburst from her son. The shock of it had her sitting up, wide-eyed.

"Don't talk that way to your mother, Ryan," Grace told him, her tone sharp. "Apologize this minute."

He swung his irate glance to Grace, then back to his mother. "No, I won't. Why do you want Alex to leave? Why'd you chase him away?"

Again, Megan reached out, the pain in her chest squeezing harder. "Ryan, listen. I wish I could explain. Maybe when you're older—"

"I don't want to listen." The first tear fell, followed by another. "I asked you to help and you wouldn't." Quivering with frustration and roiling emotions, he turned and darted out the side door.

Rising, Grace saw him streak past the window. "I'll get him."

"No," Megan said, "let him be. He has to cry it out. Like I do." Getting up, as if sleepwalking, she climbed the steps to her room and fell facedown on her bed.

Alex tossed his suitcase into the small trunk, then his briefcase. His face was fixed into an angry frown, his eyes slits, his hands clammy with nerves. He wouldn't repeat the past hour of his life for all the tea in China. Repositioning his suit coat on the passenger seat where he'd tossed it after his morning meeting, he climbed behind the wheel.

What he needed for now was to get miles away from this place. He needed time to review all he'd done and left undone, time in his own place among his own things. Time to reassess his life, to renew his purpose. Time to think of a way to persuade a very stubborn woman that she was wrong.

Turning on the powerful engine, Alex listened to the hum absently, his gaze going to the vine-covered, three-story structure. He remembered the first day he'd seen it, how nervous he'd been. His glance moved up to the third-floor windows, especially the middle one. The room where he'd spent last night wrapped in Megan's arms.

He'd been wrong, and now he was paying the price. But he didn't intend to go on paying it for the rest of his life. He'd find a way to convince Megan that his intentions had been good, even honorable, even though his methods were poorly thought out.

And the boy, God how he hated to leave Ryan. Remembering the pain he'd put on that small, innocent face tore him up. He'd make it up to Ryan and to his mother, Alex vowed as he shifted gears. As he drove out of the parking lot, he glanced again at Delaney's Bed & Breakfast.

"I'll be back," he said over the roar of his engine. "Just you wait and see."

Chapter 12

It wasn't Alex's habit to talk to himself. But there were exceptions and today was one of them.

"Damn stubborn woman," he muttered as he swung onto Highway 5 South. "It's her pride. I know it is. She refuses to listen because of her pride."

Suddenly aware that he had the wheel in a white-knuckle grip, he forced himself to relax and to ease up on the gas pedal, as well. He didn't need a speeding ticket right now to complicate his life.

Sitting back, he relived his last conversation with Megan, trying to see if he could have said something, done something differently, to make her understand. He could think of nothing, short of throwing her over his shoulder and hauling her off upstairs to her room. Maybe that's what he should have done. Despite her anger and her hurt feelings, even she admitted they were compatible in bed. Maybe after a bout of good sex, she'd have listened.

He dismissed the thought almost as soon as it formed. That wouldn't work with Megan, and they'd both feel cheap afterward. He needed to let her be, to allow her to look at their situation from all angles. She was a fair-minded person. She'd see in time that he'd been well-intentioned if a bit misguided. She'd give him a second chance. She wouldn't throw away their future happiness for the sake of wounded pride.

Would she?

Alex signaled, then pulled into the left lane to pass a lumbering eighteen-wheeler. How could he convince her that he loved her, wanted to marry her? She'd wanted that, too, she'd said. Perhaps her love wasn't really that strong after all.

No, he was certain it was. Megan was just too wounded to see the big picture right now. She'd come around in time. He'd see to it, even if he did have to resort to caveman tactics.

Grim-faced, Alex pressed down on the gas, anxious to get home.

Grace gave a short knock on Megan's bedroom door, then walked in. "Honey, are you all right?"

Sitting in the rocker and staring into space, Megan nodded. Her tears had dried up, leaving her feeling numb.

Walking into the dim room with the blinds slanted nearly closed, Grace was at least relieved that her friend wasn't crying. She sat down on the edge of Megan's bed. "I thought you might want to talk it out."

Her voice sounding as if it belonged to a stranger, Megan told Grace about the list and what Alex's father had done. And about Alex's deception. "The surgery switch wasn't his fault. But how could he stay here with us, make us care for him, get me involved, and even worse, get Ryan to open up to him, all based on a lie? He doesn't want us. He wants to ease his conscience."

Grace leaned forward. "Are you sure about that? I mean, it's hard to fake things for as long as Alex did. Maybe writing those checks and buying a dryer was atoning some. But reading books with Ryan, going to ball games, building model cars. That's a little above and beyond, don't you think?"

Megan wasn't buying. "He looked on himself as a stand-in father because he feels he got the transplant that belonged to Ryan's dad. He took it a step further and became a replacement husband, helping the poor widow woman to cope. Instead of tea and sympathy, he offered sex and household repairs. The savior of the nineties.''

"You're sounding very bitter, and maybe you have a right to be," Grace told her. "But we have to look at his intentions here. Do you think he set out to hurt you or Ryan?"

"Doesn't matter. Results are the same. A man driving maniacally doesn't set out to hurt anyone, but he usually does. Same thing."

"I think you're wrong, Megan, and I seldom disagree with you."

"You have a right to your opinion. He's charming. He won you over. But he didn't betray you." With both hands, Megan pushed back her hair. "I've said it before and I'll say it again. Alex Shephard is the wrong man for me."

"Maybe not. I think Alex is the right man for you. If not for your sake, then for Ryan's."

Megan raised her head. "You want me to marry Alex to make Ryan happy?"

"No. I want you to make yourself happy, and I have a feeling that involves being with Alex." Crossing her legs, she propped an elbow on one knee. "Listen for a minute. Alex didn't have to come back here. Once he found out about Neal spending all the insurance money, he could have just paid those mortgages off, then sent a check every month to ease his conscience. As we discovered, he can well afford it. He didn't have to help you when you were laid up with that ankle. He didn't have to sit on those hard bleachers game after game to watch a boy who isn't his because Ryan asked him to. He didn't have to build model cars or read stories or spend three days building a tree house. Or work crossword puzzles with a little old lady, which I think also shows his compassionate nature. Usually, men like him, with fat bank accounts, let their checks do their talking. Why do you suppose Alex kept coming back?''

Megan sat unmoving, thoughtful, silent.

"I'll tell you why. Because he loves you and he's nuts about your son. No other reason fits." Grace thought of something else. "Do you remember yesterday when Alex talked to Ryan about his fight with Bobby? This is the same as his advice was to the child. Alex did a terrible thing, not telling you sooner about the switch. But Alex isn't a terrible person. He didn't think things through. He made a mistake. Don't we all, occasionally?"

"When did you become his champion?"

"When I realized he cared a whole bunch for both of you."

If only she could believe all that. Megan leaned her head back. "You know what hurts the most, Grace? He...he was magic. Just being with him was magical."

Grace stood, touching the top of her friend's head gently. "Magic's powerful stuff. Hurts like hell when it disappears. I know because I've been there. But I have a strong hunch you can get that magic back, Megan. Think about it."

She drew in a shuddering breath. "I will. Is Ryan back yet? I imagine he's up in that tree house nursing his own wounds. Would you call him in, Grace? I'll be down in a minute to talk with him and get some dinner going."

"Sure, honey. Take your time."

Alex took the bypass through San Clemente and put the Porsche on cruise control, stretching his long legs. It was tension, he knew, causing his muscles to ache. He'd been holding himself as tight as a drum since leaving Twin Oaks. He needed to relax, to take some deep breaths. The doctors had warned him that too much stress could take its toll on his recovery, perhaps even cause a setback, which was the last thing he needed. He'd been doing so well that he didn't want to mess things up now.

He really wasn't hungry, yet he wondered if he should stop to eat before getting home. There probably wouldn't be anything in the fridge since no one knew he'd be there tonight.

Still, he didn't want to take the time now. He'd pop into a store near his condo and pick up a few things.

Maybe some music would help his mood, Alex decided. But as he reached toward the knob, he heard a sound from behind him. Pausing, he listened hard. Damn if that hadn't sounded like a sneeze. And there it was again.

Something wrong here. Disengaging the cruise control with the brake, he slowed the Porsche and headed for the shoulder.

"I've looked everywhere," Grace told Megan, her usually unflappable demeanor registering a frightened concern. "Ryan's not in the tree house, not anywhere on the grounds, and not at Bobby's. Nowhere in the house. His bike's still out front." She threw up her hands. "I just don't know."

Her heart pounding, Megan tried desperately to stay calm. "He never goes off without asking permission or telling me where he'll be." But he'd been so upset about Alex's leaving, more upset than she'd ever seen him.

"Mrs. K's in the lounge, said he hasn't been in there the whole day."

"All right, we have to think. You drive around, head over to the park in case he ran back there. Call out his name as you go. I'm going to check on the hillside, see if he's brooding up there somewhere. Meet me back here in twenty minutes, okay?" Outwardly, she was the picture of organized serenity. Inside, she was quietly screaming.

As Grace rushed out front to her car, Megan ran to the footpath leading up the hill. She knew that Ryan went there occasionally to look at the ocean in the distance and to daydream. He was probably there, maybe even hiding from both her and Grace, not wanting to come out until he was over his crying jag.

That was it, sure. Ryan was at the stage where tears embarrassed him, especially his own. He blamed her for Alex's leaving, so not only was he sad, he was angry, too, she thought as she climbed, stepping around the rocks. He might have to be coaxed down, reassured.

But how was she going to reassure him when she had no words to soothe herself?

"Ryan," she called out, her voice more shaky than she'd have wished. "Ryan, please come out. I'm sorry you're hurt. Let me try to explain, please." She walked on, checking behind the larger bushes, glancing around trees. "Ryan, Ryan." *Dear God, he had to be here somewhere!*

Stepping out of the Porsche, Alex whipped up the leather cover he always kept over his tiny back seat. There, huddled in the small space, was Ryan, curled up into a ball. His face tear-streaked, he looked up at Alex nervously.

"Don't be mad at me, please." Straightening from his cramped position, Ryan squirmed upright.

"Oh, Ryan." Alex didn't know whether to hug the boy or scold him. "Whatever were you thinking, climbing in there?" Offering a hand, he helped the child to climb out.

Looking alternately dejected and hopeful, Ryan stood his ground. "I didn't want you to leave. Mom wouldn't help. She wouldn't ask you to stay. So I thought if I went with you, I could talk you into going back. I mean, we *need* you at our place, Alex. It's no fun when you're not there. Mom just mopes around and...and...well, you gotta come back!"

Alex checked his watch. He'd been on the road just over an hour. Knowing Megan, she'd probably notified the police already. "You realize your mom must be frantic by now, not being able to find you?"

Ryan brightened. "We can call her when we get to your place and tell her that I got you to come back."

Hugging the boy to him, holding him close, Alex shook his head. "It's not that simple, Ryan. She's undoubtedly very worried and she's going to be mighty angry when she finds out you're with me."

"But why? She knows I'm safe with you." Innocent blue eyes questioned his.

"That's not it. You left without permission." Or would

Megan think he'd taken her son to make his point? No, surely she wouldn't.

"If I'd asked permission, she wouldn't have let me come. And I wanted to come with you. I wanted to talk you into going back. You can't leave us, Alex. *You can't!*"

Alex sat down at an angle on the bucket seat, his feet on the ground, face-to-face with the boy. "Your mom doesn't want me there right now. She's got some thinking to do and..." Damn if that didn't sound lame, especially to a small boy. "We have some things to work out."

"What things? You love her. You told me so. And I know she loves you. I never saw her act like she does with anyone but you. She's happy when you're around and sad when you're not." Something occurred to him and a frown appeared on his small face. "Is it me? Don't you want me?"

Almost roughly, Alex pulled the boy into a fierce hug. "Never, never think that. I want you all right. And I want your mom, too."

Easing back, his eyes questioning, Ryan looked at him. "Then why can't we all be together?"

Why, indeed? Boiled down in a child's simplistic terms, if they all loved one another, why couldn't they be together? Because two stubborn adults were allowing pride to stand in their way.

Alex reached for his car phone. "I have to call your mother and let her know you're all right."

"Are you going to take me back? Please, Alex, I want to be with you."

He could see that Ryan was upset, probably hungry, certainly hot and tired after hiding under that heavy leather cover for over an hour. And maybe scared. Definitely confused. It would take some time to make him understand, to calm his fears. Then tomorrow, after some dinner and a good night's rest, maybe he and Megan could talk like two reasonable adults.

"I have to take you back, but not tonight." Alex dialed the inn's number.

The phone was snatched up on the first ring. "Hello?" The voice belonged to Megan but was barely recognizable.

"Megan, it's Alex." Static from the airwaves over a busy highway squawked into his ear, but he felt she could hear him well enough. "Ryan is with me."

At the front desk where she'd grabbed the phone, thinking it was the sheriff since she'd finally given in and placed a distraught call to his office, Megan's heart leaped into her throat. "With you? How...?"

"He hid under the cover of my back seat. I didn't know he was there until a few minutes ago when he sneezed. I know you must be worried—"

"Worried? I've been frantic. Is he all right?"

"He's fine. He—"

"Bring him back, Alex. Please, hurry." Her hand on her chest where the ache still lingered, Megan drew the first relieved breath in over an hour.

"He's pretty tired, Megan, and upset. I'm almost to my condo. I'm going to keep him overnight and take him back in the morning."

"No! He's *my* son, Alex. You turn around and bring him back this very minute." Anxiety had her breathing hard again. What was wrong with the man's thick head?

Alex tried speaking slowly, calmly. "Didn't you hear what I said? The boy's beat. He's hungry, too. I'm going to get us some dinner, talk with him and have him back before noon tomorrow."

Fury rose inside her, strong and sharp. "Listen here, Alex Shephard. You have no right to keep my son from me. I've called the sheriff and—"

"You can call the marines for all I care. But you might want to think this through a bit. Your son hid in my car because he didn't want me to leave. He needs a little understanding right now, not two people squabbling. I promised him I wouldn't take him back until morning. I don't break my promises. We'll see you tomorrow, Megan." He disconnected.

"What'd she say?" Ryan asked, looking worried.

"She's still upset, but she'll be fine." He stood, indicating the passenger seat. "You might be more comfortable riding the rest of the way over there."

Gratefully, Ryan scooted over, reached for the seat belt and buckled himself in. "Is Mom mad at me?"

"No, she's mad at me, but she'll get over it." He hoped. He handed Ryan his handkerchief, which was getting to be a habit. "Here, wipe your face. And don't worry. Your mom and I will work things out. Now, what'll it be—burgers or pizza or chicken?"

"I like cheeseburgers. And fries. Is that too much?"

"Not for a growing boy." Alex smiled and slipped into gear.

In Twin Oaks, Megan stared at the dead phone in her hand. "He hung up on me," she said incredulously.

"Who did?" Grace asked, coming from the kitchen with two glasses of iced tea. She was worried about Megan. If something happened to Ryan, she'd never get over it. "The sheriff?"

"No, no. I've got to call the sheriff and tell him Ryan's been found." She turned to her friend. "He hid out in Alex's car. Can you believe it?"

"Sure I believe it. I know he's nuts about Alex. Was that him on the phone?"

Megan's lips were a thin line. "Yes, and he refused to bring my son back until morning. Says Ryan's tired and upset. Then he hung up on me."

Grace had a feeling her friend was leaving something out. "Well, makes sense to me. He's being considerate and giving you both a cooling-off period." But Megan still looked mad enough to chew nails. "You wouldn't have caught Neal doing something to inconvenience himself for the sake of the boy. No, sir. He'd have dumped Ryan back here and been on his way. Alex is thinking of Ryan's feelings. Pretty mature, I'd say.'' Strolling off, she wondered if that had been blunt enough.

Mature, my eyebrow, Megan thought. Selfish, obstinate, arrogant. He wanted things *his* way and to hell with what she wanted. She was the boy's mother, but Alex was deciding what Ryan needed. *He needs a little understanding right now.* What did he think she was going to do? Give Ryan a thrashing? She didn't believe in spankings. There were better, more effective ways of punishing children, like removing privileges.

Not that Ryan deserved drastic punishment for this, although he'd easily taken a year off her life. However, she truly understood why he'd done it. He loved Alex and didn't want to lose him. And he blamed his mother for Alex's departure. She— The ringing phone stopped her racing thoughts.

''Hello?''

The voice was deep and somewhat gruff. ''Ms. Delaney, this is Sheriff Collins. My deputy tells me you called, that little Ryan's run off and he's missing?''

''Oh, Sheriff, I'm sorry to have bothered you. We've found Ryan, thank goodness.'' She felt contrite and a shade stupid for calling for help so soon.

''No problem, ma'am. Happens a lot. Kids that age often run away to punish their parents, don't you know. Glad he's back.''

''Yes, thank you.'' Slowly, she hung up. *Kids run away to punish their parents.* Was that what Ryan was doing? Punishing her for causing Alex to leave? In the boy's mind, Megan was certain that she wore a black hat while Alex had on a big white one.

Wandering back to the kitchen, she was preoccupied with her disturbing thoughts. Of one thing she was certain: Alex would take good care of Ryan. He cared almost as much for her son as she did. He'd told her as much, and although he hadn't been honest in some ways, she believed him regarding his feelings for Ryan. All a person had to do was see the two of them together to notice the caring, the genuine affection between them. A special rapport, actually.

Sitting down at the table, she wondered what Alex would tell Ryan tonight about why he left. Would he lay the blame on her shoulders? That didn't seem like him. Would he try to explain the real situation, about the transplant switch and subsequent deception? Surely not, for Ryan was too young to grasp all that.

Standing at the sink where she was certain Megan hadn't even noticed her, so engrossed in her thoughts was she, Grace studied her friend. The tears and the trembling had stopped. Even the anger seemed to have dissipated. What was she thinking?

"What do you plan to say to him when they return tomorrow?" Grace asked, knowing she was prying, not much caring.

Megan took a sip of tea and leaned back. "I wish I knew."

"I'm full. I can't eat any more." Ryan sat back at the kitchen table and smiled. "It was great."

Finishing his coffee, Alex had to agree. The kid had polished off a big plateful and so had he. "Glad you liked it. I've been told I make the best cheeseburgers for miles around." Instead of stopping for fast food, which Alex wasn't fond of, he'd taken Ryan to the supermarket near his condo and bought the makings. "We can have some ice cream later, if you like."

"Okay." As he'd been taught, Ryan got up and began clearing his dishes.

"Just set them on the counter and I'll load the dishwasher." He, too, rose, went to the sink. "You want to watch some TV?"

"No, thanks." He glanced out the window alongside the table. All the windows in Alex's condo looked out to the sea, which was quite calm tonight. "This is a great place. I wish we lived close to the water. Do you go swimming every day?"

"Not every day." He wasn't quite sure how to entertain a young boy away from his own environment. "You want to go down and walk in the surf, get your feet wet?"

"Yeah!"

Minutes later, they were walking along a twilight beach, both barefoot. The spotty moonlight afforded a small measure of illumination. Ryan chased a wave or two and yelped when he got wet, laughing at the surf frothing around his bare ankles. It was a warm evening with a few gulls dipping low, looking for a late dinner. Ryan was fascinated.

"Haven't you ever been to the beach before this?" Alex asked.

"No. Mom keeps saying we'll go one day, but she's pretty busy. Dad used to go out on his boat a lot, but he never took me or Mom. I...I don't know how to swim, so Mom wouldn't let me go except that once when he first got it."

"Well, we'll have to get you some lessons. Or I can teach you."

Eagerly, Ryan looked up at him. "When?"

Alex kept forgetting how literally he took everything. "Soon. We'll talk it over with your mother."

They walked in silence a while, Ryan kicking at the sand. But there was obviously something on his mind. "Alex, what's going to happen tomorrow? Are you going to take me back and just leave me, then come back here?"

Unconsciously, Alex's arm slipped around the boy's slender shoulders. "No, Ryan. Your mom and I are going to have a talk and hopefully we can work things out."

Disbelief and hope mingled on the small, serious face. "You promise?"

"I promise to do my best." Ryan needed him and, surprisingly, he needed Ryan. And Megan. She would listen if it took him all day, Alex vowed.

Megan glanced at the digital clock on her nightstand. Two a.m. and she still hadn't closed her eyes. Sighing, she watched

the moonlit shadows that trailed in through the slatted blinds
of her window dance on the ceiling.

She'd gone through the motions tonight, making dinner for
herself and Grace, which they'd both barely touched. She'd
done her baking and run it over to Emily. And there at the
Cornerstone, she'd done something she hadn't planned on doing. Yet it felt right. She quit.

Emily was sorry to lose her daily delivery of baked goods,
but when she saw that Megan was serious, she wished her
well. That was one step in the right direction, Megan now
told herself. She had too many irons in the fire, was too tired
evenings. She didn't have enough time and energy left over
for her son, which was probably why he'd gotten so quickly
and thoroughly attached to Alex.

Who was she kidding? Megan asked herself as she bunched
the pillow behind her head for the umpteenth time. Ryan had
fallen for Alex just as she had, because he was good and
caring and fun and kind. A born father, Grace had labeled
him. Not just because he taught Ryan to catch and hit better,
or because he attended a few games. Not even the model cars.
It was because he was so good at reaching the boy, teaching
him things Ryan wasn't even aware he was learning.

Like the explanation of his fight with Bobby. Like instinctively knowing how much the boy would want to ride in his
Porsche. Like keeping him overnight so he could calm his
fears.

That's what parenting was about—doing what was right
even though doing the opposite was far easier. Neal had always taken the easy way out. Because he hadn't cared, hadn't
known how to be a father. Alex was a better substitute father
in a few weeks than Neal had been a real father in seven
years.

Megan shifted again. All right, so he'd come to her under
false pretenses. He'd had lots of opportunities before today
to tell her the truth, but he'd been afraid she'd overreact. And,
when he had told her, she *had* overreacted just as he'd pre-
dicted. Then she'd lashed out at him, hurling accusations,

sounding like a fishwife. She'd tuned out his explanations and nursed her hurt pride.

And she'd almost missed hearing the most important words he'd said, that he loved her and her son, that he wanted to make a life with them, be a family, have a real home. Tears came to Megan's eyes again, only this time, they were cleansing tears. She'd been wrong not to listen, not to forgive. Surely she'd made mistakes aplenty. Don't we all? as Grace had pointed out.

Tomorrow, she'd have a second chance—to let him know, to make things right, to forgive and be forgiven. "Don't blow it," she whispered out loud.

From an upstairs bedroom, Megan heard the purr of a powerful car engine pull into Delaney's lot, the sound she'd been listening for all morning. After stopping to check her hair in the mirror and add a dab of lipstick, she drew in a deep breath and ran downstairs.

She'd just reached the foyer as Ryan got out. Hesitantly, he started toward her. Megan crouched down, opened her arms wide and he ran into them. She hugged him to her, blinking back tears she'd vowed not to shed, holding him close.

"I'm sorry I worried you, Mom," Ryan said into her neck.

"It's all right, sweetie." Over his head, she looked up into eyes as green as the sea on a sunny day. "I knew you'd be all right with Alex."

Ryan pulled back to look at her. "We walked in the ocean last night. It was cool."

"Was it?" She found herself smoothing his hair, touching his wonderful face, reassuring herself he was truly back.

"His place is really neat. I slept in Alex's T-shirt last night." He looked down at his shirt and shorts. "He washed my clothes, too."

"I see that." She swallowed around a lump. "I'm awfully glad you're back. Please, Ryan, don't do anything like this again."

His face sobered. "I won't, Mom. Alex made me promise

to never worry you again like that.'' He put his mouth close to her ear. "He's so great, Mom. Don't be mad at him, please?"

Again, she raised her eyes over her son's head to Alex's watchful face. "I know, and I'm not mad anymore."

"Good." Ryan turned to Alex, excited again. "Is it time for our surprise yet?"

"Not yet, sport. Why don't you go find something to do while I talk with your mother?" He winked at Ryan.

"Okay." Spotting Grace in the doorway, Ryan grinned. "I have a secret, Grace. Only I can't tell you yet."

"Is that right? Let's go out back," she said, taking him with her so Megan and Alex would have some privacy. "Bobby's been looking for you."

"Really? Wait till I tell him about...whoops! Never mind." He rounded the corner with Grace.

Alex nodded toward the hillside. "Can we go for a walk? Have you got time?"

Straightening, Megan felt nerves skitter along her spine. "Okay." She walked around the side and started up the hill, very aware of Alex behind her. She'd rehearsed half a dozen scenarios and discarded them all. Maybe spontaneous would be best. Listen this time, she reminded herself. Don't talk. Listen.

At the top, Alex studied the rock that was Megan's favorite, the one where they'd made love just a few nights ago. "I like it up here," he said, turning to her.

Her face heating at the sensual memory her rock now represented, Megan nodded. "Me, too."

"Megan, I—"

"No, let me start." Conjuring up every ounce of courage she could muster, Megan faced him. It was all right to talk if you needed to apologize. "I'm sorry I judged you so harshly, sorry I overreacted and very sorry I asked you to leave. I was wrong. Can you forgive me?"

No one realized more than Alex how much courage it had taken her to say all that. He stepped closer now that he knew her feelings. "I should be the one apologizing. I should have been up-front with you from day one, but I was worried you'd send me away if you knew who I was right off the bat."

He knew her too well. "I probably would have."

"I thought if I waited a while, if you got to know me, you might understand. What I hadn't counted on was that, when I got to know you and Ryan, I'd be the one falling faster than anything I've ever experienced. I readily admit that love wasn't on my agenda, Megan, certainly not marriage. I'd sworn off both."

Seeing the sudden concern in her eyes, he reached out to stroke two fingers along her silken cheek. "But love snuck up on me. The night I went out with those two guys, it hit me square between the eyes. They represented the life I used to live, the one I thought I still wanted. But you and Ryan represent the life I want now. A rich, full life over one that was pretty shallow. No contest. Without you two, nothing holds much appeal."

Megan closed the gap between them, moving closer until they were nearly touching. "For me, too."

"I love you, Megan. I want you to marry me, and I promise you, I'll never deceive you again. I've learned my lesson. Will you be my wife?"

"Yes, oh, yes." Rising on tiptoe, she felt his arms close around her as he drew her into a kiss filled with promise, with love, with joy. When they parted, she pressed her cheek to his chest, listening to his heart beat. "I've learned a lot myself. You'll have to be patient with me, though. I'm still not good at trusting, but I'm working on it."

"I'm going to try like hell not to give you any reason to distrust me." He eased back, needing to bring up another subject. "I should warn you that I'll be on medication, a lot of medication, for the rest of my life. The doctors say I can lead a normal life, provided I take a few precautions, but they can't predict if this new liver will give out one day, as well."

"Life doesn't come with a lot of guarantees, Alex. I'm willing to take a chance if you are."

"Just try to stop me." He kissed her again, longer, more thoroughly. "Now about this job you have."

"I quit baking for the Cornerstone last night, if that's what you mean."

"That's a start." He didn't want her working at the inn, either. Maybe she'd consider putting Grace in charge, moving to San Diego. But making too many requests that sounded like demands would kill the still-tenuous truce they'd just worked out. All in good time, Alex told himself. He was a patient man when it came to something important and he was willing to compromise because he wanted Megan to be happy. "We can hash out the rest later."

Winding her arms around him, Megan was aware there was much to be settled yet. But with enough love, they'd work things out. She locked her hands at the back of his neck, loving the feel of him. "I missed you so much. I can't believe how much I've come to love you in such a short time."

"No more than I love you." This kiss was shorter, but just as sweet. "I think we'd better walk down and find Ryan. He worried all the way here about how you'd react to our plan."

"The two of you have a plan?"

"Yeah, to get you to marry me."

Laughing, Megan started down the path. "Your plan should please Grace. She's really on your side, you know."

That surprised him. "You're kidding. And here I thought she felt I was bad for you."

Pausing at the garden, she turned to him. "I have a feeling she's been playing devil's advocate."

"Aha!" Before Alex could say more, Ryan came bounding out the side door.

"Is it okay? Did you two make up?" His little-boy voice was high-pitched with excitement.

Alex smiled at him. "Yes, things are just fine."

"Whoopee! Can I go get our surprise now?" He was fidgeting and squirming, anxious to be off.

"Yeah, do it." Alex looked at Megan. "Now don't start

in telling me that I didn't check with you first. This is something that needed to be included in our new family.''

Skeptical but too happy to be angry at much of anything, Megan waited. In moments, Ryan came toward them walking carefully, carrying a cardboard box. Before he'd quite reached them, she heard a faint sound. "Oh, no! You didn't!"

"Look, Mom," Ryan implored her as he held out the box. Inside was a gray-and-white kitten on a yellow towel, scratching at the side, mewing his need to be free. "Isn't he great? Alex said I could name him. I'm calling him Harold."

"Harold?" Unable to resist, Megan ran a hand over the soft little head. The kitten reached around and licked her finger.

"See, he likes you." Ryan was ecstatic. "Alex said I had to take care of him and I will. I promise. You won't even know he's around."

Oh, sure, Megan thought. "Where'd you think up his name?"

"I like Harold. He just looks like a Harold." Gathering the box to his chest, Ryan turned. "I have to go show him to Grace. She loves kittens."

"I'm sure she does," Megan said, smiling. She raised a brow as she glanced up at her husband-to-be. "Harold, eh?"

"A nice, dignified name, don't you think?"

She reached up to bring his head down to hers. "What I think is that you're an old softie. And how lucky I am that you are." Closing her eyes, she pressed her mouth to his, feeling that finally she held her future in her arms.

* * * * *

PAULA DETMER RIGGS

**Continues the
twelve-book series—
36 Hours—in May 1998
with Book Eleven**

THE PARENT PLAN

Cassidy and Karen Sloane's marriage was on the rocks—and
had been since their little girl spent one lonely, stormy night
trapped in a cave. And it would take their daughter's wisdom
and love to convince the stubborn rancher and the proud
doctor that they had better things to do than clash over their
careers, because their most important job was being Mom and
Dad—and husband and wife.

For Cassidy and Karen and *all* the residents of Grand Springs,
Colorado, the storm-induced blackout was just the beginning
of 36 Hours that changed *everything!* You won't want to miss a
single book.

Available at your favorite retail outlet.

Silhouette Books

is proud to announce the arrival of

A MOTHER'S GIFT

This May, for three women, the perfect Mother's Day gift is mother*hood!* With the help of a lonely child in need of a home and the love of a very special man, these three heroines are about to receive this most precious gift as they surrender their single lives for a future as a family.

Waiting for Mom
by Kathleen Eagle

Nobody's Child
by Emilie Richards

Mother's Day Baby
by Joan Elliott Pickart

Three brand-new, heartwarming stories by three of your favorite authors in one collection—it's the best Mother's Day gift the rest of us could hope for.

Available May 1998 at your favorite retail outlet.

∇INTIMATE MOMENTS®
Silhouette®

COMING NEXT MONTH

#859 ROMAN'S HEART—Sharon Sala
The Justice Way

She claimed to remember nothing before waking up in a tree, dangling from a parachute. But when P.I. Roman Justice found the alluring amnesiac, she was holed up under his bed with a big bag of cash. He promised to protect her, but he wasn't sure he could help her find her memory without losing his heart along the way.

#860 EMILY AND THE STRANGER—Beverly Barton

When Mitch Hayden came into Emily Jordan's lonely life, he gave her reason to hope, to live…and even to love again. But he knew that if the vulnerable widow ever found out who he really was—and exactly why he had sought her out—it would break her heart…not to mention his.

#861 THE MERCENARY AND THE MARRIAGE VOW— Doreen Roberts
Try To Remember

Nathan Thorne had been hired to return wayward amnesiac Valerie Richmond to her husband and kids. But it was only after Nate kidnapped the stubborn beauty that he realized they'd both been set up, because Valerie didn't have a husband—or kids, for that matter. At least…not yet.

#862 FRIDAY'S CHILD—Kylie Brant
Families Are Forever

What Michael Friday wanted, Michael Friday got. And what he wanted was Katherine Rose. But the beautiful schoolteacher wanted more than just a passionate affair, and luck—in the form of Michael's beloved little daughter—was on her side, because what little Chloe wanted, little Chloe got. And what *she* wanted was a brand-new mommy.

#863 WHILE YOU WERE SLEEPING—Diane Pershing
Men in Blue

While she was "sleeping," Carla Terry got a makeover, traveled all the way across the country and—somehow—got involved in a murder. When she awoke she was in the arms of Nick Holmes, a perfect stranger and quite possibly her only hope of finding out why—not to mention *how*—this had all happened!

#864 CASSIDY'S COURTSHIP—Sharon Mignerey

When Cole Cassidy swept into her life, Brenna James knew he had to have an ulterior motive. What could *he* possibly want with a down-on-her-luck, bounced-one-too-many-checks waitress like herself? Well, whatever it was, he wanted it bad, because the dashing attorney was certainly delivering one very convincing case.

THE SURVIVOR

When Alex Shepherd learned that he owed his second chance at life to someone who had left behind a son—and a widow—guilt made him seek them out. But guilt was the *last* thing he felt as he looked at lovely Megan Delaney. And though she was clearly the white-picket-fence type, while he never could stay in one place for long, he found himself longing to be by her side....

Megan found Alex Shepherd's attentions impossible to resist. For some reason, the wealthy businessman was choosing to play stand-in husband—*and* father. But when the game was over, would he go back where he came from? Or was this substitute about to become the real thing?

15th Anniversary

Celebrating fifteen years of romance

Silhouette®
INTIMATE
MOMENTS®

ISBN 0-373-07855-2

07855